THE FOOTMAN AND I

THE FOOTMEN'S CLUB SERIES

VALERIE BOWMAN

JUNE THIRD ENTERPRISES, LLC

Print edition ISBN: 978-0-9893758-6-3

Digital edition ISBN: 978-0-9893758-3-2

Book Cover Design © Lyndsey Llewellen at Llewellen Designs.

For my cousin, Kate Abbott Buckley (aka MW), whose inventive imagination greatly influenced my childhood. That, and I'm pretty sure our watching soap operas every summer didn't hurt a budding romance novelist. Besides, anyone who can come up with Florida Baby Hotcycle deserves some recognition.

Let the games begin.

Every fortune-hunting female in London is after the newly titled Earl of Kendall, but he's intent on finding a wife whose heart is true. So, while drunkenly jesting with his friends in a pub one night, he has an idea—what if the ladies of the *ton* didn't know he was a wealthy earl? All he has to do is pose as a servant at his friend's summer country house party and make sure the guest list is full of beautiful, eligible debutantes. What could possibly go wrong?

May the best footman win.

Miss Frances Wharton is far more interested in fighting for the rights of the poor than in marriage, but her mother insists she attend a summer house party—and find herself a husband. Frances would rather wed a goat than the pompous man her mother has in mind, so in order to dissuade the would-be suitor, she vows to behave like a shrew. The only person she can be herself with is the kind, handsome footman she runs into at every turn. Their connection is undeniable, and the divide between them is no match for the passion they feel. But what will happen when Frances learns that the footman she adores is actually the earl she despises? In a game where everything is false, can they convince each other that their love is true?

THE PLAYERS

Lucas Drake, the Earl of Kendall

Dark-brown-haired, green-eyed, former navy hero turned earl, who needs to find a lady to make a countess. His friends cook up an insane plot to help him.

Rhys Sheffield, the Duke of Worthington
(aka Worth)

Black-haired, dark-blue-eyed, devil-may-care rake and gambler with a love of horses. He's tall, dark, and handsome and has a past with a certain lady, who may just be bent on revenge when the perfect opportunity presents itself.

Beaumont Bellham, the Marquess of Bellingham
(aka Bell)

Blond-haired, light-blue-eyed, in control of everything in his world. Bell is a spy for the Home Office, and nothing misses his notice, that is until he just might meet his match in the most unexpected of places.

Miss Frances Wharton, daughter of Baron Winfield

Brown-haired and eyed, she's determined to fight for the rights of the poor, has a tiny dowry, reads too much, and is too particular according to her mother. Frances has no interest in marriage until she meets a footman who just might change her mind.

Lady Julianna Montgomery, daughter of the Duke of Montlake

Blond-haired, light-green-eyed Lady Julianna is gorgeous,

rich, and comes from an excellent family. Once considered the best catch of the Season, she's happily engaged to the Marquess of Murdock. But when she finds her ex-flame, Worth, pretending to be a groom in the stables at a house party, she decides it's the perfect opportunity to pay him back for jilting her.

Ewan Fairchild, Viscount Clayton

Boon companion to Kendall, Worth, and Bell, and host of the infamous summer house party. Married to his true love, Theodora, whom he met when she broke her leg trying to sneak into his stables.

AUTHOR'S NOTE

The Footmen's Club Series includes the stories of the Earl of Kendall (book 1, *The Footman and I*), the Duke of Worthington (book 2, *Duke Looks Like a Groomsman*), and the Marquess of Bellingham (book 3, *The Valet Who Loved Me*).

The prologue of each of the first three books is the same scene written from each hero's point of view. Rest assured, with the exception of the prologue, no other content or scene is repeated.

If you *haven't* read the other books, the prologue will help you understand the origin of The Footmen's Club. If you *have* read the other books, the prologue will give you a bit more insight into the hero of that book.

Thanks for reading!

Valerie

PROLOGUE

London, July 1814

Lucas Drake, the fifth Earl of Kendall, was foxed. But *only* foxed, not an entire three sheets to the wind. And he should know. He spent more than a decade in His Majesty's Royal Navy. Lucas knew precisely how dangerous a situation it was to have three sheets to the wind. The sheet controls the sail, after all, and if the line is not secured, the sheet flops in the wind. If all three sails were loose, the ship would be out of control. Lucas was *not* out of control. Four mugs of watered-down ale at the Curious Goat Inn would not do that to a former sailor. He *was* foxed enough, however, to say, "I think it's time I find a wife," aloud, in the presence of all three of his closest friends.

As expected, he silenced his three companions. Worth, Bell, and Clayton immediately snapped to face him with varying expressions of alarm.

Rhys Sheffield, the Duke of Worthington, was the first to find his voice. Worth was an excellent man at heart, but his horse's arse of a father—God rest the former duke's soul—had all but ruined him. Rhys took himself and his title too seriously. Competitive to a fault, especially when it came to gaming or women—both of which he usually won—the duke enjoyed the finer things in life and projected a devil-may-care attitude that only his close friends understood was a *façade*.

Worth's reply to Lucas's statement was to wince, suck in his breath, shake his head vigorously, and say, "A *wife*? Good God, man! There's no need to rush into anything so...*permanent*."

"We're not getting any younger," Lucas pointed out.

"On the contrary," Worth replied, "at nine and twenty, we're pups. My father was over *fifty* when I was born."

The second head to turn and stare at Lucas was that of Beaumont Bellham, the Marquess of Bellingham. There was no finer patriot than Bell. The man had tried to renounce his title for a spot as a soldier in the wars against France. He'd been turned down in his request, however. Apparently, the Crown did not fancy its marquesses gallivanting across Europe being shot at. Instead, he'd settled for a position with the Home Office and did what he could by way of reconnaissance to help with the war effort on solid English soil. Bell was shrewd, detailed, and focused and was often accused by Worth of working too much. A charge Bell fully admitted to. He liked to tell Worth that *he* might try an honest day's work instead of spending his time gaming and chasing women. Worth had yet to take such friendly advice.

Bell narrowed his eyes and said, "Are you certain you're ready? It's only been two years since..." Thank God the man ended his sentence there. Lucas wasn't in any mood to discuss Emily. He never would be.

The third head to swivel toward Lucas was that of Ewan

Fairchild, Viscount Clayton. Clayton had recently got himself leg-shackled, and was just back from his honeymoon. Clayton had a mind for science and there were few things he liked better than experimenting and creating things. He was the kind of man you'd entrust your deepest secrets to. Rich as Croesus and loyal to a fault, Clayton loved his wife Theodora deeply and completely. He'd been the last one they'd all have thought would be the first to marry.

Clayton exclaimed, "Thank heavens. I cannot wait until I'm no longer the only one of us with the parson's noose around his neck."

Lucas took another long draught from his mug and wiped the back of his hand across his lips. His role in their quartet was that of the peacekeeper and confidant. The four of them had met at Eton as lads and stuck together through all manner of hurdles.

Lucas's main concern was, and had always been, duty. He'd spent his life trying to fulfill his duty to his father, his family, and the Crown. In that order. His years in the Navy had taught him responsibility, respect, and the importance of hard work. The death of his older brother Charles fourteen months ago had taught him the importance of living life to the fullest and fulfilling his promise. Before his death, Charles had been championing a bill before Parliament. On his deathbed, as consumption slowly pulled his life away, Charles had asked Lucas to ensure the bill was passed. "For the good of our estate," Charles had said. "For the good of the country." Lucas had promised his brother. If it was the last thing he did, he would ensure the Employment Bill passed.

Lucas would take a bullet for any one of his friends. He'd give his life for his country. He would walk across broken glass for his mother or sister. But finding a wife who would be true to him, who didn't want him merely for his money or his title, *that* was something he couldn't control. And he detested that fact.

Lucas glanced around at his three friends, who watched him as if he'd recently escaped from Bedlam. The rules of etiquette were different here at the Curious Goat Inn. The pub sat like a fat little duck on the corner of two streets in an area of London that was a goodly length from Mayfair, but not quite as far, status-wise, as the Rookeries. Here one could do things like get foxed, wipe the back of one's hand across one's lips, and say things like one was looking for a wife, without having to worry about mamas and maidens popping out of every nook and cranny in search of a husband with a title. Ever since he'd inherited the title, he'd been beset by such ladies at every turn.

"I'm entirely serious," Lucas continued. "I must look to secure the earldom. I fear I've been too preoccupied with the Employment Bill. I've been remiss waiting this long to find a bride."

"I certainly won't disagree with you that you've been too preoccupied with the Employment Bill," Worth drawled. "Obsessed is more like it."

Lucas shrugged. "Well, now that the Lords have tabled the vote until the autumn session, I have more time to rally the votes I need. I might as well get about the business of looking for a wife in earnest."

"I never bother to vote in Parliament," Worth drawled. "Don't happen to care for the hours. And all the arguing is downright exhausting."

Bell gave Worth a beleaguered look and shook his head. "God forbid you take an interest in your seat or any of the issues the country is dealing with."

Worth gave them his most charming grin, flashing his perfect smile that had been the downfall of many unsuspecting women. "I'm entirely confident you chaps can handle it," Worth replied, clapping Bell on the back.

"When the time comes for the vote for my brother's law," Lucas continued, addressing his remarks to Worth, "I'll drive to your town house and drag you out of bed myself."

Bell's and Clayton's laughter filled the alcove in which they were sitting.

"Let's not talk of such unpleasantness," Worth replied with a sigh. "You mentioned finding a bride, Lucas. That's much more interesting. Now, how old are you again?" The duke shoved back in his chair and crossed his arms over his chest, narrowing his eyes at Lucas.

Lucas arched a skeptical brow at Worth. "The same age you are, old man." After Eton, they'd all gone on to Oxford. They'd all taken their firsts together. They all were the same age save for a matter of months.

"Well, then," Worth declared. "You've plenty of time to find a wife as far as I'm concerned."

"That's easy to say, coming from a man who's never given a toss about securing his *own* title," Lucas shot back, giving his friend a good-natured grin.

Worth returned the smile. "I cannot argue with you there." He turned and gave the barmaid his even more charming smile, the one that brought out the dimple in his cheek, as he ordered another round of ale for the table.

"Yes, well, if you're seriously looking for a wife, Lucas, the Season has just ended," Clayton interjected. "It seems you've missed your chance. The entire *ton* is about to retire to the country as soon as Parliament closes next week."

"I'm well aware," Lucas replied with a curt nod. "The Season makes my skin crawl. Full of simpering maids and purse-eyeing mamas eager to show off their best behavior in the hopes of snaring a rich husband. I don't want to find a wife that way."

"How else do you intend to find one?" The marquess's intelligent eyes turned shrewd.

"I don't know how exactly." He took another drink, growing more confident with each sip. "But this time I intend to find a lady who loves me for myself."

He was talking about Lady Emily Foswell, of course. He never mentioned her name, but his friends knew what he'd been through. No amount of swaggering or denial on his part would convince them that he hadn't had his damn heart destroyed by her. Though until tonight, he hadn't even thought about Emily since Parliament had resumed session a few months ago. He'd been far too preoccupied with the Employment Bill.

"Yes!" Worth pounded his fist against the table. The duke's normally jovial voice filled with anger. "I think we can all agree that Lady Emily is the lowest of the low. There's no excuse for what she did, tossing over one man for another with a better title. As far as I'm concerned, she no longer exists."

Leave it to Worth to bring up a sore subject. The duke had been the most outraged of all of them by Lady Emily's behavior. And the most interested in ensuring Lady Emily knew that she'd inadvertently tossed over a future earl for a baron.

"Can we *not* discuss Lady Emily, please?" Lucas said with a groan, covering his face with one hand.

Worth's good humor returned with the arrival of the barmaid who'd appeared with their drinks. "Keep 'em coming, love," he said to her, before turning back to Lucas and adding, "I'm merely pointing out that if you want a lady who loves you for yourself, the Season and its ridiculousness are the last place you should go."

"Yes," Lucas replied with a sigh, lifting his mug into the air to salute the duke. "Didn't I already say that? The Season and its *fetes are* the last place I should go, which is why I've avoided it like the pox for the last two Seasons."

"Oh, is *that* why you haven't attended the boring balls at Almack's?" Worth replied with a smirk. "I thought it was the tepid tea and small talk. That's why I steer clear of them."

"You avoid them because they don't serve brandy and we all know it," Bell pointed out, staring fixedly at Worth, his arms crossed tightly over his chest.

Worth winked at his friend. "That and they won't give me the bank that Hollister's will."

Hollister's was Worth's favorite gambling hell. The man spent nearly all his free time there. Hollister's had given the duke *carte blanche* and he won and lost small fortunes there regularly.

Lucas scratched his chin and stared blindly at his mug. "If only the ladies of the *ton* didn't know I am an earl, I'd have a much better chance of finding a match," he grumbled. Hmm. The drink was obviously making him looser with words. Perhaps looser with thoughts as well.

Worth's laughter cracked off the wooden beams on the tavern's ceiling. "I'd pay to see *that*. An earl dressed up like a common man to find *true love*. Has a certain poetic ring to it, don't it?"

Clayton laughed too and shook his head, while Bell's shrewd, narrowed-eyed stare intensified. "It's not a *completely* outlandish idea." He tilted his head to the side.

"What's not?" Lucas had nearly forgotten what he'd said.

"The idea of pretending you're a commoner to find a wife," Bell replied.

Worth slapped Bell on the back. "Are you mad, man? You're not even *drinking*."

Bell never drank. His mug probably contained rice milk or something equally unexciting. He preferred to remain in control of his faculties, and they all knew it. He'd always been the one to ensure they all made it home safely and without unnecessary run-ins with the foot patrol or the chancellors at Oxford. The marquess leaned forward to stare directly at Lucas. "Given the right circumstances, it could work, you know?"

"Pretending I'm common?" Lucas replied, blinking. "I don't see how."

"Everyone in the *ton* knows him," Clayton pointed out. "How would he ever manage it?"

"Are you suggesting he wear a mask or alter his appearance?" Worth asked, stroking his chin, his own eyes narrowing as if he, too, were taking the idea seriously.

Lucas glanced back and forth between Worth and Bell. "You cannot be serious, either of you. Clayton's right. How would it ever work?"

"No, not a costume." Bell addressed his remarks to Worth. "I was thinking something more like the right...situation."

"Such as?" Worth replied, drawing out both words. He also leaned forward.

"You two are frightening me, you know?" Lucas replied. "You seem as if you're actually trying to plot out a way this ludicrous idea might work."

"Like a...house party," Bell replied to Worth, stroking his chin and completely ignoring Lucas's concern.

Worth inclined his head, his eyes still narrowed. "A house party, yes. I see what you mean."

"But it couldn't be just *any* house party, of course," Bell continued. "It would have to be one given by someone who was in on the experiment."

"Experiment?" Clayton perked up. "There are few things I enjoy more than an experiment, and I just so happen to be about to send the invitations to my annual country house party." Clayton's words were stated casually as if he hadn't just added a large helping of kindling to the fire that was already burning brightly with insanity.

"Experiment?" Lucas repeated numbly, blinking.

Bell snapped his fingers. "Your house party would be perfect, Clayton."

"Wait. Wait. Wait. Wait. Wait." Lucas, who sat between Bell and Worth, pushed against each of his friends' shoulders with both hands. He needed to sober up quickly. His friends had clearly lost their minds, even Bell, who was normally the level-headed one when things went too far afield. "A house party isn't going to change my identity. Ladies of the *ton* will still know who I am at a house party."

"He makes a good point," Clayton replied, sloshing more ale down his throat. Thank heavens, Clayton wasn't taking this discussion seriously, after all.

"Not if you invite only the debutantes from this Season," Bell replied, a smug smile tugging at the corner of his lips. "And not if you create the right circumstances."

Lucas sucked in a deep breath and pushed his mug out of reach. "The ladies may not know me, but some of their mothers do. More than one of them has already been to court with an older daughter making her debut." There. That was common sense, which this discussion was sorely lacking.

"That's where the right *circumstances* come in," Bell replied, crossing his arms over his chest, the half-smile still riding his lips.

Worth scratched at the dark, day-old stubble on his chin and smiled an even wider, much more charming smile than Bell's. "By God, I think you're onto something."

"I refuse to wear a mask if that's what you're thinking. That's positively medieval," Lucas declared, shaking his head.

"Not a mask," Bell replied. He settled back in his chair and plucked at his lower lip, a gesture he often made when he was plotting something.

"Or a costume, either," Lucas continued. He pushed his mug farther away for good measure. More drinking would only make this particular situation more insane.

"Not a costume...precisely." Bell exchanged a positively roguish grin with Worth.

"By God, I'm going to have the *best* time watching this," Worth added, nodding.

"Watching what?" Clayton's nose was scrunched in confusion. "I don't know what in the devil either of you is talking about any longer."

"I'm talking about Lucas here pretending to be a servant," Bell replied, still grinning like an arse.

Lucas blinked. "A servant?" Of all the things he'd expected his friend to say, those two words had been at the bottom of the list.

"Yes. It's perfect," Worth added, nodding.

Lucas turned to him and stared at the duke as if he'd lost his mind. "Perfect? Me? Being a servant? How is that perfect?"

"That still doesn't fix the problem of the ladies' mothers recognizing him. Even if he's dressed as a servant," Clayton pointed out.

"Ah, but it does," Bell replied. "That's the beauty of it. Most people don't look at servants. They don't pay attention to the majority of things beyond what they need and want. My training as a spy has taught me much about the human failure to notice details. I'd be willing to bet that not one of those ladies of the *ton* will look twice at Kendall if he's dressed as a servant and performing servants' duties. He'll be wearing livery, knee breeches, and a powdered wig, after all."

"And it has the added advantage that a servant will be in a particularly excellent position to discover how a lady truly behaves," Worth added, shoving his long dark hair off his forehead with his fingers. "I'd wager she's at her best when addressing a potential bridegroom and at her worst when addressing a servant. God knows, I've seen it time and again from my mother."

"You're both truly mad, you know that?" Lucas replied. He was becoming genuinely alarmed. Did his friends actually believe this madness would work? They couldn't possibly.

"I dunno," Clayton replied, tugging at his cravat. "But it sounds like quite a lark to me. I'm perfectly willing to offer my upcoming house party as a venue for such an experiment."

"You've gone mad too, then," Lucas declared. Bloody hell. He'd lost his final ally to madness.

"Think about it," Bell said, turning his attention to Lucas. "It has the potential to give you precisely what you want. An unencumbered look at the latest crop of debutantes behaving precisely how they would when they don't know you are watching."

Lucas narrowed his eyes on the marquess. "It's positively alarming that you don't see the problem with this plan."

Bell shrugged. "What problem? The risk is not too great. If anyone recognizes you, we'll simply ask that person to play along. No doubt they'll enjoy the game too."

"What if I find a lady I fancy?" Lucas replied. "Am I supposed to simply rip off my livery and declare myself an earl and expect she'll fall madly in love with me?"

"Not at all," Bell said. "I'm merely suggesting that you get to *know* these young ladies on the basis of how they treat servants. I've no doubt the best-natured ones will be kind and pleasant. Once you have a few candidates, you will know who to court next Season."

Lucas shook his head slowly. He pulled his mug back toward his chest. Perhaps more ale would cause this entire line of reasoning to make more sense. "You're suggesting that

I choose a future bride on the basis of how she treats a footman?"

Bell arched a brow. "How did Lady Emily treat servants?" His words were slow and deliberate.

Lucas clenched his jaw. Damn Bell. The man always knew precisely what to say. Unwanted memories flashed through Lucas's brain. Memories of the beautiful, accomplished Lady Emily snapping at her maid for bringing her lukewarm tea and dismissing a footman for catching the train of her gown in the coach door when he shut it.

"I see by the look on your face that you recognize my point," Bell drawled.

Lucas considered it for a moment. Perhaps it was the four mugs of ale he'd consumed, but suddenly the entire plan was starting to sound…good to him. Not just good, but reasonable and helpful. He'd been trying to think of a way to enter the marriage mart without having to endure the ladies who were only after his money and his title. One encounter with such a woman was enough to last a lifetime. By God, his friend may well have just stumbled upon the perfect plan!

"I'm willing to do it with you," Bell tossed out casually with another shrug.

"What?" Worth's black eyebrows snapped together over his dark-blue eyes. "Why would *you* do it?"

Bell straightened his shoulders and settled back into his chair. "Because I've narrowed down my hunt for the Bidassoa traitor to one of three possibilities."

"The man you've been hunting for the Home Office?" Worth clarified, lowering his voice.

"Precisely the one," Bell replied. "And if Clayton here will invite those three men to the house party, I will also pretend to be a servant to watch them."

Worth tossed back his head and laughed. "I should have known you had another motive all along, Bell. His Majesty's work is never far from your mind. Even when we're drinking."

Bell's grin widened. "Why shouldn't we use the opportunity for two useful pursuits instead of one? I'll admit, I was already thinking about this plan before Lucas informed us of his search for a wife, but if it helps both of us, all the better, I say. We will truly have to behave as servants, however. We'll have to wait on the guests and do all the tasks servants must do."

"Hmm. I do quite like the idea of spying going on under my roof." Clayton took another long draught of ale. "Gives the whole affair a bit of intrigue. And since I haven't been a soldier or served His Majesty otherwise, I feel it's my duty to say yes to this ruse. Not to mention my love of an experiment. Will you do it, Lucas?"

Lucas hefted his mug to his mouth and drained it. Then he wiped the back of his hand across his mouth. "Now that Bell's doing it with me, how can I refuse?"

Worth accepted yet another new mug of ale from the barmaid and flipped a coin into the air for her tip. He gave her an outrageously flirtatious grin before turning his attention back to the conversation. "I, for one, am so interested in seeing such a situation play out, not only will I attend to watch the spectacle, I will also settle a large sum on the outcome as to whether you two can pull this off. Care to bet me?" He gave them both his most competitive stare.

Bell rolled his eyes. "Everything's a bet with you, Worth."

"Perhaps, but you must admit, this is a particularly tempting bet." Worth lifted his chin toward the marquess. "Five hundred pounds say you are both outed by a keen-eyed mama within a sennight."

"I'll take that bet!" Clayton declared, pointing a finger in the air. "You'll be attending as a guest, I presume, Worthington."

Lucas's snort of laughter interrupted Worth's reply. "Of course he's attending as a guest. Our mate Worth here could *never* pass for a footman." He shook his head sympathetically toward the duke. "You couldn't last one night serving others, I'm afraid."

Worth's nostrils flared. He gathered himself up and straightened his shoulders. "I take offense to that. If you two sops can do it, surely I can."

Clayton blew air into his cheeks and shook his head, not quite meeting Worth's gaze. "Hmm. I'm not exactly certain I agree with that, old chap."

Worth crossed his arms over his chest and glared at his friend. "You truly don't think I could do it?"

"No," Clayton admitted, looking slightly sheepish. "Not if you actually have to fill the role of a servant and do real chores. No."

Worth's gaze swung to Bell. "You don't think I can do it either?" He *almost* looked hurt.

Bell shook his head. "Not a chance. Apologies, Your Grace, but you're far too used to being waited upon to wait on anyone else."

"But that's how I know how to do it properly," Worth shot back, a disgruntled expression on his face.

Lucas snorted. "I'm afraid seeing one serve and actually *serving* are two entirely different things."

Worth's eyes widened. "You're a bloody earl for Christ's sake. Why do you think *you* can serve?"

"I may be an earl but I'm no stranger to hard work. I spent years in the Navy doing chores like picking oakum and deworming hardtack. And those two tasks were pleasant compared to some of my other tasks," Lucas replied.

Worth slapped a palm on the tabletop. The mugs bounced. "Fine. One *thousand* pounds says I can make it through the entire fortnight as a servant too. Or at least I can last longer than either of you."

"Now who is being mad?" Clayton asked, waggling his eyebrows at Worth.

"I'm quite serious." Worth's jaw was locked. "One thousand pounds, gentlemen. Who will take the bet?"

"I will," all three called in unison.

CHAPTER ONE

Miss Frances Wharton winced when her mother came hurrying into the breakfast room. Mama had a smile on her face, which meant she'd received what she called "good news," or more correctly, the *opposite* of the news Frances wanted to hear. Frances shut her copy of *The Taming of the Shrew* and pushed it behind a potted flower. Mama was always complaining that she read too much.

"I've just come from Lady Cranberry's house," Mama declared. "She has confirmed that Sir Reginald Francis will be attending the Claytons' country house party next week."

Frances exchanged a look with her younger sister who sat across from her. Abigail was only sixteen years old and had not yet come out, while Frances was eighteen and had just made her debut this Season. Her mother had set her sights on Sir Reginald Francis for her. Frances had no idea why. The man might be a knight, but he was also a loud, pompous ass. Not to mention his surname was Francis. She couldn't imagine a life in which she was named Frances Francis. It presented so many *issues*.

"I'm not feeling particularly well, Mama. I'm not certain I can attend the Claytons' house party." Frances pressed the back of her hand to her forehead in as dramatic a gesture as she could manage. She'd never been much for dramatics, but usually Mama seemed to appreciate them.

"Nonsense," Mama replied, clearly unmoved this time. "You are healthy as a horse, but even if you'd come down with the plague, I'd have the servants carry you to the house party."

Frances gave her mother a side-wise glance paired with a frown.

"I wish *I* could attend," Abigail said with a long, dramatic sigh. She too placed the back of her hand against her forehead. Now, her sister always had a flare for the dramatic. Somehow Abigail's dramatics seemed so much more believable than her own. Frances made a mental note to ask her sister how to be both more dramatic and more believable at it.

"You've yet to make your debut," Mother replied to Abigail.

"I know," Abigail moaned, emphasizing her woe.

Another mental note. Moan more.

"But I would so love to attend a country house party filled with handsome gentlemen," Abigail continued.

"Filled with handsome gentlemen *and* Sir Reginald Francis," Frances mumbled.

Mama shot Frances a look that clearly indicated she did not find her daughter's jest amusing in the least. "I fail to comprehend your objection to Sir Reginald," Mama said, pointing her nose in the air.

Frances crossed her arms over her chest and drummed her fingertips against the opposite elbows. "Let's see. He's twice my age."

"Forty is hardly ancient." Mama's nose remained aloft.

"He's pompous," Frances continued, still drumming her fingers.

Mama waived her handkerchief in the air. "All men with titles are pompous. Your father was when I met him."

"He's entirely uninteresting," Frances continued, scratching her cheek.

"I don't know why you say that. He's perfectly interesting to *me*," Mama insisted.

Frances arched a brow. "He spent the better part of an hour telling me about a game of whist he played four years ago. A hand he lost, by the by. And not a particularly compelling hand."

"Oh, Frances, you're so particular." Mama gave a long-suffering sigh and pressed her handkerchief to her throat. "You must remember." Her voice dropped to a whisper as if they were not alone in their own drawing room, shabby though it might be. "You don't have much of a dowry and while I love you, you're hardly a diamond of the first water."

"Thank you for the encouragement, Mama," Frances replied, stifling her urge to laugh at her mother's egregiousness.

"I'm quite serious," Mama continued, "Sir Reginald has shown *interest*. His may be the best marriage offer you receive."

"If reciting a four-year-old tale about a card game is showing interest, I suppose you're right, Mama, but I already told you, I'm perfectly happy for you to give my dowry to Abigail to ensure *she* makes a good match."

Papa's penchant for gambling paired with his proclivity for losing had caused the family great financial distress of late, but Frances couldn't understand why her mother wouldn't be practical and double Abigail's dowry instead. It only made sense. Apparently, her mother didn't appreciate sense.

Mama waived her handkerchief in the air again. "That is madness."

"It is not," Frances replied. "Abigail is actually *interested* in finding a husband. With both of our dowries together, she might make a decent match. I don't want a husband." They'd had this argument at least a half dozen times, and her mother always dismissed it. It drove Frances mad. Mama had no concept that a young woman might actually sincerely have no desire to marry.

Mama shook her head. "Stop saying such ludicrous things. I would have the doctor pay you a visit if we had the money for such extravagances."

Frances sighed. She would not win this argument. As far as Mama was concerned, making a decent match was the only thing in the world worth thinking about. Sonless, Lady Winfield spent far too much of her time worrying over her two daughters' futures and their choices of husbands. It wasn't news to Frances that she was not exactly the most highly sought-after debutante of the Season. In addition to her father merely being a baron, and her lack of a decent dowry, she'd spent far too much time this past Season sitting with the other wallflowers. When a potential suitor did ask her to dance, she quickly frightened him off by talking at length about her plans to work with the magistrates to convince Parliament to change the poor laws. At present, she had her cap set firmly against the awful Employment Bill that would be up for vote as soon as Parliament reconvened in the autumn.

Frances had been barely more than a decade old when her father had taken her for a walk in Hyde Park and they'd seen a group of poor people protesting outside a politician's house. The small crowd had been angry and sweaty and carrying pitchforks. They were yelling about their treatment under the law. Her father had tried to hurry her past the scene, but she'd insisted upon stopping and listening.

She'd been horrified by what she'd heard. None of the crowd's complaints seemed to be outrageous demands. That day, she'd vowed that when she came of age, she'd do anything and everything she could to help them. As a debutante, she had few opportunities to change policies, but what she did have, upon occasion, was the attention of some of the most influential members of Parliament's House of Lords. During dances at *ton* balls, she'd been known to say things such as, "Did you know, Lord Sharton, that often the poor are forced to pay fines they cannot afford and are thrown back in prison where there is no hope of them ever paying them?" or "Lord Abemarle, are you aware that poor prisoners are tried for their lives with no counsel whatsoever? How can we say we live in a civilized Society when such a thing is true?"

Often her dancing partner would get a look on his face equivalent to a hare caught in a trap and hurry her back to the sidelines the moment the dance was through, never to call upon her again.

Mama had warned Frances countless times to stop being so unpleasant. That was the word she liked to use for Frances's little 'outbursts,' but Frances refused to stop. Searching for a husband held little appeal to her, but while she had the ear of some of the most powerful men in Parliament she might as well make herself useful. She'd continued to be 'unpleasant' throughout the Season until nearly every eligible chap in the *ton* all but ran from her when they saw her coming.

Sir Reginald Francis, it turned out, had been out of the country for most of the Season. He was also wealthy, according to Mama, so wealthy he apparently was willing to overlook her pitiful dowry. That was why Mama held out hope for a match with him and why Mama was so eager to cart her off to Lord Clayton's house party.

"You must promise me you'll be pleasant," Mama continued, wagging a finger at Frances.

"When am I unpleasant?" Frances winked at Abigail behind their mother's back.

"You know I'm referring to your outbursts, dear," Mama replied, dabbing at her forehead with her handkerchief.

Frances shrugged. "I simply don't see why I should be forced to take the first offer I receive."

"The first offer is usually the best offer, dear," Mama said. "Besides, to date you've had *no* offers, so I hardly think it matters in this case. I've heard from several people who know him well that Sir Reginald isn't put off by young ladies who speak up about politics and such." Mama pressed her handkerchief to her lips this time, her eyebrows dipped in worry over her gray eyes. "I can only hope that's true."

Frances frowned. She might believe such a thing was true of Sir Reginald if she hadn't already met him. The auspicious occasion had been last week at the final party of the Season. He'd talked nonstop about himself. Mama had watched her closely during their introductions and had immediately interrupted Frances when she'd attempted to bring up the Employment Bill, that hideous piece of legislation that some equally horrible member of the House of Lords was backing. A Lord Kendall. The votes were close according to Frances's sources, which was mainly the newspaper coupled with her pressing her ear against her father's study door when his friends came to visit and talk about politics. The vote had been put off, however, until the next session of Parliament and Frances had no intention of keeping quiet on the matter whenever she found herself in the company of a peer. And if she ever crossed paths with the hideous Lord Kendall, she fully intended to give him an earful.

"*I* can only hope Sir Reginald doesn't bore me to tears with talk about a faro game from a decade ago," Frances said, sighing.

Mama rolled her eyes. "Regardless, we're leaving for Devon on Friday." She turned toward the door. "I'm off to ask Albina to begin packing the trunks. Prepare yourself, and no talking about politics." Her mother turned back sharply to face her. "Do you understand me, Frances Regina Thurgood Wharton?"

Frances pointed a finger in the air. "The Employment Bill isn't necessarily polit—"

"No talking about bills. Or the poor. Or Employment. Or anything of the sort." Mama huffed.

"Fine." Frances briefly considered crossing her fingers behind her back, but that would be dishonest, and she was honest. Sometimes to a fault. "Very well, I promise not to discuss it. At least not with Sir Reginald."

"Or any eligible gentlemen of the *ton*," Mama finished, arching a disapproving brow at her.

Frances posted her fists on her hips. "Very well. Or any eligible gentlemen of the *ton*," she parroted back.

"Excellent. We might just get you married off yet." Mama smiled, picked up her burgundy silk skirts, and sailed from the room.

The door had barely shut behind their mother when Abigail turned bright blinking gray eyes toward Frances and asked quite seriously, "What are you planning to do, Frannie? You weren't crossing your fingers, I saw you. Oh, were you crossing your toes?"

Frances couldn't help her grin. Her sister knew her well. She'd loved Abigail since she'd been a two-year old peering into Abby's basinet. Frances felt responsible for her and she was entirely serious when she'd told her mother she would like nothing better than to give up her dowry to make

23

Abigail's more substantial. She would do anything for her little sister. "I might have crossed my toes if I'd thought about it," she jested. "But I promised Mama I wouldn't talk about any of the causes dear to my heart and so I won't."

Abigail leaned forward and peered at her. "What *shall* you do?"

Frances shrugged. "I have little choice. I suppose I'll have to dissuade Sir Reginald from wanting to offer for me some other way."

Abigail's eyes were wide orbs. "How do you intend to do that?" Her sister had never defied their parents in her life, and she seemed perpetually amazed at Frances's penchant for doing so.

Frances scooped up *The Taming of the Shrew* and made her way over to the window. She stared out across the street to the park while hugging the book to her chest, contemplating the matter for a moment. Slowly, her gaze dropped to the book and she held it out in front of her, letting her gaze to trail across the cover. Then she turned back to her sister and allowed a sly grin to spread across her face. The perfect idea had just popped into her mind. "By acting as if I'm the biggest shrew in the land, of course."

CHAPTER TWO

London, early August 1814

"We'll call it The Footmen's Club," Lucas declared. Three days had passed since they'd come up with their drunken idea and none of them had backed down in the harsh light of sobriety. Apparently, they were doing this mad thing and Lucas couldn't say he didn't want to. The idea seemed to make more sense the longer he contemplated it. And he'd even contemplated it with nary a drink in sight.

They'd all arrived at Clayton's town house so that his town servants could teach them the ways of Clayton's household chores. They were just finishing being fitted for their livery, an event that delighted Worth. "It doesn't matter what I'm wearing," the duke said with a charming grin and a wink. "It's all about how you wear it."

"'The Footmen's Club,'" Bell echoed. "I like the sound of that even though I intend to be a valet." Bell didn't need Clayton livery, but he was being fitted just the same in order to have clothing befitting a valet to wear for his interview.

"Who knew that knee breeches and white stockings would look so good on me?" Worth called out, completely ignoring their discussion about the title of their escapade.

"Yes. The Clayton livery is quite distinct," Clayton said. "Black coats, emerald waistcoats, white shirts, white stockings."

"You should pay me more because of my height," Worth added, smoothing his hand down the front of his shirt. "Aren't tall footmen paid more?"

Bell shook his head. "We aren't collecting wages."

"The devil we're not," Worth replied. "If I'm to perform the duties of a servant, I expect a servant's pay."

Clayton threw back his head and laughed. "Not to worry, Worth. You'll get your money. I usually hire extra staff this time of year to help with the house party. Your wages will be waiting for you after you complete your fortnight of work. I daresay you'll need every farthing you can get if you're going to pay each of us one thousand pounds when this is over."

Worth glared at him. "You let me worry about the thousand pounds. Just show me what to do and I'll do it. I intend to be a groomsman, by the by, but I like the sound of 'The Footmen's Club' too."

"Is no one to be a footman with me?" Lucas asked. "I thought we were doing this together."

Bell tugged at his cuff. "I need to be close to the men I'm watching. I intend to see to it that at least one of them is in need of a valet before the party begins."

"What are you going to do to his valet?" Clayton asked, his eyes widening.

Bell shrugged. "Don't worry. Nothing dangerous. Pay off the chap, most likely."

"Being a groomsman isn't going to be as taxing as being a valet," Lucas told Worth. "You didn't tell us you intended to be a groomsman when you made the bet."

"Have a care," Worth replied, looking a bit offended. "I need at least a sporting chance at winning. Besides, I prefer horses to people."

"Not to worry," Clayton assured Lucas. "He'll have to deal with the guests even as a groomsman. We do quite a bit of riding during my house parties."

"See there," Worth replied smugly, straightening his shoulders.

"I still say you won't be able to do it," Bell said as the tailor measured his inseam.

"I'm flattered by your faith in me, Bell," Worth shot back. The tailor's assistant was measuring his shoulders. "No padding," Worth told the man. "I don't need it."

"Very well," Lucas replied. "But I intend to visit the stables from time to time to see how you're getting on."

"Please do," Worth replied.

"I think I have everything I need, my lord." The tailor stood, gathering his scraps of materials and the string he'd used to measure. The assistant fell in line by his side.

"Thank you, Mr. Kirby," Clayton replied. "The butler will see you both out."

The tailors left the room and Clayton rang for Mrs. Cotswold, the housekeeper. The formidable lady arrived within moments. She wore a dark gown that swept the floor, a perfectly starched white apron, and a ring of keys that was attached to her waist by a belt. Clayton had already informed them that Mrs. Cotswold was the housekeeper at his estate. He'd sent for her ahead of the house party to assist his friends.

When the housekeeper entered the room, all three prospective servants stood up straight. They were queued in order of height, in front of her. She walked along the line of them and then turned to face her employer. "I'm not at all certain about this, my lord."

"I understand it's going to be difficult to think of them as servants, Mrs. Cotswold," Clayton began, "but as I've said, I give you and the other servants leave to treat them no differently than one of your own for the next fortnight."

"That's not my concern," the lady replied, her mouth tight. "The fact is, I'm not certain any of them are up to the task. The duties of a servant are many and varied and the hours are long and can be quite taxing."

Clayton pressed his lips together. He looked as if he were struggling to keep from laughing. "I understand perfectly, Mrs. Cotswold. They've all agreed to do the best they can. Haven't you, gentlemen?"

All three dutifully nodded.

Lucas stepped forward. "I'd like to thank you for taking time from your busy schedule to help us, Mrs. Cotswold. I promise to take the instruction quite seriously. I will be as fine a footman as I possibly can."

Mrs. Cotswold inclined her head to him. "Thank you, my lord. I appreciate that."

"And I've already begun my study of the tasks of a valet," Bell said. "I spoke at length with my man over the last few days. He's informed me that watching over the candles is a large part of his work. I never knew."

"The candles are only a portion of it, my lord," Mrs. Cotswold said, shaking her head slowly. She still looked highly dubious.

"I'm ready to learn," Bell replied, bowing to the austere woman.

Mrs. Cotswold turned to Worth next. He looked as if he were trying to squelch a smile. "What about you, Your Grace?" Her brow was arched, and she looked nothing but skeptical.

"All I can say in defense of myself is that I have quite a large sum of money riding on this and I hate to lose bets,"

Worth replied, staring directly over her head toward the mantelpiece.

"You've bet on this?" Mrs. Cotswold asked, her eyebrow inching even higher.

"Yes." Worth remained as still as a statue.

Mrs. Cotswold's shoulders relaxed the slightest bit. "Well, then, why didn't you say so? I've little doubt you'll be the best footman of the lot, Your Grace."

Worth cleared his throat. "Groomsman."

"Oh, so you won't be in the house?" the housekeeper clarified.

"No." Still standing at attention, Worth lifted his chin.

"That's probably for the best," Mrs. Cotswold replied. She turned away from them and all four of the men exchanged laughing glances. None of them dared to utter a sound, however, as the housekeeper turned toward them once more, her hands folded behind her back and said, "We shall begin with the basics."

"Which are?" Lucas asked.

"How to clean silver," Mrs. Cotswold replied, eyeing each of them in turn as if looking for any objections to that particular task.

The three future servants nodded in unison.

"What else?" Bell asked.

"For you?" Mrs. Cotswold replied. "How to welcome guests and valet them properly including how to see to a gentlemen's clothing and boots."

Bell nodded. "Of course."

"And?" Lucas prompted.

"For a footman? How to trim the lamps and properly wait upon the dinner table," Mrs. Cotswold replied.

"I suppose I should just totter off to the mews then," Worth said, already heading for the door.

"Not so quickly, *Rhys*," Mrs. Cotswold said.

Worth froze, a look of utter surprise stalled on his features.

The barest hint of a smile tugged at the corner of the housekeeper's lips. "You *do* realize servants are often called by their Christian names?"

Worth cleared his throat and shook off his astonishment. If a housekeeper calling him by his first name wasn't enough to stop him, apparently her admonishment was. "Of course," he replied, turning back to face her and inclining his head. "But why wouldn't I be trained in the mews?"

"In due time," Mrs. Cotswold replied, "but first there are things you'll need to learn from me."

"Such as?" Worth arched a brow.

"Such as how to put rugs around a lady's legs," the housekeeper replied with nary a pause, "which you may be called upon to do if our guests partake of a ride in a coach."

Worth frowned. "It's August."

Mrs. Cotswold nodded. "Some ladies are quite cold even in August."

"Very well." Worth sighed. "Anything else?"

"Yes. A great many things. Such as…how not to appear as if you're listening to your master's conversations." She gave them all a tight smile. "Shall we begin?"

CHAPTER THREE

Viscount Clayton's Country Estate, Devon, August 1814

Frances stepped out of the carriage at Clayton Manor and breathed a sigh of relief. No one else was in the vicinity. She might be able to make it to her rooms without an uncomfortable encounter with Sir Reginald. Albina, their maid, had already been carted away to join the other lady's maids. Poor Albina was serving as a cook's helper, a housemaid, and a lady's maid at this point. The money to pay for a full staff of servants had long ago been gambled away by Papa.

"Lady Winfield," said Lady Clayton, their beautiful hostess, who stood by the front door to greet them. "I'm so pleased you and your lovely daughter could join us."

Frances smiled at Lady Clayton and executed a short curtsy for the woman. Lady Clayton was young and lovely and seemed very nice. They'd met during the events of the Season and developed an instant liking.

"We're both ever so pleased to be here," Mama replied. "Thank you so much for your kind invitation, Lady Clayton."

"Wasn't Lord Winfield able to make it?" Lady Clayton asked, frowning.

Mama winced. "Uh. He had some business to attend to in London, I'm afraid. But we do hope he'll join us next week."

They hadn't employed a footman in an age. Thankfully two footmen from the Clayton residence were busy pulling the trunks from the top of the carriage, while Frances glanced around nervously. The longer they remained out in the open, the greater the chance Sir Reginald might spot them.

To Frances's immense relief, Lady Clayton soon led them into the manor house's large, gorgeous foyer. It smelled like lemon wax and Frances marveled at how very clean and well-kept everything looked. In addition to being far smaller, Papa's country house was dingy these days, ever since they'd had to dismiss most of the servants and sell the artwork and furniture. But there were plenty of servants here at Clayton Manor, including the two footmen who carried their trunks behind them and the formidable-looking housekeeper who stood near the bannister staring at them. Apparently, she'd returned from depositing Albina in the servants' quarters.

"Mrs. Cotswold will show you to your rooms," Lady Clayton said, gesturing toward the housekeeper.

"Thank you," Mama replied. She made to follow the housekeeper, who had already turned toward the grand sweeping staircase, before turning back to Lady Clayton. "Oh, one more thing. Has Sir Reginald Francis arrived yet?" She made it seem as if it were an afterthought, but Frances knew better.

Frances held her breath while Lady Clayton blinked as if perplexed by the question. The poor woman's brow furrowed next. "Why..." The lady tilted her head to the side thoughtfully. "Why, yes. I do believe Sir Reginald arrived early this morning."

A wide grin spread across Mama's face. "Excellent," she said, eyes sparkling. She gave Frances a knowing grin.

Trying to keep her expression perfectly blank, Frances expelled her breath and lifted her skirts. If Sir Reginald was already here, she'd best ascend to the safety of her bedchamber as quickly as possible.

She darted across the foyer, nearly tackling one of the poor footmen who was headed toward the back of the house with her trunk. No doubt he was on his way to the servant's staircase. "Please," she said in a loud whisper to the man. "Please won't you bring the trunk directly up?" She nodded hastily toward the staircase in the foyer.

The footman's face was obscured by the trunk hoisted on his shoulder, but he quickly turned his frame toward the double-sided staircase and said, "As you wish, my lady."

Frances nearly wept with relief. She was being entirely inappropriate, of course, but at the moment, she couldn't summon a care. She should also wait for her mother and the housekeeper, but instead, she plowed ahead of the footmen. She pointed up the staircase in front of them. "This way?" she asked as if it were a perfectly normal occurrence for a guest to ask for directions from footmen.

"Yes, milady," the footman who carried her trunk replied in a voice that sounded as if he were slightly amused. When Frances reached the first landing, she tried to wait for the footman to join her, but her anxiety got the better of her and she continued on up. The poor man was carrying a fortnight's worth of her clothing and unmentionables on his shoulder, she could hardly blame him for not being as speedy as she was. "I'll just...meet you at the top of the staircase," she blurted, grabbing her skirts and practically running up the final set of stairs. Once she reached the top, she glanced around in a panic. The hall was unconscionably long and filled with what seemed like dozens of closed doors that all looked alike. Terribly inconvenient.

"To the right?" she called in a voice that cracked as the footman steadfastly made his way up the steps behind her. Below Mama was still talking to Lady Clayton. Oh, what was keeping her? No doubt more prying questions about Sir Reginald.

"To the left, Miss," the footman responded. She still couldn't see his face, but Frances was once again aware of a bit of humor in the young man's tone. She did not stop to dwell upon it, however. Instead, she dutifully raced off toward the left. She'd made her way halfway down the hall when she realized that for all she knew, she'd *passed* her room.

"The end of the hall," came the footman's helpful voice. He'd made it to the second floor quite promptly for someone weighed down by such a heavy trunk.

The second footman was having a much worse time of it. He was still struggling up the staircase with Mother's trunk. Frances glanced toward him and winced. Mama did tend to hideously overpack.

Turning back to face the hallway, Frances continued her flight all the way to the end of the space, before stopping to wait for the footman. She had no choice. She had no idea which room was hers. She stood near the window, tapping her foot and biting her lip.

The footman had nearly caught up to her when a door she'd already passed opened and Sir Reginald of all people came out. Frances froze and held her breath as if that simple act alone would keep the man from noticing her should he happen to glance in her direction. Thankfully, he did not. Instead, he turned away from her and made his way toward the staircase. Even with his back toward her, she was certain it was him. She recognized his bald spot and sloping shoulders.

There was no more time to waste. Sir Reginald might turn around at any moment.

"In here?" she called to the footman in a loud whisper. She did not wait for a reply. Instead, she yanked open the very last door and darted inside. If she'd made the wrong choice, the footman would just have to come in and tell her so. A few moments later, the footman pushed open the door and followed her in.

"I'm terribly sorry if I've made a mistake with the room," she said, hurrying over and shutting the door soundly behind him. "It's just that I…" Hmm. What could she possibly tell this poor chap that would make any sense of her odd behavior?

"No mistake," the footman replied, hoisting her trunk off his shoulder and onto the floor near the window. "This is the correct room. You do seem to be in quite a hurry, however."

Frances, who'd been standing with her ear to the door to listen for Sir Reginald's receding footsteps, blinked. First, she had the fleeting thought that the footman's speech sounded quite cultured. Second, had a footman just commented upon her behavior? Well, that was certainly impertinent. Did the lad want a coin or didn't he?

Upon further reflection, however, she supposed she couldn't blame him for acting oddly after the way *she'd* behaved. At any rate, Mama would be here soon, and no doubt would be seriously displeased to find Frances alone in the room with a footman.

She needed to pay the chap and send him on his way. Still listening at the door, her back turned away from the servant, she fumbled for her reticule that dangled from her wrist. The reticule contained a bit of pin money that might tide him over.

She stuck her gloved hand into the small bag until she felt the outline of a coin. She pulled it out to look at it. A half-pound. Good enough. Clutching the coin, she turned to look at the footman who stood not two lengths behind her and... sucked in her breath.

Good heavens. This was no lad, but a full-grown man, and perhaps one of the tallest and certainly most handsome she'd ever seen. He had intelligent dark-green eyes, and a face that looked as if it had been carved into marble. Dark eyebrows, a perfect nose, wide shoulders, and full, masculine lips. Unconsciously, she pulled the coin up to her lips and exhaled, staring at him as if he were a statue come to life. Good heavens. Seems somehow she'd managed to close herself into a bedchamber alone with God's gift to footmen.

CHAPTER FOUR

Lucas narrowed his eyes on the pretty young woman he'd just helped. She was leaning back against the closed bedchamber door, one gloved hand pressed to the wood, the other holding a coin near her rosy lips. Was it his imagination or was she shaking? He'd never seen a young lady in such a hurry before. She'd acted as if the devil had been on her heels. Now she was standing there in quite a state, her bosom heaving with her deep breaths, her skin flushed a lovely shade of pink.

He'd seen her look at him. Twice. Then her eyes became deeply focused. She was staring at him. There was no mistaking it, and the look on her face was utter surprise.

For an awful moment he wondered if she recognized him, but he quickly discarded the notion. He didn't recognize *her*. He was quite certain he would have remembered her if they'd been introduced.

He'd spent the better part of the morning hauling trunks upstairs for a variety of young women and their mamas, but this was the first young woman who'd caught his attention so thoroughly. Not only because she was beautiful—and she truly was, with dark-brown hair, a pert nose and lovely dark eyes that hinted she was up to something— but she'd mostly managed to catch his attention due to her unexpected behavior. She'd certainly been the first young lady to abandon Mrs. Cotswold and her own mother and rush up to her room ahead of him. Not to mention asking him to follow her up the grand staircase. At first, he'd simply guessed she had a desperate need to use the privy, but when Sir Reginald Francis emerged from his room, she'd turned ashen white and leaped into the first bedchamber she'd come across. What precisely was the matter between the young woman and Sir Reginald? Or was she merely painfully shy and doing her best to avoid all other guests? The way she was looking at him, however, made him seriously doubt she was at all shy.

Lucas's suspicions were confirmed when the young woman stepped toward him and said, "Would you mind very much peering out the door and ensuring that a man about five inches shorter than you, with graying hair at the temples, a bald spot, sloping shoulders, and probably a smug look on his face is no longer in the corridor?"

Lucas had to bite his lip to keep from laughing outright. That was a description of Sir Reginald if ever Lucas had heard one. In addition to being unpredictable, this young woman was also humorous. Both of which made her interesting. Interesting and a bit mysterious. But why was she hiding from Sir Reginald? He was hardly worth the intrigue.

Lucas smiled at the irony of his own thought. *He* was hiding from Sir Reginald too. In fact, Lucas had been slightly worried earlier when he'd noticed Sir Reginald's coach pull up. They knew each other from Parliament. One glance and Sir Reginald might recognize him in an instant. Unless, of course, Bell was right, and the upper crust rarely noticed servants.

Regardless, Lucas had made a mental note to ask Clayton why the devil he'd invited the knight to the house party. Clayton had been under strict orders to keep the guest list to a minimum to reduce the risk of recognition.

There would be time to discuss Sir Reginald with Clayton later, however. At the moment, Lucas fully intended to humor this poor young lady. If she needed a confirmation that Sir Reginald was no longer in the corridor, Lucas would be happy to provide her with one. Of course, Mrs. Cotswold hadn't taught him anything about the propriety of peering after guests in the corridor, but he was already quite certain he shouldn't be alone in a guest room with a young lady, so what did a bit of peering matter?

He moved closer to the door and the young woman hurriedly stepped aside, but not before he caught a whiff of her perfume. A light and airy flowery scent that made his head reel.

"Pardon me," he said, clearing his throat again. Why did this young woman's presence make his throat tight?

Her lips rounded into a small O and she stepped farther sidewise from the door. "My apologies." She glanced away, blushing slightly.

He'd made her blush? That was adorable. Lucas stepped forward, turned the handle, and opened the door a crack. He peeked out into the corridor. James, the other footman, who was carrying the mother's trunk, was entering the bedchamber next door. Otherwise, the hall was empty. The girl's mother must still be speaking with Thea downstairs. Lucas briefly wondered at a woman who hadn't even seemed to notice that her daughter had run up the stairs and disappeared. The entire situation was quite strange. He felt slightly sorry for the young woman.

Lucas shut the door again and turned back to her. "He looks to be gone," he reported.

The young woman heaved a sigh and leaned back against the wall, letting her head tip toward her right shoulder. A lock of dark hair had escaped her bonnet and it lay on her shawl. He wanted to wrap the lock around his finger, see if it felt as soft as it appeared.

"Oh, I'm so glad. Thank you. Thank you very, very much," she exclaimed.

"Was he...bothering you, my lady?" Lucas couldn't help but ask. Mrs. Cotswold would no doubt disapprove of a footman being so nosy. But *façade* or not, he was still a gentleman and a gentleman always protects a lady. But who was this young lady, and what danger did she face from Sir Reginald of all people? The man could be a pompous ass, but harmless otherwise, as far as Lucas knew. Though the knight had certainly been a thorn in Lucas's side over the summer. Sir Reginald had been teetering between defense of the Employment Bill and rejecting it, which meant Lucas had spent the better part of the last few months trying to convince the knight of the bill's merits.

Normally, Lucas would have been pleased to find one of the men he still needed to convince at the same house party. It would give him more of an opportunity to make his case, but at this particular house party, it would be nothing but embarrassing if Sir Reginald recognized him, which was entirely possible, powdered hair or no. Lucas would definitely have to steer clear of the man.

"He wasn't bothering me...yet," the young woman replied with what looked to be an irrepressible grin. "But that's why I wanted to get away from him so quickly. I'm certain he shall bother me in future."

Lucas was torn between smiling and frowning. This young woman had a fascinating way with words. Everything she said was unexpected. He found himself looking forward to her next sentence. But he didn't like to hear that she predicted trouble from Sir Reginald. Had the knight said or done anything ungentlemanly toward her?

"Would you like me to tell him to stay away from you, my lady?" As soon as the words left his mouth, Lucas realized how impertinent they must sound. As an earl, Lucas had every right to say such a thing, but as a footman...it was another matter entirely. Blast. He wasn't off to the best start at this charade, was he? Not to mention, he could hardly tell Sir Reginald to stay away from her while dressed as a footman. For the first time all morning, Lucas was seriously doubting the intelligence of The Footmen's Club experiment.

The young woman took a step closer to him. She seemed to study his face. "That's very kind of you, Mr. ....?"

"Lucas," he blurted. Damn. Now she'd think that was his surname. What was it about this young woman that had him so flustered? Normally, he was much more self-possessed than he was acting at present.

"Mr. Lucas," she replied, "but I don't think that's necessary. I can handle Sir Reginald on my own. As long as I see him coming first," she added with a whimsical laugh.

"As you wish, my lady," Lucas said. He'd been there long enough. He should leave before her mother arrived and found them in the room together unchaperoned. He cleared his throat and gestured toward the door the young woman was once again blocking.

"Will there be anything else, milady?" he asked in his most obliging tone. Mrs. Cotswold had drilled into him that a proper servant never left a room before asking if there would be anything else.

"Oh, I..." The young lady blushed again, and he found himself wanting to touch her soft-looking skin.

"Well, then, I'll just..." He gestured toward the door.

"Oh, yes, yes, of course." She blushed an even deeper shade of pink. His hand was on the door handle when she said, "Wait, I—"

He turned and knocked her outstretched hand, which apparently had held some sort of a coin because it fell to the wooden floor with a smack.

They both bent to retrieve it at precisely the same moment. He said, "My apologies," while she said, "Oh, dear."

They knocked heads with a hearty *thunk*. He was the first to scoop up the coin while they both profusely apologized to one another as they lifted themselves up, rubbing their skulls. He made to hand back the coin and she pushed his hand away. The warmth of her fingers burned him even through her glove.

"No. No. Keep it. That was meant for you," she said, still blushing profusely.

"I couldn't possibly take it, milady. Not after having nearly knocked you to the floor."

"No, please. You've earned it. Thank you for your discretion about Sir Reginald," she added, with a nod.

"My pleasure, milady." Lucas hated to take her money. He felt like a scoundrel, but the longer he waited, the more chance they would have of being discovered together. Worth's words rang in Lucas's ears. The duke had been all for taking monetary gifts from guests. Worth had said he looked forward to it. In fact, he'd bet the Footmen's Club that he would get more gifts than any of them. That was a bet Lucas and Bell could hardly refuse. Worth was the least likely of any of them to be paid for exemplary service. They'd readily agreed and now it was the thought of the bet that had Lucas sticking the coin in his pocket. That and the fact that were he a real servant, he'd gladly accept the gift. No use appearing unnecessarily suspicious.

"Thank you, milady. I must go." He patted the coin in the pocket of his emerald waistcoat.

"No, thank *you*," she replied. "It's the least I could do."

Lucas pulled open the handle. "Would you do me one favor, my lady?" he asked, knowing he was being wholly inappropriate but unable to stop himself.

She blinked at him. "What favor?"

"Will you tell me your name?"

Her eyes widened with surprise. "My name?"

"Yes, I do hope you don't think it too forward of me." Suddenly, he felt awkward for asking. But his purpose had been twofold. First, he truly wanted to know her name so he could make some discreet inquiries about her and her family. Second, he'd decided that asking an inappropriate question might just be the best way to discover how she truly felt about servants, and thereby gain a glimpse into her character. If she was churlish to servants, he was about to find out.

She pushed the curl off her shoulder and a wide smile appeared on her face. "I suppose it's only fair to tell you my name after you've been so kind to share yours," she replied. "I'm Frances, Frances Wharton."

"Thank you, milady." He bowed. There. Not only had she not been offended by the question, she'd bestowed a gorgeous smile on him. So far at least, Frances Wharton seemed like a nice young lady indeed.

Lucas left the room and pulled the door closed behind him. He hadn't exited a bit too soon, either. James was just coming out of the other bedchamber and Lucas joined him on his way back down the staircase to see to the next coach.

Pulling it from his pocket, he tossed the coin in the air and caught it in his fist. Frances Wharton? She hadn't used the word 'lady,' yet she must be of the Quality or she wouldn't have been invited to the house party. Not to mention she was dressed as a lady, spoke like a lady, and had been treated like a lady by Thea. Interesting, then, that she hadn't included that word when telling him her name. She also hadn't felt it necessary to blurt out her father's name. Wharton? Hmm. Seemed Lucas knew a baron with that surname. A grin spread across his face. Yes, indeed. Frances Wharton might just be one young lady to keep an eye on.

CHAPTER FIVE

That night at the long table in Lord Clayton's elegant dining room, the empty seat to Frances's right caused her no end of worry. Her mother sat on the other side of the void, watching Frances while smiling and nodding like an inhabitant of Bedlam. Mama clearly knew something that pleased her about the seat's future occupant. Which could only mean one thing. Sir Reginald was on the way. The theory stood to reason. He wasn't occupying any of the other seats at the dinner table and Frances's fervent wish that he had taken ill and would not be coming at all was dashed when Lady Clayton said in a loud voice for the entire table to hear, "Sir Reginald should be here any moment."

Frances's heart sank. She had already tried to feign illness before dinner, believing that to be a much better alternative than pretending to be a shrew. Being a shrew would involve theatrics and was certain to be tiring, while feigning illness involved lying in one's bed and reading, and what could be better than that?

Despite Frances's fake coughing, back of her hand to her forehead, and plenty of moan-sighing, her mother would have none of it. Mama had ordered Frances to dress for dinner and prepare to be charming and friendly. Mama had also reminded Frances she was not, under any circumstances, to mention anything about either the Employment Bill or politics of any sort.

Frances had reluctantly allowed poor, beleaguered Albina to help her dress, all the while seriously doubting whether she could be charming *or* friendly, let alone both, particularly if Sir Reginald was her dinner companion. How would she ever pretend to be interested when the man began telling a story about his feet or something equally mind-numbing? Abigail had always been good at listening to other people's boring stories and feigning interest. Frances, however, tended to alternate looks that had been described by her mother as a trapped fox and a sleepy parson. But Frances couldn't help it. Boring stories were boring stories and Sir Reginald Francis had proven himself to be a successive offender.

For the thousandth time, Frances wondered why her mother simply didn't give up on her and save the dowry money for Abigail. Abigail was charming. Abigail was friendly. Abigail was looking forward to marriage and running a household and having a family. Abigail never wanted to discuss politics. Abigail was much more like the other young women at the house party. It was beyond ill luck that Abigail wasn't the elder of the two of them.

Frances glanced around at the other occupants of the dining table. It was mostly comprised of young ladies and their mothers. In fact, now that Frances considered it, the table was noticeably lacking in eligible gentlemen. Not that she minded as far as courtship was concerned, but she suspected the other young ladies had (like Mama) come here hoping to find more eligibles. Frances mentally shrugged. Normally, she'd be interested in talking politics with the eligible gentlemen, but since she'd already promised Mama not to broach the subject, she supposed it didn't matter how many eligibles were here. She seriously doubted the other young women and their mamas felt the same, however.

Frances took another surreptitious glance around the table. There were several lovely young women here. She recognized each one of them. Like her, they were all the outcasts of the Season. The ones who hadn't made matches at least.

With one notable exception.

Lady Julianna Montgomery.

Lady Julianna was the daughter of the Duke of Montlake and the sister of Frances's friend, Mary. Lady Julianna was gorgeous, with blond hair and light-green eyes. She was also tall and thin and proper. In fact, she was so wealthy, popular, and beautiful that the *Times* had followed her debut and subsequent courtships. Abigail and Mama had been positively on tenterhooks reading the stories. Frances remembered bits and pieces of their gossip. Apparently, the year before last, when Lady Julianna had made her debut, there had been rumors that she'd caught the eye of the elusive Duke of Worthington, but no one had truly believed that. Worthington was dashing and exceedingly handsome by all accounts, but he was also an established rake and a notorious gambler. He'd never been one to frequent the events of the *ton*. Still, the rumors had been given some credence. After all, if Worthington *was* planning to finally marry, Julianna Montgomery certainly would be the sort of young woman who could manage to bring him to the altar. Surprisingly, Lady Julianna had remained unattached her entire first Season, but this past Season, she'd made an excellent match. She'd become engaged to the Marquess of Murdoch. The marquess was young, rich, handsome, and the heir to the Duke of Murdoch, his childless uncle.

Frances took a sip of wine and eyed Lady Julianna from behind her glass. The blonde was here at the house party with her mother and younger sister, who'd just made her debut this Season and had yet to secure an engagement. Lady Julianna was everything Frances was not. Regal. Poised. Charming. Gorgeous. How she managed to always keep a serene and inviting look on her face, Frances would never know. No doubt about it, Lady Julianna was a diamond of the first water. Surely her dowry was indecent. And Frances was entirely certain that Lady Julianna never did anything inappropriate such as bringing up politics to potential suitors. No wonder the Marquess of Murdoch had come calling.

When Lady Julianna suddenly turned and met Frances's gaze, Frances nearly dropped her wine glass. She quickly looked away. Perfect. Now she'd been caught staring at Lady Julianna Montgomery. What more rude behavior could she display this evening? She glanced at the clock that rested on the mantelpiece in the center of the long room. That clock had to be the slowest contraption in history. She sighed under her breath. She'd be forced to sit here for at least two more hours, if not three. These sorts of formal affairs were ever so lengthy and tedious. Especially when the talk was as trivial as it was at present. Mama was chatting with the woman on the other side of her about Sir Reginald's imminent arrival. Frances was already bored, and the knight hadn't even made his appearance.

The only thing that was keeping the evening from being completely wasted was the fact that the extremely handsome footman who'd helped with the trunks and asked for her name this morning was serving the table. Frances had been unable to keep her gaze from him all evening. Was it her imagination or had he just glanced at her? Lucas was his name. Mr. Lucas. He'd been awfully kind to her. He'd even tried to give her back her coin. She'd never known a servant to do such a thing. She'd also never known a servant to be as handsome and well-built as he was. In addition to being tall, his broad shoulders filled out the black jacket he was wearing perfectly, not to mention his—Good heavens, her cheeks were heating. Mama would have a conniption if she knew the impure thoughts Frances was having about a footman. She hid her smile behind her napkin and tried not to glance at Mr. Lucas. Much.

Moments later, Sir Reginald came hurrying into the dining room. "I'm *awfully* sorry to be late, my lady," he said to their hostess, "but I received a letter from the *Prince Regent*, and well, one does not wait to read a letter from Georgie." He pretended as if he only meant Lady Clayton to hear, but his words had been loud enough to reach the entire dining room.

Frances couldn't help it. She glanced at Mr. Lucas. Had he just rolled his eyes? That was interesting. She took another sip from her wine glass to keep from smiling again.

Sir Reginald soon located the empty chair to Frances's right and proceeded to seat himself. He was just about to open his mouth to speak when Mama leaned across Frances to say, "My dear Sir Reginald, you must tell us what the *Prince Regent* said in his letter."

Frances didn't miss that Mama had also emphasized the words *Prince Regent* and nearly toppled out of her chair in her attempt to garner Sir Reginald's attention.

A self-satisfied smirk popped to the knight's thin lips as Mr. Lucas settled a napkin on his lap. Sir Reginald didn't spare the footman so much as a glance, Frances noted with some distaste.

Sir Reginald cleared his throat. "Why, he asked how I'm getting on at the house party and wanted to know if I'd like to come to dinner at *Carlton House* upon my return," Sir Reginald announced, his voice raised again for the entire table to hear.

"Did you hear that, Frances?" Mama asked nodding more. "Sir Reginald has been invited to *Carlton House.*"

Frances did her best to smile and nod also, but she was certain both looked pained and awkward. Why did they keep emphasizing the words Prince Regent and Carlton House? Frances had never given a fig about the prince and wasn't about to start now. The man was almost always on the wrong side of every political issue she'd ever taken an interest in.

"I intend to write back and invite him here, with Lady Clayton's blessing, of course." Sir Reginald smiled and nodded toward Lady Clayton who raised her wine glass and inclined her head and said, "Of course, Sir Reginald. Of course."

Mama nearly squealed. She pressed one hand to her chest. "The Regent! Coming here! Why, just think of it, Frances."

A great deal of talking and excitement bubbled throughout the room at the news that the Prince Regent would be invited to join them. Frances glanced at Mr. Lucas who had pursed his lips and raised his brows in the semblance of being mock-excited about the news too. She smothered her laugh behind her napkin again just before Sir Reginald turned to her and said, "My dear Miss Wharton, it's lovely to see you again. I still recall our fascinating discussion of whist the last time we spoke."

"I recall it, too," Frances managed to croak, while Mama smiled approvingly. Frances glanced at Mr. Lucas when she said it and was convinced she saw the hint of a smile hovering at his firm lips. Goodness, that man was handsome. Was it hot in the dining room of a sudden?

"Yes," Mama added, "Frances has mentioned your fascinating conversation about whist more than once." Mama leaned so far over toward Sir Reginald, that Frances had to grab her wine glass to keep it from toppling and lean so far back in her chair as to risk falling out of it. In fact, as the chair tipped back, Mr. Lucas appeared to right it for her.

"Be careful, Frances," Mama whispered under her breath, a false smile still plastered to her face for Sir Reginald's sake.

Frances shot Mr. Lucas a thankful look and lifted her wine glass to her lips again. She was quite certain Mama might smile herself into insanity if she kept it up at this rate.

When Frances resumed listening to the conversation, Sir Reginald was still talking about whist. Frances watched the knight from the corners of her eyes. Did he truly believe his whist story had been fascinating? From the wide smile on his face, he looked as if he believed Mama. Frances fought the urge to shake her head. Some people were far too quick to believe flattery.

Moments later, Frances found herself looking around the room to catch Mr. Lucas's gaze again, but apparently he had left. He was probably on his way to the kitchens to retrieve the next course. Frances had the strangest feeling of being left alone. She glanced around the table again. When her gaze fell on Lady Julianna, the woman gave her an encouraging smile. Frances returned the smile just before Sir Reginald cleared his throat again.

"I hope you don't think it too forward of me to say, Miss Wharton, but I've had my eye out for you all afternoon," the knight announced.

"Have you?" Frances drawled, clutching her wine glass as if it might somehow save her from the conversation. "I'm sorry to hear that."

She earned a scowl from her mother for that pronouncement.

Her words didn't appear to affect the knight in the least,

however. He kept talking as if he hadn't even heard her. "Yes, but when my man arrived from London with the mail and there was a letter from the *prince, well,* ..." Sir Reginald let the sentence die away.

Reading the letter was more important than looking for me, Frances mentally finished for him, biting her lip to keep from smiling. She wished Mr. Lucas had been in the room to hear this last bit. Sir Reginald could be quite entertaining if one had enough wine and the correct perspective.

"Oh, do tell more about the *prince's* letter," Mama encouraged Sir Reginald. She looked as if she was about to shred her napkin with excitement. Frances continued to clutch at her wine glass as if it were the last connection to sanity.

"Of course there was quite a bit more in the *prince's* letter," Sir Reginald continued obligingly, "but one doesn't become a confidante to the *prince* by telling his secrets." The man dabbed at his lips with his napkin while giving Frances a knowing look.

Frances glanced away in misery. She searched the room. There were four footmen in total waiting on the dining table and two of them had been busy removing the soup bowls while Mr. Lucas and the fourth man had left the room. The two of them soon returned carrying a large silver platter upon which sat a roasted goose. They laid the platter on an empty sideboard and began helping the other two footmen lay out plates. Frances had never paid much attention to the comings and goings of servants at meals such as this one, but tonight she found herself watching Mr. Lucas's every move. Soon after he finished with the plates, he was busy going from person to person offering slices of roasted goose, while two of his cohorts carried the platter. She watched his progress, as a funny feeling roiled in her belly the closer he came to her.

"Milady?" he asked, bowing when he finally reached her seat. "Roast goose?"

"Yes, please," she responded, not looking at him, and desperately hoping that neither Mama nor Mr. Lucas himself could tell she was blushing. Drat. She'd never blushed over being offered roast goose before. *She* was the goose.

She was served quickly and efficiently before Mr. Lucas and the platter moved on to Sir Reginald while Mama asked, "Sir Reginald, how often do you dine with the *prince?*" Mama's eyes were sparkling in a way that made Frances worry. It was official. Mama's interest in the knight's friendship with the prince bordered upon obsession.

"Oh, quite a bit, I'd say," Sir Reginald replied, another smirk on his face.

Frances glanced at Mr. Lucas, who arched a brow this time. He obviously doubted Sir Reginald's lofty pronouncement. Frances fumbled to get her napkin to her lips before she laughed out loud.

"Does the prince enjoy whist?" she finally managed to ask Sir Reginald.

The knight's eyes widened. Frances wasn't certain if he was pleased that she'd asked him a question or pleased that he had more opportunity to talk. Both, perhaps? "He does indeed, my lady."

For the next three quarters of an hour Frances sat listening to Sir Reginald and her mother carry on a lengthy conversation about the Prince Regent's card-playing habits, while she sipped her wine and used her fork to poke at her goose.

When Sir Reginald launched into a story that seemed to miss no detail about his travels to Clayton Manor, replete with an exhaustive description of each time they stopped to change horses, how his back ached whenever he emerged from the coach, and (perhaps most fascinating) how much mud appeared to be clogging up the roadways of late, Frances decided she could take no more. She might not have succeeded in feigning illness, but nothing was stopping her from feigning shrewishness. She'd no sooner decided to make a scene that would (hopefully) horrify Sir Reginald and (mercifully) give her an excuse to leave the dining room, then she looked up to see Mr. Lucas pouring more wine in her glass.

There it was. The perfect opportunity. One didn't look a gift horse in the mouth.

She glanced at Mr. Lucas and winked, hoping against hope the looks they'd seemed to exchange all night weren't merely in her imagination. She'd sorely regret it if Mr. Lucas misunderstood, but she'd be certain to apologize to him later regardless.

She bumped Mr. Lucas's arm, causing the wine to spill on both the tablecloth and her skirts and immediately leaped to her feet. She frantically swiped at her stained gown with her napkin. "Clumsy oaf!" she called in the most entitled, shrill tone she could muster. "Look at my skirts. They're ruined!"

Mr. Lucas turned his body away from the table so that only she could see him. For a horrible moment she thought she'd been completely wrong and he didn't understand that she'd done this on purpose.

He bowed to her, the light in his eyes signaling that he was in on the ruse. "Sincere apologies, my lady. I'll fetch something to clean the gown immediately."

"No need," she replied, still feigning a shrill tone. "The gown is ruined. I'll just retire to my room and let my maid see to it."

Mama, who'd barely had enough time to comprehend what had happened, turned as red as an apple. "Frances, what in heaven's name has got into you? Lower your voice." Mama was intently watching Sir Reginald for his reaction to the scene, a fake smile pinned to her face.

Lady Clayton stood and came sailing over. That lovely lady apologized quietly and escorted both Frances and Mr. Lucas quickly from the dining room. Frances had barely taken two steps toward the door when she heard Sir Reginald say to Mama, "I like a woman with spirit. And that footman *was* a clumsy oaf."

Confound it. Was she actually *attracting* the ass with this behavior?

As soon as they reached the corridor Frances turned to apologize to Mr. Lucas, but Lady Clayton had already ordered him to return to the servants' hall in the basement and remain there for the rest of the evening. Oh, dear. Frances had no way of knowing for certain if he realized she'd done it all on purpose. She would have to go looking for him later.

CHAPTER SIX

Frances *Wharton*, Lucas thought two hours later as he stood leaning a shoulder against a wall down in the servant's hall. Thankfully, no one had seemed to recognize him before Thea had removed him from the dining room earlier. He'd turned his back upon the table immediately and Thea had quickly carted him away, along with Miss Wharton.

He'd stayed downstairs to watch the butler complete his duties and to ask some questions about tomorrow's plans. He'd learned quite a bit about life in service since he'd come here, and to his delight most of Clayton's servants seemed pleased to teach him. Probably on Mrs. Cotswold's orders, but still, he appreciated their help and their not acting put out by his presence. Of course, a few of them kept forgetting they weren't supposed to call him "my lord," but he quickly reminded them. His presence in the servants' hall made one of the housemaids blush earlier. He hoped he hadn't embarrassed the poor girl too much.

Service was more difficult than Lucas had imagined. He'd spent his evening rushing up and down a great many stairs while balancing elaborate platters full of food. Not only had his physical skills been put to the test, but so had his mental ones as he'd been kept quite busy trying to recall in which direction to serve the soup tureen, on which side of each guest to stand while serving, and precisely how long he should wait at each seat before moving to the next to ensure he wasn't going too slowly. Ensuring he didn't spill any food on the guests or the table was its own feat. He would have made it through the first evening without incident if Miss Wharton hadn't purposely bumped into his arm.

By far his greatest fear of the evening, however, had been that the diners who knew him—and there were a handful— would suddenly look at his face and recognize him. Amazing, really, how correct Bell had been. The marquess had said none of the members of the *ton* would give Lucas a second glance when he was dressed in livery while wearing a powdered wig, and by God, none of them had. Except, that is, for Miss Wharton, who kept glancing at him. He knew she was glancing at him because he kept glancing at her. At first he'd been worried for her when Sir Reginald took the seat next to her. Particularly when the blowhard had begun by announcing to the table that he was friendly with the Prince Regent. In fact, he'd practically shouted the words "the Prince Regent" so the entire table could hear.

And calling the prince "Georgie"? *That* was enough to make one physically ill. The table's occupants had seemed impressed, however. Especially Lady Winfield. Lucas had no idea why. Carlton House was famous for its lavish dinners, but it was hardly much fun. Why, Lucas usually tried to get out of any invitations to dinners at Carlton House (and he'd received a great many over the years). It was awkward there, in the past due to Mrs. Fitzherbert's presence, and the conversation always revolved entirely around the prince.

Lucas much preferred the company of his friends at the

Curious Goat Inn to the stuffy confines of Carlton House. However, Sir Reginald's friendship with the Regent was one reason Lucas was interested in securing the knight's vote. The man was a cohort of the Prince and the Prince was influential with a score of MPs. If Lucas could manage to sway that loyal group of royalists to his cause, he'd have the vote on the Employment Bill all but guaranteed. Lucas would have to continue to court his favor, though, if he were going to win over Sir Reginald and his cronies.

Yes, tonight Lucas had felt sorry for Frances Wharton. He couldn't help it. He realized why she'd been in such a state trying to hide this morning. She was avoiding Sir Reginald at all costs. The moment the knight sat down, she looked as if she wanted to flee. Lucas had made it his business to hurry over to provide Sir Reginald with his napkin. Any worry about Sir Reginald looking up at him and recognizing him was quickly squelched. The older man didn't so much as spare him a glance. Sir Reginald was much more interested at staring down Miss Wharton's *décolletage*. That had been difficult to watch. He'd wanted to punch the leering knight in the gut.

But being invisible had its benefits. Lucas was beginning to enjoy himself actually. It was as if he had a sort of magic or something. The feeling was both alarming and freeing at the exact same time. It truly perplexed him that not one of the diners (save for Miss Wharton and Thea) had made eye contact with him. On the other hand, he could overhear comments he'd never have a chance to hear as a guest at a dinner table.

He'd also made it his business to closely watch Miss Wharton's interactions with Sir Reginald. Lucas came around often enough with wine refills that he was able to hear some of the mind-numbing conversation Sir Reginald was treating poor Miss Wharton to. Lucas could have sworn

THE FOOTMAN AND I

there was an entire conversation about mud. He and Miss Wharton had shared more than one look, both rolling their eyes over the knight's tales.

At one point in the evening, the pained look on poor Miss Wharton's face made Lucas want to pour the entire tureen of turtle soup in Sir Reginald's lap. But she soon responded with a saucy comment or two that made Lucas smile and her mother blanch. He'd learned more about Frances Wharton tonight. The young lady clearly wasn't one to demur and apparently, she was quite comfortable with speaking her own mind. Lucas would have liked to have heard more of Miss Wharton's witty comments, but too often his duties called him from the room when he and James needed to hurry downstairs to fetch the next course.

Thea had been drinking wine tonight, probably to keep from laughing at him. She'd been simultaneously horrified and delighted by the idea of The Footmen's Club. Clayton had had to talk her into it in the end, but once she'd agreed, she was entirely immersed in the plot and endlessly amused by it. She, too, appeared nonplussed to discover that not one person at the dining table had recognized Lucas. Granted, given their guest list, there were only a handful of people present who had met him before, and that ass Sir Reginald was the surest choice, but he was so busy talking about himself and his closeness to the prince, he hadn't glanced at the servants at all.

Clayton had sat at the other end of the table, dutifully ignoring Lucas. In fact, Clayton had done such a good job of ignoring him it was almost odd. When Lucas finally got to him to serve the goose, Clayton waved him away. He'd have to have a talk with him about not acting too obvious.

Lucas had frozen after Miss Wharton had used him to spill wine on her gown. Would that be the way everyone recognized him? Her calling him out for being a "clumsy oaf"? The hint of a smile played around the corners of his mouth. She wasn't a terribly good actress, poor woman. She'd delivered her lines far too formally. But it had been a good enough show to fool Sir Reginald, and clearly removing herself from the knight's presence had been her goal.

Thea and Clayton had been in stitches when they'd come downstairs an hour after the dinner party had ended. They pretended as if they needed to have a word with Lucas for his clumsy behavior. He'd good-naturedly taken the ribbing from the other servants too. They'd all told him it was a rare servant who didn't make some sort of mistake and it was just too bad that he'd managed to spill wine on the biggest termagant at the party. Of course, Lucas wasn't about to give Miss Wharton's secret away and tell them all she'd only been pretending to be angry. It wasn't his secret to tell.

But the fear of being caught pretending to be a footman had been real. Once he'd been safely belowstairs, he'd had the thought for the hundredth time since he'd come here: perhaps he was going about this entire wife-finding business the wrong way. Perhaps he needed to throw himself on his mother and sister's mercy and have them pick out a bride for him. They'd offered often enough. He'd been reluctant to take them up on their offers because he knew his mother would pick a girl with a large dowry from the best family without a thought to how the girl regarded him or how he thought of her. His sister would merely pick out one of her friends, which might work better than his mother's method, but certainly had its own drawbacks. Surely there were better ways to find a wife than this. But he couldn't deny that his visit here hadn't been in vain.

He'd spent some time tonight while serving dinner glancing over the other prospects, but his gaze kept returning to Miss Wharton. She was the one who captured his attention, whether it was the look on her face that indicated she was fantasizing about clouting Sir Reginald over the head with the soup tureen, or replying to the knight's boring comments with clever ones the man didn't seem to understand.

"I heard ye had some excitement up in the dining room tonight," Mrs. Claxton, the cook, said as she came out of the kitchens for the night, wiping her hands on her apron.

Lucas bit his lip and tilted his head. He knew perfectly well that servants were not supposed to gossip about their employers and their employers' guests. He also knew perfectly well that nearly all servants did gossip about their employers and their employers' guests. It made him feel a part of the club, the real club of servants, to be trusted by Mrs. Claxton with such a statement. If she thought he would tell Clayton or even Mrs. Cotswold that she'd been gossiping, she never would have said such a thing to Lucas.

"Indeed, I did," Lucas replied, pulling away from the wall and walking with Mrs. Claxton toward the servants' staircase that led up to the sleeping quarters. He would spend his night in a small room on the men's side of the fourth floor. He'd insisted on being a servant in every way possible. Bell would be up there too. Worth, however, was sleeping above the stables with the other groomsmen and stablehands.

"Turns out I'm a 'clumsy oaf,'" Lucas continued, grinning at the cook.

"I'd have liked ta have seen it," Mrs. Claxton said, shaking her head. "And I'd like even more ta see what that gel would say if she ken who ye really was."

Lucas gave Mrs. Claxton a warning look.

"I know. I know. It won't be coming from my mouth. But I can't help wishin'," Mrs. Claxton finished, chuckling.

They were just about to climb the stairs when a bundle of green satin came hurtling down toward them. Lucas had to grab the young woman wearing the satin about the waist to keep her from falling face-first onto the cobblestone floor.

When he'd finally stood her up and ensured she was steady on her feet, he realized he'd just caught Miss Wharton.

"Oh, dear," she said, a blush quickly traveling from her chest to her hairline. "I'm terribly sorry. I wanted to make it down here before you all had gone to bed."

Mrs. Claxton and Lucas just stared at her. A small group of the other servants who were also done with their duties were gathering behind them, staring at Miss Wharton as if a unicorn had just emerged in their midst.

"Can we help ye, milady?" Mrs. Claxton asked, her brow wrinkled. "Would ye like somethin' ta eat? I can send up a maid—"

"Oh, no, no, no," Miss Wharton said, pressing a hand to her collar bone. "Nothing like that. I just wanted to see Mr. Humbolt, the butler, and the footmen who were serving in the dining room this evening."

Lucas glanced at her warily. He'd assumed she'd knocked his hand causing him to spill on purpose, but he may have been entirely mistaken. Was she here to call him another name? Or worse. Had she somehow discovered who he was and come to demand an answer for his charade?

Mr. Humbolt cleared his throat and stepped forward from the back of the small crowd while James and the other two footmen stepped forward as well. Because Lucas was already standing next to her, he merely bowed. Bowed, and hoped that no matter what Miss Wharton said, none of the servants mentioned that he was an earl. They'd all been carefully instructed not to speak of it in front of anyone, least of all the debutantes, but the nagging fear was still there in the back of Lucas's mind as he said, "At your service, milady."

She blinked at him as if she hadn't yet recognized him

standing there. "Oh, my. It's you." Her mouth formed a small, surprised O.

"It's me," he echoed, letting the brief shadow of a smile cross his lips. He had to admit he was intrigued again. What was she doing down here at this time of night?

She nodded vigorously and looked at Lucas, James, the other two footmen, and Mr. Humbolt in turn. "Please accept my apology," she said, "for my behavior in the dining room earlier this evening. I had quite a good reason to act that way, but I certainly didn't mean to be rude to any of you."

"Think nothing of it, my lady," Mr. Humbolt quickly responded.

Lucas took his cue from James who merely nodded and bowed to Miss Wharton.

"Yes, well, er, thank you." Her gloved hands were folded in front of her and she was pulling at her fingers nervously. She turned to Lucas. "And I owe you a special apology for calling you a 'clumsy oaf,' Mr. Lucas. Of course, you are neither clumsy, nor an oaf."

"I'm not certain you know me well enough to judge that accurately, my lady," he replied with a grin.

A hush fell over the servants who'd all just seemingly witnessed a footman say something quite impertinent to a houseguest. They all seemed to hold their collective breaths until Miss Wharton smiled, laughed, and said, "Be that as it may, Mr. Lucas, I greatly appreciate your service at table this evening and I do hope I did not cause you any trouble with Lord Clayton."

"None he can't handle," Mr. Humbolt replied, a twinkle in his blue eyes.

Miss Wharton nodded. "Well, then, I had better get back upstairs," she finally said as the entire group of servants continued to stare. "Again, I'm awfully sorry for the way I behaved."

She lifted her skirts, turned, and was gone nearly as quickly as she came. Lucas stared after her scratching his chin. *That* was interesting.

"Well," Mrs. Claxton said, her hands on her hips. "If that ain't a first. Ain't never seen a lady come down here ta apologize ta a bunch o' servants a'fore."

CHAPTER SEVEN

The next morning, Frances slowly opened one of the large wooden doors that led into Lord Clayton's library. At dinner last night, before Sir Reginald had arrived and bored her into acting like a shrew, Lord Clayton had mentioned he owned a collection of books on the history of law. Frances wanted to know about the poor laws. Had there ever been another bill similar to the currently proposed Employment Bill? Had such a bill been struck down? If so, what argument had been made to convince the House of Lords to vote against it?

She might not be at liberty to discuss the poor bill with any of the noblemen at this particular house party, but she certainly intended to have every bit of knowledge on her side when next she encountered some unsuspecting lord at an event between now and the vote. The delay of the vote until the next session of Parliament gave her more time to bend the ear of every MP she came across. As soon as this blasted house party was over.

"Thank heavens," she breathed to herself, briefly closing her eyes after she peeked in to find the room empty. She slipped inside and quickly shut the door behind her. Hopefully, none of the other guests would come to bother her. She was most likely quite safe from Sir Reginald, she thought with a wry smile, there was little chance of him looking for something to *read*. No doubt he was otherwise occupied with his correspondence with *the Prince Regent*.

She made her way to the center of the enormous two-story room. It was packed with books lining gorgeous oaken shelves from floor to ceiling. There was a fire burning low in a huge fireplace across the room and the dark green velvet curtains had been drawn, letting in the morning sunlight. She breathed in deeply. The familiar scent of paper and ink hit her nostrils. What a lovely, lovely room. She spun around in a circle until she was dizzy.

Libraries had always been her favorite rooms in any house. She'd been without one for some time now since Father had been forced to quietly sell most of his collection to pay his creditors. Lord Clayton's library was a dream come true, however. It had a staircase leading up to a second row of bookshelves that lined the top of the room on three walls. The fourth wall was covered with glass windows from floor to ceiling and looked out over a flowering garden behind the house with a meadow in the distance.

Frances took a few minutes to quietly look around the grand space. Hmm. She bounced the tip of one finger against her chin. The collection was larger than she'd even imagined. She should have asked her host precisely where the *law books* were kept. They could be anywhere.

Why, she might search through these books all day and still not come across the ones she wanted. Perhaps she should go looking for Lord Clayton to ask. Wait. No. That wouldn't work. The male members of the house party had all planned a ride this morning. They weren't home at the moment.

Frances plunked her hands on her hips and looked around, squinting at the farthest reaches of the room. She quickly spotted a group of similar-looking large brown leather volumes taking up an entire set of shelves in the far corner on the ground floor near the windows. The sheer size of the collection and the dimensions of the individual volumes made her think they must be important. She would begin her search there. She dropped her pink shawl on the dark green velvet settee in the center of the room and headed straight for the corner.

She'd barely made it halfway when the door to the library opened. She spun around, squelching the urge to run and hide. She was not a child found in a room she wasn't allowed inside. She was a guest and had as much right to be in this room as anyone else. She could only hope whoever was entering the room was not someone who would want to talk. Talkers could be so tiresome at times. When one was intent upon reading, for instance.

She saw the back of the intruder before she saw his face. When he swiveled around, letting the door shut behind him, she realized why he'd entered backward. Both of his arms were filled with small logs. But she recognized his face immediately. It was her footman!

Well, not precisely *her* footman. The poor man didn't belong to her or anything of the sort, but she'd come to think of Mr. Lucas as someone special since their initial meeting in her bedchamber yesterday morning and her scene in the dining room last night. She was delighted to see him now. Especially since they were alone.

She'd worried all night that perhaps he had been aghast at her behavior in the dining room. She'd been hasty when she'd done it. He might well have got in trouble for spilling wine upon a guest. Hadn't Mr. Humbolt implied that Mr. Lucas had got a scolding from Lord Clayton? Frances intended to find Lady Clayton this afternoon and set the record straight. Last night Frances had hurried downstairs to deliver an apology and had been relieved to see Mr. Lucas.

Well, at first she was embarrassed that he'd had to catch her fall, but then she was relieved. Then, she'd blushed profusely after realizing he'd had his arms around her waist. In fact, she'd replayed the moment in her mind again and again until she'd fallen into exhausted slumber.

For some reason it had been important to her to apologize to him most of all. She could only hope he didn't think *too* badly of her now. But here was an unexpected opportunity to apologize once more...privately.

"My lady," he said as soon as he saw her standing there. "My apologies for the interruption."

"No interruption," she replied. For the second time she realized his speech was cultured. She took a tentative step toward him. "Mr. Lucas? That is your name, isn't it?"

He lowered his gaze to the floor and nodded. "I've come to stoke the fire," he announced, making his way toward the large fireplace with the wood in his arms.

"Of course." She swallowed. "Don't let me keep you."

He continued toward the fireplace and set the logs on the floor next to it.

Frances watched him. The law books could wait. Mr. Lucas was far more interesting at the moment. There was something about him that made him stand out from all the other footmen she'd ever encountered. No, not just footmen, all other *men*. It wasn't just his looks, which were quite extraordinary. It was also the way he carried himself, the twinkle in his eye, as if he knew things he wasn't telling. He seemed a bit irreverent too. She liked that about him. She liked it a great deal.

He took off his jacket and laid it aside. Clad only in his white shirt and emerald waistcoat, he squatted down and began to place the logs on the fire one-by-one. His back was toward her and she stared at him egregiously, completely unable to stop watching the muscles work in his shoulders as he lifted each log.

Oh, dear. What was happening to her? She'd never had such impure thoughts about any man before, let alone a man she barely knew. One she should leave be for half a score of reasons.

Even though she told herself to turn and walk away, she couldn't bring herself to do it. As a result, when he finally stood and turned, she nervously spun in a circle in an effort not to be caught staring. She nearly ran into the desk that she'd quite forgotten was directly behind her. With an *oomph*, she fell back onto the highly polished dark wood floor. She landed on her elbows and her bum; the breath knocked from her chest.

He was at her side in a flash, gently placing his hand on one of her elbows and helping her to stand. His deep voice sounded in her ear. "Are you quite all right, my lady?"

Several silent awkward moments passed before she was able to drag enough air back into her aching lungs to speak. "Ye...Yes, I'm fine," she eventually managed. She pressed a hand to her throat and hoped that her blush didn't make her too awfully red. "I'm more embarrassed than hurt, to be honest." She gave him a tentative smile, which he immediately returned, his white teeth flashing.

She bit her lip and glanced away. "After last night and now this, you must think I'm terribly clumsy." She smoothed a hand down her middle and then righted her skirts.

"Not at all." He let his hands drop away from her and she frowned, continuing to stare at him.

He stood at attention; his brow furrowed. "May I help you with something, my lady?"

Dear heavens. Why did she have to be such a complete

ninny in front of this man? She stared up at him at a loss for words, searching his handsome face as if she needed to memorize it. "No, nothing.... It's just that... It's just that I..." She barely knew what she was trying to say and every second that ticked by made the whole thing that much more uncomfortable. "I wanted to thank you again for helping me yesterday," she finally blurted, "in the bedchamber, I mean, and to apologize again for my atrocious behavior at dinner last night." There. At least she'd managed to apologize again. Even if she'd just made a mess of the words.

His lips quirked. He opened his mouth to say something, but then closed it again promptly.

She narrowed her eyes on him. "What?" She turned her head to the side to watch him from the corners of her eyes. "What were you about to say?"

"Nothing, my lady." He shook his head slightly, still standing at attention.

"No, please say it," she prompted. Oh, dear, perhaps he wasn't telling her because he thought she was silly. She couldn't bear it if he thought she was silly. Anything but that.

"It's not my place to say anything, my lady," he continued. His posture remained rigid as he looked past her head toward the windows. The picture-perfect footman on the job.

Hmm. Obviously, she'd have to do some prodding if she were going to get him to tell her his true thoughts. No doubt he felt as if he couldn't be honest with her because she was a guest. "You're wondering why I caused you to spill the wine on purpose?" she prompted.

He inclined his head to the side. "I have my suspicions."

She eyed him carefully. "Which are?"

He finally met her gaze, but his back remained ramrod straight and his arms remained folded behind his back. He stood with his feet braced apart, almost as if he were standing on the deck of a ship. "My guess is that you were eager to leave the room," he said.

She couldn't help the smile that popped to her lips. "Was I that obvious?"

He inclined his head. "You seem to have quite an aversion to Sir Reginald, my lady."

Frances laughed. She'd never had such a candid and inappropriate conversation with a servant, but for some inexplicable reason it felt as if it was the most normal thing in the world to be standing with this footman in his employer's library discussing why she disliked the suitor her mother had chosen for her. She bit her lip. "I suppose you must think I'm terribly ungrateful."

His chin inched slightly higher. "Why would I think that, my lady?"

She sighed. "Because Sir Reginald is an excellent prospect, or so my mother tells me. I should be flattered that he's paying me attention, instead of fleeing from it."

Mr. Lucas dropped his gaze. The look on his face was no longer one of amusement, it was more like...empathy. "I'm certain that's not for me to say, my lady. But I will say that it seems to me it might not be the best choice to marry a man whose surname is the same as your Christian name."

Frances gasped. "That's precisely what I've been saying," she replied, laughing again, delighted that she'd finally found someone who agreed with her on the topic. "Mama refuses to listen."

"Well, she should listen," he replied. "It seems as if it could cause a variety of problems."

Frances blinked at him as if he couldn't be real. She'd never met a man who thought the way she did. The men she met tended to either say things she heartily disagreed with or things that bored her silly. She honestly couldn't recall talking to a gentleman who'd truly made her *laugh* before.

She'd already laughed multiple times in Mr. Lucas's presence. It felt odd but wonderful.

"I couldn't agree with you more." She gave him a tentative smile. "But even if his name was different, I fear I wouldn't be interested in Sir Reginald."

Mr. Lucas cleared his throat and shifted on his feet. "That's none of my business, my lady. I—"

Oh, dear. Had she made him uncomfortable? She hoped not. She clasped her hands together in front of her and took a deep breath. For some reason it was important to her to make Mr. Lucas understand that she wasn't some spoiled, ungrateful little debutante. "It's not that I think I can do better," she blurted. "I'm certain Sir Reginald will make a fine match. I just...hope it won't be with me."

For the first time, Mr. Lucas let his body relax and he stared at her with a serious look in his eye. "Any gentleman of the *ton* would be lucky to have a lady like you at his side, Miss Wharton."

She gazed at him for a few minutes. Oh, heavens. The man was a dream. What a perfectly lovely thing to say. She wanted to sigh. She wanted to thank him. She wasn't certain either would be appropriate.

She swallowed and straightened her shoulders. "I know it must be difficult for you to appreciate my feelings," she continued, forcing herself to carry on with her explanation. "It's different for my class."

"How so?" He tilted his head to the side. His dark-green eyes seemed to look into her soul.

She splayed her hand in front of herself as if it might help explain. "As a servant, you are allowed to marry as you desire. You don't have to worry about silly things such as dowries and titles and families. It's all quite a lot of nonsense, I assure you."

His brows shot up. Was it her imagination or had the hint of a smile come back to tug at his lips? "Indeed, my lady."

She rubbed a hand across her eyes. Oh, dear. She must sound like the biggest ninny in the world complaining about her privileged life to a man who was in service. What had she been thinking when she said all of that? Clearly, she was an awful, thoughtless person. She wouldn't blame him if Mr. Lucas turned his back and never spoke to her again.

"I'm terribly sorry," she added, casting her gaze to the expensive rug that covered the floor. "I know I must sound daft." She shook her head. "The fact is that my mother's choice of a suitable husband for me and mine are not aligned. Regardless, I'm certain *you* don't wish to hear about it. No doubt you're quite busy today."

Mr. Lucas walked back over to where he'd left his coat. He bent over and scooped it from the floor and, heaven help her, she watched the seat of his breeches the entire way. He turned back to face her. "On the contrary, my lady. I've never seen anyone go to such lengths to avoid another person." He pulled the coat over his broad shoulders. "If you don't mind my asking, why don't you wish to marry Sir Reginald? The gossip in the servant's hall is that he's quite wealthy."

Frances nodded so vigorously a few curls came loose from her chignon. "Oh, he's wealthy," she said with a sigh. "But, unfortunately, I don't love him."

CHAPTER EIGHT

One of the large doors to the library creaked open and Lucas and Frances scattered apart like dice thrown on the deck of a ship. Lady Winfield stepped into the room, scanning the space until her gaze alighted upon her daughter.

"How did I know I would find you here?" she said to Frances, an exasperated tone in her voice.

Lucas turned back toward the fireplace. The older woman may not have recognized him at dinner last night, but he'd met Lady Winfield before, and he didn't dare do anything to call attention to himself. He was already jabbing at the fire with a poker by the time the lady reached her daughter's side.

"Do you need something, Mama?" he heard Frances ask.

"Yes, come with me. The gentlemen will return from their ride soon and we may be able to catch Sir Reginald's attention if we go for a walk through the garden."

Lucas turned his head to see Lady Winfield already marching toward the door, obviously expecting her daughter to fall into step behind her.

"Sounds delightful," Frances said in an exaggerated voice, which indicated it sounded anything but. She glanced back at Lucas who gave her a quick wink.

Frances rolled her eyes and mouthed, "Cannot wait," to Lucas's amusement, before following her mother from the room.

Lucas watched Frances go, blinking as if she were a figment of his imagination. Had he heard her correctly? He could have sworn the lady had mentioned *love*. In fact, it sounded as if she prized it over a marriage of convenience. Truly? Or was she only opposed to the match because she didn't happen to fancy Sir Reginald?

Setting the poker aside, Lucas glanced at the settee near where she'd been standing. A pink shawl lay atop the piece of furniture. He jogged over to it and picked it up carefully, rubbing the fine fabric between his fingers. He lifted it to his nose. It smelled like her. He closed his eyes. He'd been affected by that flowery scent from the first moment he'd been in the bedchamber with her yesterday morning. Peonies.

He'd have to find her and return the shawl. He wasn't certain how or when, but he'd figure out a way. Carrying the shawl back over to the fireplace, he stared into the increasing flames. He'd already decided that he was beginning to like Miss Wharton. She was funny, she was intelligent, and she obviously didn't fancy herself above speaking kindly to servants. She'd apologized to him not once but twice.

For the first time since all this had begun, guilt began to creep into his conscience. If he did come to have feelings for this particular young lady, what would he do? Show up at the events of the *ton* this autumn and introduce himself to her as the Earl of Kendall? That would go over like a rowboat in a hurricane. He could hardly expect that she would fall into his arms. No. She'd be angry with him for lying to her, and she would have every right to be.

The Footmen's Club experiment had already got convoluted. Damn it. Why had he thought this charade was a good idea again? Oh, yes. Ale had been involved. At the moment that's all he remembered.

Somehow in his imagination before he'd come here, he'd seen himself as merely being cleverly disguised as a servant and doing nothing more than observing the young women who were potentially looking for suitors. The plan had never been to *interact* with them and certainly not as much as he already had with Miss Wharton. She was certain to recognize him in future.

Clearly, he had not thought through his strategy well enough. If he had any hope of salvaging the game, he needed to stay away from Miss Wharton. At least far enough away to keep from, say, having another *private conversation* with her. He stared down at the shawl in his hand. He glanced around for a few moments before he strode over to the large desk near the back wall. He opened one of the bottom drawers and laid the shawl inside. *If* Miss Wharton happened to return to the library tomorrow and *if* he saw her again, he would merely return her shawl to her. He would *not* have another long conversation with her. That would only be asking for trouble. The last thing he needed was trouble.

Also on the subject of potential trouble, Lucas had made a decision. He might as well use his time at the house party effectively and find a way to speak privately to Sir Reginald about the Employment Bill. Such a meeting would be no small feat. It would require Lucas to change his appearance and dress as a nobleman. He'd have to remove the livery and the powdered wig, and hopefully find Sir Reginald alone or in the company of only males, so as not to alert the female portion of the guest list to the appearance of the Earl of Kendall. That would only make for awkwardness as the bevy of matrons went about trying to toss their eligible darlings in his path, the avoidance of which had been the entire reason for his charade as a footman in the first place. It would be damned inconvenient to be both the Earl of Kendall and Lucas the footman at the same party, but Lucas refused to squander the opportunity to speak to the knight. He would simply have to work out the details when the time came.

Lucas's thoughts were interrupted when the door to the library opened again and Bell strolled in. Ostensibly, Lucas had come to the library to deliver more logs to the fireplace, but that had mainly been an excuse to be here at this hour to meet his friends. They had all agreed to convene to discuss their first day as servants. Thankfully his friends had been late. Wait. No. Bell was never late. Lucas glanced at the clock that sat on the desk. Bell was precisely on time.

Clayton entered next, directly upon Bell's heels. "Good morning, Lucas," the viscount called in his most jovial tone.

Lucas clicked his heels together just as Mrs. Cotswold had instructed him and promptly bowed. "My lord."

That sent Clayton into a fit of laughter. "Good God, man. You don't need to carry on the charade when it's just us."

"On the contrary," Bell interjected. "It only stands to reason that he would behave as a footman as long as he's in this home. I know from experience it's much less trouble than switching from role to role. That can be confusing and cause mistakes."

"Yes, well, speaking of that—" Lucas began, intent upon telling his friends of his plan to shed his servant's garb and speak to Sir Reginald.

"I heard you nearly got sacked on your first night," Bell interrupted, a slight grin on his lips.

Clayton was smiling too. "Yes, Lucas, we can't very well employ a footman who spills wine on ladies' gowns."

Lucas folded his arms behind his back and braced his feet apart. Very well. He'd been expecting this ribbing all morning. "I suppose I should be grateful that Thea didn't sack me."

Clayton laughed. "Honestly, I cannot believe you lasted an entire evening. I was quite certain Thea would ruin it all at the dinner table last night by bursting out with laughter."

"She did a fine job of acting," Lucas replied. "She even reprimanded me for my behavior." He chuckled.

The three men made their way to a large wooden table and chairs that sat near the wall of windows. They each took a seat. As Lucas took his, he glanced outside to see Frances and her mother poking around the flowers as if they were actually interested in horticulture. Frances looked miserable, while her mother craned her neck, obviously searching for Sir Reginald.

"It seems you both know how *my* evening went, how was yours, Bell?" Lucas asked, doing his best to focus on his friends instead of watching Frances in the gardens.

"A success, I'd say." Bell's sharp ice-blue eyes met his. "I didn't spill anything on Lord Copperpot."

"The man you're valeting?" Lucas asked.

Bell replied with a nod. "So far I believe I've been quite convincing. To all save one person, at least."

"Oh, do tell, who might that be?" Clayton leaned forward and waggled his brows.

"Only the most exasperating lady's maid I've ever come across," Bell replied.

Lucas arched a brow. "A lady's maid, you say?"

"Yes, she's given me no end of hassle," Bell replied, a frown on his face. "She's the most distrustful chit I've ever known—and I'm a spy for Christ's sake."

"Doesn't believe you're a valet, Bell?" Clayton asked, chuckling.

Bell rolled his eyes. "I don't think she believes I'm a male, let alone a valet."

"Well, you can't blame her, can you? It's not as if you aren't playacting," Lucas added.

Bell braced one elbow on the table and frowned. "Be that as it may, I've never known anyone to take such an instant dislike to me."

"Feelings hurt, Bell?" Clayton asked, giving him puppy-dog eyes.

"Hardly," Bell scoffed.

"Is she one of our lot?" Clayton asked next.

"No," Bell replied, "apparently she came with Lady Copperpot. She's the daughter's maid."

Clayton shrugged. "Well, I can't do anything about her behavior then, unless you'd like me to have a word with Lady Copperpot."

"No. Nothing that drastic. She's merely an annoyance. I'm entirely certain I can handle her." Bell shook his head. "Meanwhile, Kendall, how is your wife search progressing? Any prospects yet?"

Lucas opened his mouth to mention Miss Wharton, when Bell continued. "I haven't had time to do much research on any of them, but I do know of *one* young woman whom you should steer well clear of."

"Who's that?" Lucas asked.

"One Miss Frances Wharton."

Lucas snapped shut his mouth. "Why?"

"Isn't she the one who acted like a termagant at dinner last night?" Clayton asked. "A young lady who screams at servants is hardly the type of wife you're looking for, Kendall. Besides I hear her father is destitute. No dowry there."

Lucas cleared his throat and looked toward the door, desperate to change the subject. "What's keeping Worth? Have either of you heard if *he* made it through the night?"

"Oh, you know Worth," Clayton replied. "He's always the last to make an entrance."

As if he'd been summoned by his friends' words, the Duke of Worthington came sauntering into the room. He glanced around to ensure the four of them were alone before saying in a booming voice, "Did someone call for a groomsman?"

"We were just talking about you," Clayton said as Worth joined them at the table.

"Not to worry, gentlemen," Worth replied with a grin. "I'm still in the game. My identity has not yet been revealed." He crossed his arms over his chest and gave them all a smug smile.

Clayton sighed. "Blast. There goes one hundred pounds."

Worth arched a dark brow. "Whatever do you mean?"

Clayton pulled a purse from the inside pocket of his coat, removed a handful of bills, and tossed them toward Bell. "I made a side bet with Bell that you wouldn't last the first night."

"I am hurt by your lack of faith in me," Worth replied, batting his eyelashes dramatically in Clayton's direction. "And thank you, Bell, for believing in me," he said to the marquess, who pocketed the money and bowed his head toward Worth.

"I take it no debutantes have come out to the stables yet then, Worth," Lucas said with a laugh.

"One," Worth answered. The brooding tone of his voice made Lucas glance at him twice.

"Really?" Bell asked, his voice taking on a clearly interested tone. "Who?"

Worth leaned back in his chair, balancing it on two legs,

his arms dangling along his sides. "Oh, only one Lady Julianna Montgomery."

Bell's eyes widened and he whistled. "Lady Julianna Montgomery?" he echoed. "The young lady you jilted two years ago?"

CHAPTER NINE

Frances told herself she wasn't *truly* hoping she'd see Mr. Lucas when she went to the library again the next morning. But she couldn't help the tug of disappointment in her chest when she opened the door and found the room empty. Servants' tasks were scheduled, were they not? Had she been a fool to expect he might return with more wood for the fire again today?

She hurried over to the corner where she suspected the law tomes were housed, intent on seeming as if she was quite busy indeed if Mr. Lucas *did* enter the room. When five entire minutes had passed with no sign of him, she found herself dejectedly staring up at the large volumes, completely unable to remember what she was looking for.

When the door opened a few moments later and Mr. Lucas strode in with his arms full of small pieces of wood, her heart thumped so hard in her chest that it hurt.

She swung around quickly, her rose-colored skirts swishing against her ankles. "Good morning," she called, immediately regretting the loudness of her voice.

Her mother was constantly berating her for being loud,

but Mr. Lucas didn't seem to mind. A wide smile covered his face. His reply was equally exuberant. "I wondered if you would be here again, my lady."

She lifted her skirts and made her way toward him. "Disappointed? Or pleased?" That was an awfully flirtatious thing to say, but she simply couldn't help herself.

"Pleased. Definitely pleased." He inclined his head toward her before continuing his path to the fireplace and setting down the logs.

She joined him there, standing a few paces away, while he removed his coat and tossed the logs onto the fire just as he'd done yesterday. She sighed. She could watch this all day.

"I trust you had a more relaxing dinner last night," Mr. Lucas said without turning to look at her. "I noticed you somehow managed to be seated nowhere near Sir Reginald."

"That was no coincidence," she replied with a laugh. "I had tea with Lady Clayton yesterday afternoon and told her my plight."

"You spoke with Thea...Lady Clayton?" Mr. Lucas cleared his throat.

Frances narrowed her eyes on him. Had he called Lady Clayton by her Christian name? That was odd. "Yes, we had tea and a nice chat. She agreed to seat me elsewhere last night. She sympathizes with me, dear lady. It turns out her father wanted her to marry a man she didn't love either."

Mr. Lucas glanced up at her and nodded. "Yes. If she hadn't broken her leg spying on Lord Clayton's horse, things might have gone quite differently for her."

Frances eyed Mr. Lucas again. That was also odd. How did he know so much about his masters' personal lives? And what was that about spying on a horse?

"Or...uh...so I've heard. In the servants' hall," he finished, returning his attention to the logs and the fireplace.

Oh, that was how. Now it made sense. He'd heard idle

gossip. Stood to reason. Many servants loved to gossip about their employers.

Frances sighed. "Yes, well, Lady Clayton took pity on me and sat me elsewhere last night, but Mama was nearly apoplectic about it so I'm certain she's asked Lady Clayton to rectify the situation this evening. I'm afraid I'll be sitting next to him again. But don't worry, I promise not to cause you to spill wine on me this time."

Mr. Lucas turned his face up to her, an unhappy look upon it. "Would you believe me if I told you I'm disappointed?"

She laughed. "You *want* to spill wine on me, do you?"

Mr. Lucas shrugged. "Makes for a more exciting evening than simply going from person to person asking if they'd like more goose."

Frances laughed again. "I'm not certain which of us has the more tedious evening ahead. Do you know what it's like to make small talk with the most boring group of people?"

Mr. Lucas's crack of laughter shot across the room. "Are they all that bad then?"

"The ones I find myself seated next to, yes. Last night I sat next to Lady Rosalind Cranberry and all she wanted to talk about was the fabric she'd recently purchased for hair bows. Bows. For hair. Can you imagine?"

Mr. Lucas shook his head. "Very well. I admit. That doesn't sound interesting in the least."

"It's not. I assure you." Frances sighed.

"Is there no gentleman here whom you fancy?" he asked next, standing and dusting off his hands.

Frances's cheeks burned. "Well, I—" She couldn't exactly burst out with the word 'you,' no matter how desperately she was thinking it. It was inappropriate for a score of reasons.

Mr. Lucas cleared his throat. "I only mean yesterday you

mentioned love. Does that mean you expect to find love before you marry?"

"If I marry at all," she replied with a wistful sigh. "Yes, I suppose I'm naïve enough to believe that love is an essential part of marriage."

Mr. Lucas scooped up his coat again and pulled it over his shoulders. She was only disappointed that he didn't happen to be facing the opposite direction. The man's backside looked as if it had been carved from stone. "Pardon me, what was that?" Drat. He'd just said something she'd completely missed.

"I said, if you'll pardon my forwardness, my lady, I must say it's rare to hear such a thing from a lady of your...station."

"My station?" she repeated. "You mean you believe all ladies of the Quality are interested in marrying for money or status?"

A funny look covered his face, one that told her that's precisely what he had thought. "My apologies, my lady, I didn't—"

Frances waved away his apology. "It's all right," she said with a smile. "There's no reason whatsoever that you and I shouldn't be honest with one another, Mr. Lucas. For example, I envy you your freedom of choice."

It was his turn to look surprised. "Freedom, my lady?" He crossed his arms over his chest and cocked his head to the side. He looked unbearably handsome that way and whatever soap he used was making her head spin. She wanted to lean up to his neck and sniff him.

"I know it sounds strange," she replied, "but you at least have the freedom to marry. Servants are allowed to marry whomever they choose. Whomever they *love*."

"Ah," he said. She had the fleeting thought there was a bit

of disappointment etched in his handsome features. "I see. You're in love with someone other than Sir Reginald."

She couldn't help her laughter. "No." She shook her head, still smiling. "No, I'm not. But I'm not in love with Sir Reginald." She shrugged. "The truth is I'm not particularly interested in marriage at all."

He blinked. "To anyone?"

"That's right." She pushed one of the errant curls behind her ear.

"What if you fell in love?" Mr. Lucas asked, studying her face intently now.

She laughed at that too. "I suppose you could say I have my doubts that will happen."

He continued to search her face. "Why's that?"

"Well, my mother has trotted me out in front of most of the gentlemen of the *ton* this year and they're all the most boring lot of overbred stuffed shirts you could imagine." She rolled her eyes.

He cocked his head to the other side. There was that irrepressible grin of his again. "All of them?"

"Yes." She waved one hand in the air. "The ones I've met are all self-entitled horses' asses. But that's not the worst part."

His eyes widened and he leaned toward her, clearly interested. "What is the worst part?"

"The worst part is they all act as if I should fall at their feet if they deign to speak to me. It's as if the smallest bit of attention from a gentleman with a title should make me swoon dead away as far as they are all concerned."

He looked as if he were fighting a laugh. "A title doesn't make you swoon?"

She rolled her eyes once more. "Far from it."

"I see. What about footmen?" He winked at her.

Her eyes went wide and she put her fists on her hips. "Why, Mr. Lucas, are you *flirting* with me?"

He took a step closer and looked down at her with those intense green eyes. "Of course not, Miss Wharton. *That* would be inappropriate."

She wanted to fan herself. She wanted to take another step toward him and touch him. She wanted him to...kiss her. She stood there watching him, staring up into his face for what seemed like endless seconds until he stepped back, shook his head as if dispelling the charged air between them and asked, "Does Sir Reginald have nothing that redeems him in your eyes?"

Trying to get her breathing back to rights, she tapped her cheek and thought for a moment. "Not unless I can convince him to reject that hideous Employment Bill."

CHAPTER TEN

Lucas strode out of the library. Blast and damnation. What in the devil's name was happening? Things were not progressing well with Miss Frances Wharton. Not only were his friends set against her, based on what Clayton and Bell had said yesterday, but apparently, she was set against the Employment Bill of all things. Not to mention she'd indicated she wasn't interested in marriage. How had he got himself into this situation?

Lucas had never encountered a young woman of the Quality who wasn't interested in marriage. Perhaps their mothers were *more* interested, but the young ladies all certainly seemed to be as well. Had Lucas actually managed to find a woman who believed in true love but was singularly uninterested in marriage? Would she ever change her mind? Did he want her to? Not to mention, she'd just delivered a diatribe about how singularly uninterested she was in gentlemen of the Quality. He hardly believed he'd win her over by declaring himself an earl in her presence.

And the Employment Bill. How had he managed to find the one female who gave a toss about the bill? And who just so happened to be on the *opposite side* of the matter from him? If he didn't know any better, he'd think his friends were playing a trick on him. Putting the one woman he'd been interested in at the house party up to telling him his brother's bill was 'hideous.' Only it was too ludicrous even for his friends to conceive of. No. Lucas had brought this insanity upon himself the moment he'd agreed to be a part of this charade and he deserved every moment of ridiculousness that ensued.

But the one thing he'd never counted on was the guilt. The guilt that was steadily mounting. Every time he spoke with Miss Wharton, the deeper he sank into his pack of lies. He'd told himself yesterday that he wouldn't speak to her again. He'd promised himself that even if she happened to be in the library again today, he would be polite and proper, return her shawl and leave the room promptly. None of that had happened. Instead, he'd found himself ludicrously pleased to see her again and had quickly struck up yet another lengthy conversation with her. Poorly done of him to say the least.

He'd even managed to forget to return her shawl. Or perhaps he chose not to remember to do it. He was a fool. The proper thing to do, of course, would be to cut off all contact with her immediately and take himself away from this house party. But even as he had the thought he knew he wasn't about to do it, for two reasons; one, he was loath to miss the opportunity to speak to Sir Reginald about the Employment Bill, and two, now he truly wanted to ask Miss Wharton to explain her arguments against it.

Surely Miss Wharton had heard incorrect rumors about the bill. What else could explain her stance against it? Why, the codicils in the bill were meant to *help* people, assist the hardworking gentlemen who had to run large estates and keep the people who worked for them employed. Men like himself and Frances's own father would be forced to turn away new tenants if the bill didn't pass. Who would want that?

Lucas was certain Miss Wharton didn't understand the details. Perhaps after hearing her out, he could explain it to her in a way that would make her see reason. Yes, that's exactly what he would do. Despite his guilt *and* his surety that continuing this charade would end in his own misery, Lucas found himself looking forward to his next meeting with Miss Wharton. It was too late to try to stay away from her. She'd seen him enough and talked to him enough to recognize him in London. He'd just have to bring more logs for the library's fireplace tomorrow morning and see what happened next.

But first he *had* to speak to his friends. He needed their assistance for his meeting with Sir Reginald. Yesterday, they'd been interrupted by a guest who'd entered the library right after Worth had announced that his erstwhile *fiancée* had discovered him in the stables. The four men had been forced to scramble and look as if it was perfectly normal for the host and three random servants to be sitting together in the library. Clayton stood and began issuing orders, while the other three had scattered in opposite directions. Last night, Clayton sent word to change their meeting place to a storage room in the servants' hall belowstairs. There they would have more privacy and less chance of interruption.

Lucas took the servants' stairs down the basement two at a time. He'd spent so long speaking with Miss Wharton this morning that today he was the tardy one. His three friends were already in the small storeroom when he entered.

"Busy with footman duties today, *Lucas*?" Worth asked, arching one dark brow.

Bell stood in the far-right corner facing the others, leaning a shoulder against the wall, his arms crossed over his chest. Worth sat atop a keg on the left wall bouncing one leg, while Clayton stood near the door, his back pressed to the wall. The viscount shut the door as soon as Lucas entered and took a seat at the small table in the center of the room.

"Something like that," Lucas muttered, sliding into a seat across from Clayton.

"Is everyone still a servant as far as the guests know?" Bell asked. "I am."

"I am, too," Lucas replied with a nod, but he refrained from saying more.

"I still am," Worth declared. "With the exception of Lady Julianna, that shrew."

"Yes," Bell said, stepping forward. "What exactly happened there, Worth? You never said."

Worth groaned and rubbed his eyes. "Of all the house parties in all the world, why did Lady Julianna Montgomery have to pick *this* one? And by the way, Clayton, I'm none too pleased with you for inviting her here. If I didn't know better, I'd say you were out to sabotage my odds."

"On the contrary, I had nothing to do with it," Clayton replied, leaning back in his chair. "I asked Thea about it last night. She told me that Lady Julianna's mother and sister were invited, and at the last minute they sent word that Lady Julianna would be accompanying them. It was too late to write and ask them not to. Besides, what excuse could poor Thea have possibly given?"

"Yes, well, she might have let *me* know Julianna was on her way. The chit loves horses. I could have made myself scarce."

"A groomsman making himself scarce in the stables is hardly good form," Clayton replied with a laugh. "Besides, Thea had quite forgotten your history with Lady Julianna, and she hadn't told me the girl was coming. When you mentioned it yesterday it was the first I'd heard of it."

"Regardless," Bell interjected. "Do tell what happened when she saw you, Worth."

"Yes," Lucas added, leaning forward and propping an elbow on the table. "She had to have recognized you."

"Of course she recognized me," Worth declared, pulling up his boot. "The chit isn't blind. Not to mention I'm not exactly someone to forget." He sat back and gave them all a wicked grin.

Bell rolled his eyes. "Go on, what happened?"

Worth's smile didn't diminish. "I managed to convince her to go on a ride with me without sounding the alarm."

"And then what happened?" Lucas asked, turning in his chair to see more of Worth. His memory of Worth's history with Lady Julianna amounted to some gossip in the papers and then Worth saying he'd dodged a bullet. As far as Lucas knew, they'd never actually been *betrothed*.

"Let's just say I managed to convince her to keep her mouth shut," Worth replied, smoothing his hands down both sleeves of his jacket.

"How?" Bell asked, his sharp, narrowed eyes searching Worth's face.

Worth cleared his throat. "My charm?"

Bell arched a brow. "Truly?"

"Very well. I'd rather not say," Worth replied.

"Oh, you can't do that to us, Worth," Lucas said with a groan.

"I can and I will," Worth retorted. "We all spoke about this. One or two people knowing who we are is perfectly acceptable. The *rest* of the party just can't know."

"Agreed," Clayton said with a nod. "As long as Lady Julianna keeps it to herself, I suppose you're still officially in the game."

"Thank you." Worth inclined his head toward their host and gave the other two men a smug smile.

"I can only imagine what you had to do to get her to agree to remain silent," Bell said, whistling. "If memory serves you were *persona non grata* with her the last time you two spoke."

"*Wrote* is more precise," Worth replied, "and no amount of prodding shall make me tell you, though I admire your subtle efforts, Bell. And for the record, the *non grata* was quite mutual. Now, let's speak of more pleasant things, shall we? Any wifely prospects, Kendall?" The duke blinked at Lucas.

Lucas tugged at his cravat and scrunched up his nose. What was there to say? "No," was the first word on his lips. Frances Wharton had certainly intrigued him, but he wasn't prepared to *marry* her at this point and there were definite things about her and her family that made her a poor choice. There was, however, something he did want to discuss with his friends. "I have yet to find my future bride, but I do need your help with something."

"Yes?" Clayton asked, leaning forward.

Lucas cleared his throat. "Since Sir Reginald Francis is here and—"

"Sir Reginald?" Bell interrupted. "I haven't seen him. What's he doing here?"

"That's a question I'd like to know the answer to also." Lucas leaned back in his chair, crossed his arms over his chest, and stared directly at Clayton.

"I couldn't help it," Clayton replied, lifting his chin. "I always invite Sir Reginald. He's thick as thieves with the Prince. I hardly want to get on the bad side of their ilk."

"But you might have warned me before I had to serve him at dinner," Lucas replied.

Worth whistled. "*That* must have been something."

"I admit," Clayton said with a wince, "Thea and I wanted to see if Bell's theory was correct. Would you *truly* be over-looked when dressed as a servant, Kendall? And you were.

Sir Reginald never even glanced at you. By God, it was amazing." Clayton clapped his hand against his knee.

Bell tugged at his sleeve. "I told you so."

"Indeed, you did," Lucas replied. "But what if Sir Reginald *had* looked at me?"

"Then you would have lost the bet the first night, old man," Worth said, hopping off the keg, and slapping Lucas on the back. "That's the entire game."

"I suppose I may have had the chance to talk him out of it like you apparently did with Lady Julianna," Lucas replied.

"A fine attempt," Worth replied, "but I still refuse to tell you what I said to her."

Lucas shrugged.

"So, Sir Reginald is such a blowhard he didn't even notice you serving him dinner, Kendall," Bell continued, shaking his head.

"Didn't even notice him when Kendall spilled wine on his would-be *fiancée*," Clayton added.

"Whose would-be *fiancée*?" Worth asked, his brow furrowing.

"Sir Reginald's," Clayton replied. "Apparently, he's set his sights on Miss Wharton."

"Miss Wharton?" Bell echoed. "The termagant?"

"There's another termagant here?" Worth asked. "I thought Lady Julianna was the only one at this party."

"Miss Wharton isn't a termagant," Lucas blurted. "She was simply trying to dissuade Sir Reginald and I, for one, cannot blame her."

His friends' heads all swiveled to look at him. And from the looks on their faces he might as well have just declared that he was sprouting two heads. It reminded Lucas of the night at the Curious Goat when they'd hatched this insane plot to begin with.

Clayton cleared his throat. "I believe I speak for all of us when I ask, how exactly do you know *that*, Kendall?"

Lucas pressed his lips together while he quickly thought of and discarded several replies. Now he'd gone and done it. There was hardly a graceful way to explain how he happened to know that Miss Wharton had only been pretending to rant at a servant two nights ago at dinner.

"I spoke with the lady, afterward. She...apologized," he offered.

"Apologized?" The look on Clayton's face was that of pure shock. "You mean she sought you out?"

Lucas nodded. "Yes, she came down to the kitchens after dinner and apologized to all of us."

"But how do you know she's trying to dissuade Sir Reginald?" Bell pressed.

Lucas tugged at his neckcloth again. By God, this was becoming more complicated by the moment. "She told me."

"What?" Worth nearly shouted. "The lady actually *told* you she isn't interested in Sir Reginald's suit?"

"That's right," Lucas replied. It was too late now. He'd begun down this road and he needed to see it through.

"But she still thinks you're a footman, correct?" Bell clarified, frowning.

"Correct," Lucas replied.

Clayton shook his head. "Why in the world would she discourage his suit? She's without a dowry and Sir Reginald seems to be the only one interested."

That wasn't something Lucas intended to answer. "Be that as it may, she told me herself."

"When she apologized to you for yelling at you in the dining room?" Bell asked.

Lucas nodded. "That's right."

"I still would like to know how she happened to mention

to a *footman* that she wasn't interested in a gentleman's suit," Worth prodded.

Lucas took a deep breath. Very well. He might as well out with it. "We've become…friendly. I see her in the library in the mornings."

All three men's brows shot straight up.

Worth found his voice first. "A lady being friendly with a footman?" Worth nearly snorted. "Well, isn't that perfect?"

"It's not perfect, it's awful," Lucas mumbled.

"Why? I thought you were looking for a lady who would be nice to servants," Worth continued.

Lucas shook his head. "I was, but now that we've actually spoken a handful of times, how in the world am I ever to meet her as Lord Kendall? She'll recognize me."

"Oh, I see. That does create a problem, doesn't it?" Clayton said, pressing a finger to his top lip.

"I say that is a problem for another day," Bell added, plucking at his bottom lip. "I wouldn't worry about it now, Kendall. These things have their ways of resolving themselves."

"I don't know about that," Lucas replied, "but I do know I'd certainly like to stop discussing it." He pulled off the hot wig and ran a hand through his hair. "Now, can we speak about something else?"

"Yes, what would you like to speak about, Kendall?" Clayton answered gamely.

Lucas settled back into his chair. "I'm going to need your help with something, all of you."

"What's that?" Clayton asked, leaning forward again and looking quite interested.

"I need to speak privately with Sir Reginald and when I do so it has to be as the Earl of Kendall."

Clayton snorted. "So, what, you intend to run back and

forth between rooms pretending to be Lucas the footman in one and Lord Kendall, the earl, in another?"

Lucas scrubbed the back of his hand against his forehead. "Something like that."

"Oh, I cannot wait," Clayton replied, laughing and slapping his hand against the table. "How quickly can you change clothing between courses?"

Worth's crack of laughter bounced off the walls of the small room. "Yes, and remember, the game will be lost if you show up as the Earl of Kendall in your livery."

"Or accidentally pour Sir Reginald's wine when dressed as the earl," Clayton added.

Bell turned to lean his back entirely against the wall and expelled a deep breath. "Oh, Kendall, you *do* know how to complicate things."

CHAPTER ELEVEN

The next morning Frances could barely sit still on the tufted stool in front of the mirrored dressing table in her guest bedchamber. Albina was busy curling her hair with hot tongs. The maid had recently finished applying the slightest hint of rose-colored rouge to Frances's cheeks. She'd also already dabbed her favorite peony-scented perfume behind both ears. The butterflies winging around in her middle made her feel more like she was preparing for a ball than dressing in a simple yellow gown to take a stroll to the library.

But Mr. Lucas would be in the library again today. She was certain of it. Just as certain as she was of the fact that she was looking forward to spending time with him again. It made no sense. It wasn't as if she could have a future with him. Even if she wanted to. Her parents would never allow it. And besides, hadn't she always been the one dead set against marriage? *Not* that she wanted to marry Mr. Lucas. Why, she'd only just met the man. Heavens, no. But he certainly was handsome, and funny, and charming and—

"Ouch!"

"I'm sorry, Miss. It were an accident," Albina said, wincing and scrunching up her nose.

Frances rubbed at her right cheek, the one that Albina had just accidentally glanced with the hot tongs.

Frances met the maid's gaze in the looking glass. Albina's eyes were wide with worry. "Please don't tell yer mum, Miss Frances. She'll be displeased with me, fer certain."

Frances left off rubbing her cheek and gave the maid an encouraging smile. "No, of course I won't tell her, Albina. It's all right. Don't worry."

Albina expelled her breath and her eyes lost their troubled look. She resumed her ministrations on Frances's *coiffure*.

Frances continued to watch the maid in the looking glass. Albina was medium height, with blond hair and sky-blue eyes. She was pretty enough but usually had a vacant expression on her face. She did her work thoroughly and never complained, however, which was why the maid was one of only two servants Frances's family had left. She'd already stepped in to be a lady's maid to all three women in the house and clean and help cook. What more could they ask of her? The poor girl had nothing to worry about from her mother's quarter. They needed her desperately. Hmm. Perhaps Albina was afraid for her job for just that reason. They'd let go of all the rest of the staff except their cook. No doubt Albina thought she could be next on the chopping block.

For the hundredth time in as many days, Frances silently cursed her father. The man couldn't leave a gaming table alone. She'd heard the late night conversations her mother and father had in the bedchamber when their voices were raised. Her mother begged her father to stop gambling, while her father insisted he'd win the next time and all would be put to rights. Her mother was wasting her breath. Father had no intention of stopping. Their lives had changed little by little as they'd sold off household goods and let go of staff. Frances had come to realize that her mother's displeasure and their reduced style of living weren't the only two consequences of her father's choices.

More and more men had begun coming to the door of their London town house at all hours. Mama and Abigail hadn't noticed. The men usually arrived after they'd all retired for the evening, but Frances's bedchamber window was directly above her father's study. She'd been privy to the sound of raised voices and angry-sounding threats on more than one occasion. She'd never mentioned any of the episodes to mother or Abigail. She didn't want to worry them. What sense was there in that? But she guessed Father's situation was even more dire than Mother seemed to believe.

"What do ye plan ta do today, Miss Frances?" Albina asked, shaking her from her thoughts. The maid had finished curling her hair and was busy pinning the curls into place.

Frances sighed and did her best to sound nonchalant. "Oh, I thought I'd go to Lord Clayton's library again today."

Albina shook her head and grimaced as if she smelled curdled milk. "I don't see how ye can stand all that readin'."

Frances chuckled. "Reading is one of my favorite things to do."

"I know, Miss," Albina replied, setting yet another curl with a hairpin. "But it just seems so borin'."

Frances smiled at the maid in the looking glass. "You should try it more, Albina. I'd be happy to work with you on reading just as I've helped you learn to write." In fact, Albina had come to her late last summer and asked Frances to teach her how to write. No one had been more surprised than Frances, but she'd spent three hours a day, morning, noon, and night with the maid and the young woman had made considerable progress quickly. Albina was a quick learner and a diligent student.

Albina kept her gaze focused on her task. "I know. I know, Miss. So ye've said many times. Maybe someday I'll take ye up on it. Fer now, I'll just stick to writin' though."

Frances concentrated on keeping her head steady to make the maid's job easier for her. "How are the other servants treating you, Albina? Downstairs, I mean. Lord Clayton's servants." Frances had to admit, she wondered if Albina knew anything about Mr. Lucas. For instance, did he have a wife? She'd never even contemplated that possibility before this morning.

"It's the regular lot," Albina replied with a sigh. "Can't say they've been particularly nice ta me, but I also can't say they ain't been helpful neither."

Frances nodded. Not exactly useful gossip, but at least her maid was being treated well.

Albina finished with the last pin and pressed her hands against Frances's head to tamp down the entire coiffure. A sly smile crept across the maid's face. "There is one chap, though."

Frances leaned toward the looking glass, suddenly quite interested. "Yes?"

"I must say I've taken a fancy to 'im," Albina said, still smiling.

Frances smiled too. "Really? Albina, I've never heard you say such a thing before."

"He's a right fine sight ta look at, 'e is. Works fer Lord Clayton as a footman."

Frances's stomach dropped. She forced herself to ask the question even though she feared she already knew the answer. "What's his name?"

Albina stepped back, clamping her hands together in

CHAPTER TWELVE

As expected, Lucas found Frances in the library later that morning. She was sitting at the table near the windows with a large book spread out in front of her.

"Good morning, Mr. Lucas," she called, the moment he walked through the door.

"Good morning, my lady," he replied. Blast. He'd meant to bring her shawl. He'd taken it upstairs with him last night, intent upon bringing it with him this morning so he wouldn't forget to give it to her. But he'd been distracted earlier, firing off a note to Sir Reginald, asking the knight to meet him in one of the drawing rooms tomorrow afternoon. He'd sent the note along with one of the other footmen to deliver to Sir Reginald and left Frances's shawl lying on the desk in his bedchamber. Lucas would just have to bring it tomorrow.

He quickly completed his normal chore of loading up the fire before sauntering over to the table where Frances sat. He peered over her shoulder. "What are you reading?"

"Today, it's Shakespeare," she replied, closing the book so he could see the title. "Did you know I got the idea to act like a shrew in front of Sir Reginald by reading Shakespeare?" she finished with a laugh.

"*The Taming of the Shrew?*" he asked, then immediately wanted to kick himself for making a literary reference. Would Frances wonder how a footman knew Shakespeare?

She didn't seem to think anything about it, however, when she replied, "The very one."

He glanced at her. A small red welt had formed on her cheek near her ear. "What happened to you?"

She self-consciously rubbed at the welt. "Oh, it's nothing. A mishap with a curling utensil."

"I see," Lucas replied. "Well, your hair style looks lovely despite the mishap."

She blushed as he lowered himself into the chair next to her and asked, "How was your conversation at dinner last night?"

Just as Frances had predicted, she'd been seated next to Sir Reginald at the dinner table the previous evening. Lucas had heard a great many references to the Prince Regent's future visit coming from the knight's oversized mouth. Otherwise, the meal had been quiet, and yet again, no one had recognized Lucas.

Frances rolled her eyes. "Sir Reginald went on and on about the prince's imminent arrival."

"Yes, I heard the prince is coming on Monday," Lucas replied.

Frances nodded. "Not soon enough for Sir Reginald, I assure you."

Lucas laughed. "Do you expect the dinner conversation to worsen after the prince's arrival?"

She shrugged. "I cannot see how it will improve. As I said, there's nothing more boring than dinner conversation at a *ton* event. Absolutely no one wants to talk about what I want to talk about and the few people who do aren't at this particular party."

Lucas leaned one elbow on the tabletop, eyeing her intently. "What is it that you'd like to talk about, my lady?"

Frances opened her mouth to speak, but quickly shut it.

"What?" he prodded. "You were about to say something. What was it?"

She leaned forward and lowered her voice to a conspiratorial whisper. "May I tell you a secret, Mr. Lucas?"

He nodded. "Of course, but why the secrecy?"

Frances's gaze darted back and forth, and an adorable smile popped to her lips. "Because I'm not supposed to be talking about this at Lord Clayton's house party. I promised my mother."

"Talk about what?" Lucas prodded, on tenterhooks waiting to hear what she said next.

Frances appeared to contemplate the matter for a few more moments before a wide smile spread across her face. "Wait a moment." She blinked several times. "I promised Mama I wouldn't speak about politics or the poor laws to any *gentlemen* at this party. I never promised Mama I wouldn't speak about it with a footman."

"Speak about what with a footman?" Lucas replied, his eyes narrowing.

Her smile widened. "You asked what I liked to talk about, Mr. Lucas. The answer is politics. And I'm perfectly able to keep my promise to my mother and discuss both politics and the bill with you." She clapped her hands together. "Oh, I knew I liked you since the moment you first helped me avoid Sir Reginald," she declared before promptly blushing again.

"Wait. You're interested in politics?" he asked, furrowing his brow.

"Yes, politics, laws. Decisions that are being made that

affect everyone. Things that really matter in this country. Unlike hair bows." She punctuated her speech by pounding one fist atop the table.

He rested his chin on one propped-up hand, fascinated by this discovery about her. He'd never heard her speak so emphatically. "'Things that really matter' such as?" he prompted.

"Such as the Employment Bill for one thing." A frown covered her face.

Lucas's brows shot up. "The Employment Bill?"

"Yes, did you know there is a bill that will be voted on by the House of Lords when they return to Parliament this autumn? A very important law."

Lucas expelled his breath. How much did he dare reveal to her about his knowledge of the law? He chose his words carefully. "I believe you mentioned that before. What do you know about it, Miss Wharton?"

She eyed him up and down, pursing her lips. "Spoken like a true male, Mr. Lucas."

He chuckled. "My apologies, my lady, it's just that I haven't known many women who were interested in such things."

She tucked a curl behind her ear and crossed her arms over her chest. "And I haven't known many footmen who were either, so I suppose we're both guilty of being surprised for no reason."

"Fair enough." He narrowed his eyes on her. "But I'm curious. Tell me. Are you for or against the law, my lady?"

She shuddered, closing her eyes briefly. "Against it, Mr. Lucas, completely, entirely, unequivocally *against* it. As you should be!"

His dropped his chin to his chest and scratched the back of his neck. "Is that so?" Blast. Blast. Blast. Damn and blast.

She wasn't just against it. No, she had to be 'completely, entirely, unequivocally' against it.

"Yes." She nodded vigorously. "Frankly, I don't see how anyone with a heart beating in his chest could be for it. In fact, I came in here to look up the history of such laws. I've every intention of researching the history of similar laws in order to sway more of the vote against it." She turned in her seat to face the enormous collection of books. "I've simply no idea where to begin."

"First, tell me what you don't like about the law," he prodded.

"Well, for one thing it gives more rights to the noblemen running large estates, and less to the poor tenants and farmers. It puts more money in the pockets of men who are already quite wealthy. It does nothing for servants and the working class but give them even fewer options to find work without references from what may well have been awful employers."

Lucas swallowed. All of those things were true when looked at from a certain point of view, but he saw each of those issues in a completely different light. "Is there anything you like about the law?" he asked tentatively.

She tapped her fingertips along the tabletop for a few moments before saying, "Honestly, the only good it does is repeal of some of the harshest conditions of the trade acts."

The Trade Laws were archaic laws that gave the working class almost no rights. The repeal of the worst parts of the trade acts was one of Lucas's favorite parts of his brother's bill. At least he and Miss Wharton could agree on that.

Lucas stood. "Follow me," he said, starting toward the opposite side of the room. "I know where the law tomes are."

"You do?" Her voice held a note of surprise.

Damn it. He hadn't stopped to consider that it might

seem odd that a footman knew where certain books were in his master's huge library. He thought it best to change the subject. "May I ask how you intend to sway the vote?"

Frances continued to follow him. Her voice was tinged with resolution when she said, "I may be a mere female, Mr. Lucas, but I am often in the company of the men who make such decisions and it would be derelict of me not to use my time in their presence to attempt to influence their votes."

Lucas remained silent as he made his way to a small nook in the wall hidden from view from the rest of the library. He stepped inside, and she followed him.

"My goodness," she exclaimed, spinning in a small circle and smiling. "I hadn't realized this alcove was here."

Lucas pointed up. The books of law were stacked to the ceiling on both levels of the room.

Her gaze followed his finger and she smiled. "Oh, Mr. Lucas, thank you. I never would have found these if you hadn't shown me." She hesitated a moment before narrowing her eyes again. "I do hope you don't mind my asking, how did you know these were here?"

He glanced away and scratched at his temple. The blasted powdered wig made his head itch. He needed to think more before he did certain things. But being in her company made him carefree (or careless, more like). Thankfully, he'd already invented his answer on the walk over. "I spend a lot of time in this room. I like to read. Lord Clayton doesn't mind as long as my chores are finished."

"A footman who likes to read?" As soon as the last word left her lips, she clapped her hand over her mouth. "Oh, my goodness. I'm terribly sorry. That was hideous of me," she mumbled behind her fingers.

Lucas shook his head. "Please, no apologies, my lady." He could only hope her guilt would keep her from asking more questions.

"It's just that..." she continued. "Oh, I do hope I don't insult you, but...I have noticed your speech is quite cultured and I wondered how..."

Lucas leaned a hand against the solid wooden frame of the nearest bookshelf. "How I'm a footman if I'm educated enough to speak this way and read law tomes?"

She bit her lip and shook her head. "When you put it that way it does sound awful. I'm terribly sorry. I beg your pardon."

"No, don't be sorry," he replied. "Let's just say my family and Clayton's family have long been friendly. He did me quite a favor by employing me as a footman, however." There. That was true, yet vague. The perfect answer.

"Of course," Frances said. "I feel foolish for asking you to explain."

"Think nothing of it my lady, truly." He could hardly blame her for saying something rude to him when he was merely pretending to be a footman. As far as he was concerned, he was guilty too. Once again, he decided changing the subject was probably the best thing to do.

"Well, here they are." He splayed his open palms toward the books. "May I help you find any one in particular?"

"No. I shouldn't keep you any longer. I'm quite happy to poke about until I find the one I need."

"Very well." Lucas watched her. She seemed to want to say something else, but she'd hesitated.

"May I ask you something, Mr. Lucas?" she finally ventured.

He nodded. "Of course."

"Have you met my maid...Albina? Downstairs perhaps?"

Lucas bit his lip while he contemplated the question. He'd met many servants downstairs, both those who were employed by Clayton and those employed by the guests, but he didn't seem to recall the name Albina. "I don't believe so. Why?"

"Oh, it's nothing." Frances shook her head and waved her hand in the air dismissing it. "Nevermind. Wait. I do have one more question."

He blinked at her. "Yes?"

Her cheeks heated. "You're not...married are you? Or otherwise engaged?"

His brows snapped together in a frown. "Of course not."

She breathed a sigh of relief. "Thank heavens."

Lucas smiled at her comment, then made to step past her back toward the entrance to the alcove. But she moved to the side at the same moment he did, and they bumped into each other. Her head tipped back, and his chin tipped down. Their lips were mere inches apart.

He couldn't move. He watched intently as she tucked a fallen curl behind her ear, then she lifted her gaze to his and he studied the flecks of gold in her dark orbs. His hand moved slowly of its own accord to gently cup her elbow. Her breaths increased, causing her chest to rise and fall faster. He stepped infinitesimally closer, the scent of peonies driving him mad.

He licked his lips in anticipation of the kiss.

Her tongue darted out to run over her lips as well.

He sucked in a breath. Somewhere in the back of his head, he knew he'd be crossing a line if he didn't turn and walk away right then, but he couldn't make himself leave her.

"Must you go so soon?" she asked, her voice a trembling whisper.

"I suppose I could stay a bit longer," he replied, his own voice husky. "If you'd like to convince me to."

In answer, her hands moved up his shirtfront and wrapped themselves around his neck, pulling his head down to hers. "I would like to," she breathed.

Lucas needed no further invitation. His lips met hers, a warm press at first until he opened his mouth and slanted it across hers. His tongue slid between her lips and she moaned in the back of her throat.

Lucas went hard instantly. He pulled her body tight against his and ravaged her mouth with his. He couldn't get enough of her. She was soft and tasted like spring, and the scent of her perfume made him want to taste her. She wrapped her arms more tightly around him as the kiss intensified. He wanted to press her back against the bookshelf, wanted to grind himself against her, but he didn't want to scare her. She might be questioning her decision to kiss him already and any sudden movement from him might well cause her to push him away.

His hands moved down her back. Lower and then lower again. Until he pulled her against him even more tightly, a groan emanating from his throat.

Time seemed to spin as he held her and kissed her, never wanting it to end. A voice calling from somewhere in the garden intruded, making Lucas quickly come to his senses. He slowly pulled his mouth from hers and moved his hands up to cup her face. Her eyes were still closed, and her lips were pink and swollen.

He pressed a kiss to her forehead and stepped back.

She opened her eyes. Her breathing was heavy, and she looked at him as if he were some sort of exotic creature standing in front of her instead of a flesh and blood man. She lifted her fingertips to her lips and softly touched them.

Confusion marred her lovely brow. "I...should probably go," she whispered.

Lucas nodded. He was desperately hoping his raging cockstand would diminish before he was forced to leave the alcove. He cleared his throat and tried to think of something else. What? What? He shook his head. Oh, yes. "Before you go, may I ask you something about what you said earlier, regarding the Employment Bill?"

She nodded, closing her eyes again briefly as if still trying to make sense of what had just happened. "Of course," she finally offered.

Lucas leaned a shoulder against the bookshelf. "Did I understand you to say that you attempt to speak with members of the House of Lords to convince them to vote against the bill while you are at parties with them?"

Her eyes focused on his face and she slowly raised a single brow. "Don't look so aghast. Men have been doing the same thing for centuries. I'm not naïve enough to believe that many important decisions aren't made in a gentlemen's study over port and conversation while a ball is happening in the ballroom."

Lucas shifted his weight to the opposite leg. Thankfully, his cockstand was quickly subsiding. "I cannot argue with you there, my lady, but tell me, you said you don't see how anyone with a heart beating in his chest could be for the bill. Why do you think that?"

"Countless reasons!" Her words were nearly shouted. She cleared her throat and took a deep breath. Her next words were delivered in a much more moderate tone. "I mean, I could list a solid dozen reasons off the top of my head, but the biggest is that it only benefits the wealthy."

He knew that was patently untrue. Charles would have never authored such a bill. But Lucas sensed he needed to reply carefully, so Frances would listen without feeling as if he were like so many others who had attempted to stifle her opinions.

A bell chimed.

Lucas stepped out of the alcove and glanced at the clock that sat on the desk nearby. "We both must go now. But I *would* very much like to discuss this more. Will you meet me here tomorrow, say, one hour earlier?"

"I suppose I could do that." A small smile popped to her lips. "If you promise to kiss me again."

This time a smile made its way to *his* lips. "I suppose I could do that."

CHAPTER THIRTEEN

The hour Frances spent in the quiet library with Mr. Lucas the next morning was the most enjoyable hour she'd spent since arriving at the house party. He was witty, he was kind, he was intelligent, and he was every bit as irreverent as she'd first guessed him to be. Best of all, the man actually *listened* to her. She sat there, going on and on about the evils of the Employment Bill, and instead of making an excuse and hurrying from the room, he sat next to her and looked into her eyes as she spoke. He asked questions to clarify certain points, and he nodded and murmured to demonstrate that he was paying attention.

Mr. Lucas had proven himself a more well-behaved gentleman than any of the titled lords of the *ton* she'd met. None of the gentlemen of her acquaintance truly paid heed to her words the way Mr. Lucas did. Oh, they humored her, and patted her on the hand, and sent her off to sit with the wallflowers again while they found other amusements, but not one of them had appeared to be truly contemplating her points when she'd enumerated the reasons why the Employment Bill was so awful.

Once Frances had made her case, she stared hopefully at Mr. Lucas, fully expecting him to agree with her on all points. After all, how could one not see the truth in the arguments she'd made? But instead of readily agreeing with her, he said something entirely unexpected. "If I were to guess what a nobleman might say in response," he began, "I suppose he would say it would behoove him to support the bill so that he could fulfill his duties to the many people who rely upon him."

Frances stared at him as if he'd just turned into a dragon. "What are you talking about?"

He shrugged. "If I were a nobleman, I might say the bill was helping by lowering the cost of wages and ensuring I didn't have to employ someone who wasn't holding up their end of the agreement. I'd be able to employ more people and fulfill my commitments to those who already work for me."

Frances rolled her eyes. "Honestly, has Lord Clayton been telling you this drivel?"

Mr. Lucas cleared his throat. "Is it not true that men like Lord Clayton have obligations to fulfill? Surely your father has mentioned it to you if you've spoken to him about the bill."

Frances clenched her jaw. "My father has never fulfilled an obligation in his life." The words flew from her mouth before she had a chance to examine them.

"I'm sorry to hear that," Mr. Lucas said, giving her a look that did indeed indicate he was truly sorry. There was no pity in his gaze, however. Good. She detested pity.

She shrugged. "No need to be sorry. It's harsh but true. Our lands are mortgaged and we've dismissed most of our servants." Frances knew she shouldn't be telling anyone these things, but somehow, she felt safe with Mr. Lucas. Somehow, she felt as if she could tell him anything and he wouldn't judge it.

"If that's the case, then the bill would help to put more money back in your father's pocket," Mr. Lucas continued.

Frances pressed her lips together tightly. "My father's pocket is empty because he's gambled everything away. I'd rather put money in the pocket of the hardworking servants he's forced out onto the streets."

Mr. Lucas's voice lowered, and a note of regret sneaked in. "Is it that bad?"

She lifted her chin and looked away. She refused to cry but she had to blink back tears. "We have only Albina and Mrs. Wimberly left."

He leaned forward and touched her hand. Fire shot up her arm. "I'm sorry, Frances."

It was the first time he'd called her by her Christian name. She wanted to do the same. She blinked away the tears once more. "It's fine. We'll be fine." She tried to paste a fake smile on her face. "It occurs to me, I don't know your Christian name."

He glanced away, not meeting her gaze and waited a few moments before he said, "Lucas is my Christian name."

She frowned. "What? Why didn't you tell me? Here I've been calling you Mr. Lucas all this time."

"I thought it would be too forward of me to correct you. Not to mention I shouldn't have given you my Christian name to begin with."

"What's your surname then?" she asked.

He glanced away. His gaze scanned the room. "Uh, it's... Wood. Lucas Wood."

She nodded. "Well, that's easy to remember. Now, Lucas, you must tell me, you cannot possibly be in favor of the bill."

He scratched the back of his neck. "There are many aspects to it that perhaps you, I mean, *we* don't know about."

Still sitting, she pressed her fists to her hips. "Oh, please don't tell me that. I've heard it all before. Mention an aspect of the bill and I'll tell you precisely how much I know about it."

They spent the next half hour poring over every single point of the law. Frances had to admit that for a footman, Lucas was quite well versed on the details of the legislation. For every one of her arguments, he brought up a counter point that a nobleman 'might' argue.

"You're far too influenced by your employer, I fear," she finally announced.

"Why do you say that?" His brow furrowed once more.

She tossed up a hand in frustration. "Lucas, you're in service. Don't you see how this bill does nothing but keep you and your future children in service?" She blushed. "My apologies. I am making assumptions about you. Such as that you intend to have children."

"I would very much like to," he replied quietly, searching her face.

She felt her blush deepen. Good heavens, why had she mentioned his nonexistent children? "Well, then, can't you see how such a bill does nothing for your good?"

Lucas looked out the window, slowly drawing one finger in a circle along the desktop. "I suppose you're right."

"Of course I'm right. The House of Lords has the power to defeat this law, but they only vote in favor of themselves and their own purses."

His gaze met hers again. "You're not in service, my lady, can you tell me why you're so interested in seeing it defeated?"

"Because," she said quietly, turning to stare out across the garden and meadow beyond the windows. "I care about fairness and what is right. I care about other people more than myself and my own interests."

Lucas's voice lowered. "You think anyone espousing the bill only cares about their own interests?"

Her nostrils flared. "I don't see how they cannot. It certainly isn't helpful to the hardworking people who've been in their employ for years, sometimes generations."

"I'm certain some members of the House of Lords do oppose the law," he pointed out.

"Not nearly enough," Frances replied. She still wasn't entirely certain if Lucas was for the bill or if he was just arguing the point in order to rile her, but either way there were few things she liked better than discussing the laws.

He clasped his hands in front of himself and steepled his fingers. "Do you know the members of Parliament who are for and against the law?"

"No," she replied. "But I can guess at some of them and I understand there are still a handful who are as yet undecided. Those are the men I intend to look for the next time I'm in Society."

Lucas looked as if he were about to say something but shut his mouth before finally saying, "You truly think you can sway them?"

"I've no idea but I know I must try," she replied with a resolute nod.

"You're certain you're right, aren't you?" he asked, narrowing his eyes on her.

"I'm beyond certain."

He appeared to contemplate that for a moment.

She wanted to grab him and shake him. Instead, she leaned toward him. "Lucas, do you hear me? Am I making you think?"

He looked lazily into her eyes and his gaze focused on her mouth. Oh, God. He was going to kiss her again...and she wanted him to. "You're making me think about all sorts of things." He leaned closer, closer and his eyes began to close. Frances leaned closer too and when their lips touched, he immediately came out of his chair, pulling her atop him onto the thick carpet on the floor next to the table.

He rolled atop her and pressed himself against her while showering her face and neck with kisses.

This was madness. Someone might come in at any moment and find them, but Frances couldn't make herself care enough to stop. Instead, she wrapped her arms around his shoulders and held him to her, her legs parting as far as they could beneath her skirts.

His mouth slid down to her neck and he nuzzled her ear before lowering his kisses to her *décolletage*, and finally pulling down her gown to free one breast. When his lips closed around her nipple, she went completely mindless. His insistent tongue brushed the sensitive peak and his lips tugged at it, pooling heat between her legs. "Lucas," she cried softly against his ear. He shuddered and pressed himself more tightly against her. She could feel the outline of him through his breeches, pressing against her most intimate spot. He rubbed against her in a way that made her want to call out.

Then his mouth moved back up to hers and her fingers pushed up into his hair, knocking his wig to the ground beside them. She stared at him. His hair was dark. She liked that. She liked that very much. She'd guessed as much from the color of his eyebrows, but seeing him without the wig, the man was even more handsome.

The briefest hint of guilt flashed through her brain. Not guilt at her own shameless behavior, but guilt at the fact that Albina had told her she fancied him. If she were in her right mind, she would let him go. She should not be doing this. She should encourage a match with Albina. But she also couldn't help but think that she'd had a moment with him before Albina had ever even met him and oh, it was so difficult to think with his mouth on her neck like that.

Lucas rolled over, pulling her atop him. They bumped into the table. One of the smaller books that had been opened near the corner of the table fell to the floor not an inch from their faces and their laughter over the silliness of that caused them to stop kissing.

Lucas rubbed his nose against hers. "I suppose that's our cue to stop."

She sighed, her hands still around his neck. "I suppose so."

He rolled to the side, scooped up his wig, jumped up and then helped her up. They both spent a few moments putting their clothing to rights before he pulled out the chair for her and she resumed her seat as if the last few moments had never even happened.

He took his own seat again as well.

"Well, then, now, where were we?" she asked with a giggle, unable to stop staring at him. By God, the man was so handsome it nearly hurt to look at him. She'd no idea why he found her appealing. She certainly wasn't the female equivalent in looks.

Lucas cleared his throat. He'd replaced his wig, but it did look a bit worse for the wear. She leaned over to help him adjust it back into place. "Thank you," he said. "I've found this a chore to get used to."

"What?" she asked, frowning.

"Oh, er, uh. It's a new wig. I'm accustomed to my old one." He cleared his throat. "By the by, what about the law's owner? Do you know who he is?"

She narrowed her eyes until she could barely see out of them and spoke through clenched teeth. "Oh, yes, I know the name well. I detest the man and if I ever lay eyes on that *bastard* Lord Kendall, I intend to tell him precisely what I think of his revolting Employment Bill."

CHAPTER FOURTEEN

F rances hurried back up to her room after her
rendezvous with Lucas in the library. She supposed
what they were doing each day qualified as a
rendezvous and God help her, she had no intention of stopping their interludes.

With a clear head she could see she wasn't being entirely
disloyal to Albina. Albina hadn't even met Lucas, after all,
according to him. She merely fancied him from afar. Of
course, the right thing to do would be to tell Albina that she
was already smitten with the man herself, but that was out of
the question. How in the world would she explain to her
maid that she'd been meeting a footman in the library and
kissing him each day? She doubted Albina would tell Mama,
but there was no guarantee, and besides, it wasn't a story
Frances wanted spread about. Albina had been known to
gossip upon occasion. No. This particular secret was one
Frances intended to keep to herself. It was wrong, and it was
illicit, and it was the most fun she'd had in an age. She only
wished Abigail was here to share it with. Abigail could keep a
secret.

Frances pressed a hand to her throat as she made her way up the winding staircase to her bedchamber. Heavens, when she got to her room, she would have to check the looking glass for love bites. She'd heard other young ladies at parties speak of such things, but she'd never been privy to such salaciousness. Now, she was doing her best to pull her curls over her neck to hide what might well be a mark from a lover. She shuddered, remembering the feel of Lucas's mouth on hers, his lips on her neck, his tongue on her breast of all scandalous things. Ooh, she couldn't wait for him to do it again. She bent her head and stared at the ground to hide her smile.

Lucas was more than just handsome. In addition to their lovemaking, she'd also been stimulated by their discussion. It was the first real conversation she'd had with an adult male where she truly felt as if they were equals. All the other gentlemen she'd spoken with about politics wanted to dismiss her views as quickly as possible, have a servant fetch her more tea, and talk about something boring like the last play at the theater or the lovely artwork on the wall next to them.

For a time, she'd been concerned that Lucas might actually be in *favor* of the Employment Bill. He seemed to defend it quite vigorously. She'd heard that the law's creator, Lord Kendall, was friendly with Lord Clayton. Perhaps Lucas knew the earl from having served him when he came to visit. Regardless, she'd decided that Lucas couldn't possibly be in favor of a bill that did absolutely nothing to help his own class. She guessed that he enjoyed the discussion as much as she did and wanted to provide her with the means to make her arguments. It had been quite chivalrous of him when she stopped to consider it.

She'd made it to the second floor's landing and was nearly halfway down the hall to her bedchamber door when another door opened, and Sir Reginald emerged. Frances froze, hoping he might not see her and continue on past, but apparently, luck was not on her side at the moment. Instead, Sir Reginald made a grand show, stopping, and bowing, and doffing his hat.

"There you are, Miss Wharton. You look as lovely as ever," he boomed.

Frances wondered if her lips looked swollen from kissing Lucas and if a love bite was, in fact, visible on her neck. She started to giggle.

"Are you quite all right, Miss Wharton?" Sir Reginald looked genuinely worried for her.

"Oh, yes, I'm…fine…quite…fine," she said, in between giggles. She pressed her fingertips to her lips to keep from laughing more. It was just so comical to see Sir Reginald after what she'd just done in the library with Lucas.

"Are you going to the picnic lunch with the other ladies?" Sir Reginald asked, thankfully willing to change the subject.

"Oh, er, yes, I believe I am," she replied. She pinched the inside of her arm to stop laughing.

"Very well," the knight bowed again, "then I shall see you at dinner this evening?"

Frances wanted to say, "I hope not." Instead, the thought just made her giggle more. "Yes, dinner," she replied noncommittally.

"I do hope we're able to go for a ride," he said. "Perhaps tomorrow afternoon?"

Frances was just about to open her mouth to say she was otherwise occupied tomorrow afternoon when Sir Reginald snapped his fingers. "Wait. No. Not tomorrow. I'm meeting with Lord Kendall tomorrow afternoon."

Frances stopped laughing. She narrowed her eyes on Sir Reginald. "Kendall? Did you say Lord Kendall?"

"Yes, the Earl of Kendall. Do you know him?" Sir Reginald asked as he plucked at his ornate cuff.

Blood pounded in Frances's temple. "I've never met him. I wasn't aware he was at this party."

"Oh, he hasn't been," Sir Reginald replied. "He's only coming for a day or two. He's fast friends with Clayton, don't you know?"

"Yes, I'd heard as much." Frances forced herself to breathe properly, while a hundred thoughts flew through her mind. Lord Kendall—*the* Lord Kendall—would be *here*? At this house party?

"From what I understand he's arriving any moment now," Sir Reginald added.

"Is that so?" A slow smile spread across Frances's face. If that blackguard the Earl of Kendall was coming here, she intended to give the man a piece of her mind. "What time are you meeting him?"

CHAPTER FIFTEEN

ow that he was at the house party as the Earl of Kendall, Lucas had been given a bedchamber on the second floor with most of the other guests. Bell met him there that afternoon to serve as his valet. As Bell helped him change from the Clayton livery into his buckskin breeches and emerald-green coat, Lucas couldn't help but replay the entire conversation earlier with Frances in his head. She'd been so knowledgeable and discerning when she spoke about the Employment Bill.

Clearly, she'd formed her own steadfast opinion on the matter and Lucas was both duly impressed and utterly frustrated. There was little chance she would change her mind. In fact, many of her points had made Lucas question his own logic. He'd been so dedicated to ensuring the bill passed because of his promise to his brother. He knew all the talking points, had repeated them at length to his compatriots in the House of Lords, and he'd believed them, by God. Every word of them. Only when Frances had asked him if he could see how such a bill did nothing for his own good, guilt had weighed on him. He'd had to remind himself that he was playacting. But playacting would be a poor excuse if he ended up hurting Frances because of it.

And while he was thinking about guilt, that particular emotion had doubled and then tripled within him after the kisses they'd shared. The first time he'd kissed her, his guilt had been minimal. It wasn't the most noble thing to do, to kiss a woman who didn't know who you truly were. But he'd quickly dismissed that doubt when she'd responded so enthusiastically. The second time they'd kissed, he'd gone a bit farther, risked a bit more, and it had been pure bliss, until she'd announced that she detested the Earl of Kendall. *That* had made it all too clear that he was nothing more than a liar.

This charade may have begun as a lark, but it was turning into something all too serious. His lies were multiplying. It made it worse that in the middle of lying to her about who he was and what he stood for, he'd gone and kissed her. Such bad form.

He had absolutely no excuse for his behavior. He had no right to speak to her, let alone kiss her. She hated him. Well, she hated Lord Kendall, who he really was. She didn't know her friend Lucas, the footman, was the same man she detested.

How would he ever explain himself to her? How could he? She'd been busy pouring out her heart to him and he'd been her sworn enemy all along. It didn't matter that he didn't *know* he'd been her sworn enemy. He knew it now and he was still not telling the truth. He had to figure out a way to make this right. At the very least he had no right to kiss her and he would not do it again.

"How do you stand the guilt?" he asked Bell, who was currently helping him into his right boot. Bell was serving as his valet for two reasons. Lucas's own man hadn't come with him for obvious reasons, and Bell was interested in practicing his skill at valeting every chance he got.

"What guilt?" Bell asked with a laugh.

"You never feel guilty? You're a spy. You lie for a living."

Bell straightened at that accusation and gave him a blank stare. "I do what is necessary to fulfill my duty to the Crown."

Lucas expelled his breath. "No matter what I tell myself, I'm not doing this for a noble pursuit. I've told so many lies I don't recognize myself any longer."

Bell contemplated the matter for a moment. "I suppose it helps that most of the people I have to lie to are either lying to me as well or guilty of something."

"Yes, well, Miss Wharton hasn't lied to me and I doubt she's guilty of anything," Lucas replied, sliding his stocking foot into the boot. "This entire experiment—as Clayton likes to call it, it's not at all what I imagined it would be."

Bell grabbed the other boot and held it out for Lucas to step into. "Because you're falling in love with Miss Wharton?"

Lucas's jaw dropped. "What? No, I—"

"That's what you wanted, isn't it? To find true love? I do admit it's turned a bit dubious given the fact that you're spending time with her and she knows you as a servant, but it's not insurmountable, you know? I was right about the dowry though, wasn't I?"

Lucas nearly growled. "Yes, you were right about the dowry. If only I gave a toss about a dowry. I began this thing looking for a *true* wife. I never thought about the fact that I would need to be a *true* husband. Even if I was madly in love with Miss Wharton, I couldn't have her now if I wanted her. All I've told her is a pack of lies. This entire idea was ridiculous to begin with. I should go back to London and marry the first lady my mother points to."

Bell's laughter filled the room. "Where's the fun in that?"

"There may be no fun, but there is no guilt either." Lucas groaned.

Bell shook his head. "Guilt isn't the worst feeling, Kendall."

Lucas put his fists on his hips. "Oh, really, what's worse?"

Bell shrugged. "Regret."

Lucas tipped his head back to look up at the ceiling and expelled his breath once more. "It doesn't matter any longer. I've made my decision. This afternoon I'm speaking to Sir Reginald about the Employment Bill. This evening I intend to keep to myself in the servants' hall and far away from the dining room. Tomorrow morning I'll say good-bye to Miss Wharton, and then I'm leaving."

A sly smile spread across Bell's face. "If you're not in love with her, why say good-bye?"

"Don't make me dismiss you on your first day as my valet," Lucas nearly growled.

Bell's laughter was interrupted by a knock at the door.

"Come in," Lucas called, still shrugging into the coat Bell had just held out for him.

The door opened and one of Clayton's footmen, Arthur, entered. He held a silver salver with a note lying on it.

"For you, my lord," Arthur said, bowing to Lucas.

"Thank you, Arthur." Lucas flipped him a coin. "That will be all." He pulled the note from the salver and set the plate on a nearby table.

"From Clayton?" Bell asked nonchalantly as he folded and placed Lucas's livery in the wardrobe.

Lucas shook his head. "No. You won't believe who it's from."

"Read it," Bell prompted.

Lucas took a deep breath and spoke aloud the words he'd just hastily read to himself.

Lord Kendall,

We have not met, but I have something important to discuss

128

with you as it pertains to your Employment Bill. I've been informed that you are joining the house party and would like to request a few moments of your time. I appreciate that you're a busy man and I thank you for your consideration.

    F. R. T. Wharton

"From Miss Wharton?" Bell asked, arching a brow.

"It must be," Lucas replied. "I assume she used her initials so that I might believe she's a male."

Bell frowned. "What does she think you'd do when you discover you're meeting with a young woman instead?"

Lucas shrugged. "My guess is that she intends to worry about that when the time comes."

Bell shook his head. "Miss Wharton should take care. She has to know it's inappropriate of her to ask for a meeting alone with a man."

Lucas nodded. "No doubt that's why she didn't sign her Christian name. Blast. What am I to do with this?" He held the note aloft.

Bell pursed his lips. "I could meet her and pretend to be you."

"No!" Lucas nearly shouted. "No more playacting. This entire affair is convoluted enough as it is."

Bell laughed. "Very well. But if you change your mind, do let me know. I'm something of an expert at pretending to be people I'm not."

Lucas glanced at his friend. "Yes, as to that, how's it coming with the lady's maid you mentioned?"

A low growl was Bell's only answer.

That was interesting. Bell never lost his cool. Lucas would have to poke into that story more when he had time to ask additional questions.

Lucas checked his pocket watch. He had to admit it was nice to wear his own clothing again, have his own items at his disposal. "I'm late. I must get downstairs to meet Sir Reginald." He strode to the door. "Thea promised to take all the young ladies and their mothers out for a picnic this afternoon in order to clear the house of them while I'm downstairs."

"Clever," Bell replied, still putting away Lucas's other set of clothing.

Lucas opened the door and stepped into the hallway.

"What do you intend to do about Miss Wharton?" Bell called after him.

"I've no earthly idea," Lucas called back.

CHAPTER SIXTEEN

F rances was pacing in Lord Clayton's conservatory when a trio of young ladies from the party came traipsing through.

"Miss Wharton, there you are. Have you heard?" the first young lady called.

"Heard what?" Frances replied. She'd been enjoying the solitude of the pretty space, but she quickly realized she'd made a mistake coming here.

"The Earl of Kendall is here," the second young lady announced, her voice positively breathless.

"Oh, I do hope he'll be coming to dinner," the third conjectured, practically squealing.

That's precisely why Frances had been pacing. She'd sent a note to Lord Kendall's room not an hour ago, but she'd yet to hear back. She'd skipped the picnic, somehow managing to convince Mama that she had a megrim. The appearance of the three young ladies obviously meant she wasn't the only one who'd skipped the picnic.

She'd defied her mother in sending that note. She was in the wrong, no question, but she'd carefully weighed the arguments for and against speaking to Lord Kendall and had decided she might never have such an opportunity again. Lord Kendall did not often attend the same events she did. She'd made up her mind soon after her encounter with Sir Reginald in the corridor. Besides, what her mother didn't know wouldn't hurt her. Frances did, however, promise herself that her talk with Lord Kendall would be the only time she broke her promise to her mother.

Frances had been pacing for another reason as well. Sir Reginald had told her he was meeting with Lord Kendall at four o'clock, but she'd failed to ask where. The estate had over a hundred rooms. They could be in any one of them.

She must practice patience. Too bad it had never been her strong suit. Even if she'd been able to find where Sir Reginald and Lord Kendall were meeting, it would hardly be well-mannered of her to barge in on their private conversation.

Frances refused to be put off by the man, however, and Lord Kendall seemed like just the sort of arse who would put her off. Especially if he realized she was a female who wanted to discuss the Employment Bill with him.

She'd taken a chance by signing her note with her initials. He would assume she was male, of course. A man like him would never guess a female would do such a thing. Of course, since she was an unmarried woman, it was inappropriate of her to request a meeting with him alone. But it was important enough to risk being accused of an impropriety. She would not remain in his company long. What she intended to say to him would be brief. She'd practiced it in the looking glass a hundred times during the Season, preparing for the day she might unexpectedly meet Lord Kendall at a *ton* event. Such an opportunity had never presented itself, but she hadn't forgotten her speech.

"I heard something about Lord Kendall's arrival," Frances

replied to the three young ladies, doing her best to seem as if she could not care any less.

The first young lady stopped and stared at her. "You're not excited?"

"Should I be?" Frances asked, blinking at them innocently.

"Have you *seen* the Earl of Kendall?" the second young lady asked.

"No, why?" Frances ventured. "Have you?"

The three ladies looked at each other. "Well, no, but the rumors are that he's extremely handsome and of course he's highly eligible."

Frances blinked at them some more. "Is that why you all are making such a fuss?"

All three of them raised their eyebrows simultaneously and looked back and forth at one another with wide eyes as if they could not believe what they were hearing.

"He's not just supposed to be *handsome*, Frances. They say he looks like *Adonis*," the first one said.

"And he's not just eligible," the third lady said, "he's second only to the Duke of Worthington in eligibility."

Frances nodded and did her best to pin a believable smile to her face. "Well, then, for your sakes, I do hope he makes it to dinner."

No use telling them they were excited over a horse's ass. The ladies giggled and continued chatting and strolling down the path while Frances rolled her eyes. She slipped behind a nearby orange blossom tree to find much-needed solitude.

The three debutantes may have dressed up their news in solicitude, but Frances knew better. They were being disingenuous. She knew as well as they did that she was hardly a debutante who would turn the head of the second most eligible man in the *ton*. She was passable pretty at best and her dowry was a pittance. Even if the Earl of Kendall wasn't a horse's backside, she was hardly planning to compete with the lovely rich girls with whom she'd just spoken to garner his attention. Not to mention Lord Kendall was the last man on earth she'd want to marry. For heaven's sake. She was more likely to step on his foot than flirt with him.

Besides, the man she *had* been flirting with recently just happened to look like Adonis as well. No doubt Lucas would make the Earl of Kendall seem like a troll. During the Season, Frances had determined that other young ladies tended to inflate the looks of many of the bachelors based on the size of their pocketbooks and the prestige of their titles.

She'd been told many an eligible gentleman was exceedingly handsome only to see him and wonder what the fuss was about. The only thing she wanted from the Earl of Kendall was a minute or two of his time. Only the longer she went without hearing back from him, the more anxious she became. She had hoped to hear back before he met with Sir Reginald. She'd sneaked from her room, leaving Albina to pretend as if she were still sleeping off her megrim. She'd asked the maid to come find her if a reply arrived from Lord Kendall.

Frances was tempted to sneak down to the servants' hall to find Lucas. It was a ludicrous notion, but she couldn't stop herself from wanting to see him again, even sooner than tomorrow morning. The happiest hour of her day was the time she spent with him in the library. At the moment she was a bundle of nerves and seeing him would calm her. She knew it.

A twig snapped behind her and she turned to see Albina coming down the path toward her. Frances's stomach lurched.

"Albina!" she called, waving from behind the orange blossom tree. "I'm here."

Albina's head swiveled until her gaze alighted on Frances

and then she nodded, picked up her skirts, and hurried over. She didn't appear to have a note in her hand.

"Did he send a reply?" Frances blurted, wringing her hands.

Albina shook her head. "No, Miss. I'm afraid not."

Frances's stomach lurched back to its original location. "Oh," she said, attempting and failing to disguise the disappointment in her tone.

"But I think I can help, Miss," Albina continued.

"How?" Frances asked, searching the maid's face.

"I was talking to one of the other maids downstairs," Albina said, "and I learned where the Earl of Kendall's bedchamber is."

Frances's eyes went wide. "Truly?" She wanted to leap for joy. There was no way the man would be able to escape her if she staked out his bedchamber. "Albina, you darling, that's perfect. Where is it?"

"On the second floor, the sixth door on the right at the top of the staircase," Albina replied, a proud smile on her face.

"You're certain?"

"That's the direction Lord Clayton's maid gave me," Albina replied.

"Thank you, Albina." Frances lifted her skirts and started off down the mulched path toward the front of the conservatory. "I intend to go there immediately and stay until he returns."

CHAPTER SEVENTEEN

Dressed impeccably as the Earl of Kendall, Lucas made his way to Clayton's blue drawing room at precisely four o'clock. The knight had replied to Lucas's invitation, ensuring he wouldn't miss it. Bell's question continued to ring in his head. "What do you intend to do about Miss Wharton?" What did he intend to do about Miss Wharton, indeed.

He would have to write her back of course, but he'd no clue what he would say. He obviously had two choices. He could accept a meeting with her and confess all, but risk her eternal hatred. Or he could reply that he didn't have the time for a meeting at present. She wouldn't be pleased with that answer, but she already had a bad opinion of him. He doubted it could get much worse. It truly came down to whether he was ready to admit to the lies he'd already told her and hope there was some possible way he could explain it all to her. Even if she was forgiving about his pretending to be a servant, he doubted she'd be as forgiving when she learned she'd kissed a man who was working against her.

Blast. Why the devil did this entire thing have to be so complicated?

He grabbed the door handle to the blue salon and took a deep breath. He would decide what to do about Frances later. At the moment he had a knight to persuade.

Sir Reginald was already sitting in the room when Lucas entered.

"Good to see you, Sir Reginald," Lucas intoned, striding toward the older man. The door closed behind him.

"Likewise," Sir Reginald replied, standing to greet Lucas.

They shook hands.

Tea was being served by Clayton's servants, but Lucas marched directly to the sideboard. "Would you care for something stronger, Sir Reginald?"

"By all means," was the knight's reply.

Lucas splashed brandy into two glasses and made his way back toward the seating arrangement in the center of the room. Sir Reginald sat on the settee in front of the window while Lucas took a seat on a chair at a right angle.

"Thank you for meeting with me," Lucas said. He used the opportunity to take a good look at the man. The lines near Sir Reginald's eyes were well-defined as were similar lines in his forehead and at the sides of his mouth. He was balding. His shoulders sloped. There was no doubt about it. Sir Reginald was not a handsome specimen of a man, but he wasn't entirely repellent either. A lady could do worse, Lucas supposed. Even as he had the thought, he realized how awful it sounded in his head. If he were Frances, would he want to give himself for life to someone who could charitably be described as *not entirely repellant*?

"I must admit, I was surprised to receive your note, Kendall," Sir Reginald began. "I didn't realize you would be here."

"I hadn't intended upon coming," Lucas replied. "My

plans changed at the last minute." At least that much was true. He much preferred to be telling the truth for once.

"Clayton says you don't intend to stay long," Sir Reginald continued.

"That's correct, which is why I'm pleased you could meet with me this afternoon."

"My pleasure," the knight said, taking a tiny sip of his brandy before setting the glass aside on the table next to the settee.

"It's too bad you're not staying," Sir Reginald continued, "the party has been quite a crush. *The Prince Regent* is coming on Monday."

"I heard," Lucas replied, "you must give him my best."

"I will," Sir Reginald said, "but you may miss other happenings as well. For instance, I just might find a bride here this week."

The words hit Lucas like a punch to the gut. He forced himself to keep his face blank as he asked the question he already knew the answer to. "Really? Who is the fortunate lady?"

"Well." Sir Reginald puffed up his chest and smoothed his hand down the front of his plum-colored coat. "Nothing's settled yet, you understand, but I've become partial to Miss Frances Wharton."

"Baron Winfield's daughter?" Lucas continued, biting the inside of his cheek, hard.

"Yes, his eldest. She's a bit headstrong, apparently fancies herself knowledgeable about politics." He chuckled condescendingly, rolling his eyes. "Can you imagine? But it's nothing a good husband shouldn't be able to quell. She's a pretty enough chit."

"I hear Winfield is in debt. Are you certain there's a dowry there?" It was a horrible thing to say, but Lucas couldn't help himself. And *quell*? Had the man truly just said *quell*? He clearly didn't know Frances if he thought he would be able to *quell* her opinion on politics.

Sir Reginald waved a hand in the air. "Makes no difference to me. In fact, I've reason to believe that's why the family's interested. No doubt I'd be looking at a much older bride if a hefty dowry was my aim. I already have more money than I know what to do with." The knight had the audacity to wink. Lucas *quelled* the urge to punch him in the jaw.

"You're *certain* she's interested?" Lucas asked, narrowing his eyes on the older man. He shouldn't have asked that question either, but he couldn't stop himself once more.

"I don't see how she couldn't be," Sir Reginald said, coughing into a handkerchief he'd pulled from his lace-covered sleeve. "The chit doesn't have many options."

The grin the knight gave him revealed crooked, yellowed teeth. Lucas shuddered for Frances's sake. No wonder Frances thought all the men of the *ton* were pompous, boring asses. This man was sitting here talking about her future as if she had no say in it.

"I see," Lucas replied woodenly. He had to change the subject before he knocked the man unconscious. He shook his head. "At any rate, the reason I asked you here was to—"

"Allow me to guess." The knight gave him an obsequious smile. "You want to discuss the Employment Bill."

Lucas grinned at him and took a swig of brandy. "However did you know, Sir Reginald?"

The knight sighed and waved his hand in the air again. "Seems that's all you want to discuss with anyone these days, Kendall. You're garnering quite the reputation for being preoccupied with that bill."

"My apologies if my conversation has turned monotonous." Lucas gave the knight a tight smile. He had to tread carefully with the man. One rude word from him could send Sir Reginald and the entire group of Royalists, who'd yet to declare their intentions as to the vote, scattering to the opposition. "Have you had any more thoughts on the matter since the last time we spoke?"

Sir Reginald settled into his chair and ventured another sip of brandy. "Honestly, I have not. I know it's not what you want to hear, but it's the truth."

Lucas nodded. "Fair enough. If you haven't yet made up your mind, I am happy to discuss the finer points of the bill."

"I know you are, Kendall, and that's the problem," Sir Reginald said with an impatient sigh.

Lucas furrowed his brow. "What do you mean?"

"I mean you're more interested in the bloody details of the bill, while I'm more interested in the—" he waved his hand in a circle, "—details of, say, what's in it for me if I vote the way you'd like me to." Sir Reginald's obsequious smile returned.

Lucas clenched his jaw. He was not naïve enough to believe these types of discussions didn't happen when it came to politics, but it still made his stomach turn when he encountered it.

"One would hope you'd vote according to your conscience," he replied, doing his best to keep his temper in check. "As I said, I'm happy to discuss the points—"

"One would hope, wouldn't one, Kendall?" Sir Reginald turned up his nose. "But I'm telling you that I'd be more interested in some sort of a bargain."

"What were you thinking, Sir Reginald?" Lucas asked, merely to have the pleasure of knowing what exactly the man wanted from him. "You've already said you have more money than you know what to do with."

"I don't want money, Kendall." A dark gleam shined in the knight's eye. "I want something much more elusive."

"And that is?" Lucas prodded.

The knight rolled his eyes. "Power, of course."

Lucas frowned. "Power? What could I possibly do to—?"

The knight plucked at his sleeve. "Everyone knows you're thick as thieves with the Duke of Worthington."

Lucas clenched his jaw more tightly and blew out a deep breath instead of doing what he wanted to do, which was to explode from his chair with equal parts disgust and affront. "You're thick as thieves with the Prince Regent," he managed to ground out.

Sir Reginald tossed a hand in the air and chuckled. "Georgie doesn't have any *power*. Everyone knows that. He's a regent for Christ's sake. We pat him on the head and tell him he's a good boy and he plans another dinner party and builds another palace. No. I want to be the Chancellor of the Duchy and I'll need the vote of every duke in Parliament if I'm to win."

Lucas stared at the man as if he'd lost his mind. Powerful didn't begin to describe the position. The Chancellor of the Duchy administered the estates and rents of the Duchy of Lancaster, which was essentially a great deal of the Sovereign's income. The Chancellor of the Duchy was one of the most senior positions in Parliament.

Lucas finally found his voice. "You want to be the Chancellor of the Duchy of Lancaster?"

"Precisely."

It was all Lucas could do to keep from standing up and striding out of the room without a backward glance at Sir Reginald. But he needed more information first. "What if I'm unable to convince Worthington to vote for you?"

The knight pursed his lips unpleasantly. "Then I will be unable to vote for the Employment Bill. And more importantly, I'll be unable to convince my *friends* to vote for it."

So *this* was why Sir Reginald had refused to pick a side all these months. He'd been holding out for the perfect opportunity to spring this trap on Lucas.

"I see." Lucas stood. He needed to get away from the man immediately. "I plan to be here two more nights. I'll give you my answer before I leave."

"Excellent," Sir Reginald replied. "I look forward to hearing your decision."

Lucas made his way back to his bedchamber on the second floor with ground-devouring strides. Every few paces he was tempted to stop and punch his fist through a wall. His regard for Clayton and the well-being of his home was the only thing that kept him from it.

The Royal Navy had been a place filled with honor and dignity. Yes, he'd seen unfair acts, but there was also pride and accountability. There was equity and there was loyalty. Politics were completely different.

The world he found himself in since inheriting the title was a cesspool of secrets and lies. His brother had the stomach for it. Lucas did not. Sir Reginald and his scheming ilk made Lucas sick, and the thought of that man touching Frances made his skin crawl. She deserved so much better than the bloated knight.

Lucas took the steps up the grand staircase two at a time, thankful that the foyer was empty at the moment. As soon as he made it to the second-floor landing, he turned to the right to head toward his room and stopped dead in his tracks.

Standing directly across from his bedchamber door, with her arms folded across her chest, was none other than Frances.

CHAPTER EIGHTEEN

Frances had been standing in front of the Earl of Kendall's bedchamber door for the better part of a quarter hour. She felt perfectly silly and was entirely aware of how inappropriate she was being, but she no longer cared. This wasn't about her reputation or what the guests at the house party thought of her. She was doing this for the working classes, the maids like Albina and the footmen like Lucas. They deserved better than what the Employment Bill would give them. Even if it didn't change the outcome of the vote, Frances intended to tell the bill's creator exactly what she thought of his self-serving nonsense.

She'd already come up with an excuse if anyone were to happen by and see her outside Lord Kendall's door. She would pretend she was horribly lost, and had been certain she was waiting for her friend Mary Montgomery. Mary was one of the ladies at the party who she liked a great deal. Of course, Mary's room wouldn't be on this side of the floor, but that's where the part about pretending to be lost came in. After all, who could possibly blame a poor young woman for her confusion on a floor with so very many doors that looked exactly alike?

The pacing she'd begun in the conservatory earlier continued in the corridor outside Lord Kendall's room. She was mentally rehearsing her speech over and over. She intended to tell him what a money-loving, self-serving, classist ass he was. Had he ever stopped to consider the lives of the poor? Had he ever looked at his own valet, or his own cook and wondered what their lives must be like? Had he ever considered how his bill would make things more difficult for them? No. No, he had not and the reason he had not was because he didn't care. He didn't care about anyone but himself and his lot, the men who were in charge of everything and always had been. The men who made the rules for everyone else but ensured those rules benefitted only themselves. She would inform Lord Kendall that he was the lowest of the low for proposing that law, and she hoped when he laid his head on his pillow at night that the suffering of every single one of the downtrodden people he'd be making things worse for would keep him awake as it should.

She nodded her head determinedly. Oh, she was quite certain he'd bumble and fumble and come up with some asinine excuse as to why she shouldn't worry her pretty little head over such things. He'd give her a condescending smile that would reveal yellowed teeth and foul breath. Adonis, her foot! No doubt his hygiene was worse than Sir Reginald's. He was probably a bloated, bleating windbag who looked as if he'd crawled out from under a bottle of liquor, most likely an expensive bottle, but that hardly mattered.

She'd been posted in front of his door for no more than a few minutes when Mary's older sister, Lady Julianna, came floating up the staircase. She was wearing a lovely white gown with a gauzy, embroidered overskirt and looked as if she'd just stepped off the pages of a lady's fashion periodical.

Frances watched in horror as the engaged woman glanced her way, took another quick look, and proceeded to glide toward her.

Frances bit her lip and looked in both directions. It would be awkward to use her excuse that she was waiting for Mary, but what other choice did she have?

"Oh, Miss Wharton, not you, too?" Lady Julianna said as soon as she'd come within earshot.

Frances blinked and glanced in the opposite direction. Lady Julianna had said her name, but was it possible she'd been mistaken? There was no one behind Frances, however, and she was forced to turn back and face Lady Julianna as that woman came to stand directly in front of her.

"'Not me,' too?" Frances echoed, her brow furrowed.

Lady Julianna gave her a conspiratorial grin, stepped forward, and looped her arm around Frances's. She tugged her gently into a walk beside her. They headed toward the lady's end of the corridor.

"Don't tell me you didn't know you were standing in front of the Earl of Kendall's bedchamber door?" Lady Julianna whispered as soon as they'd taken a few steps.

Frances felt herself blanch. She was torn between denying it and asking how Lady Julianna happened to know which door was his.

"It's... I... Well... How did you know?" Frances finally blurted. Very well. She wasn't a particularly good actress, was she?

Lady Julianna's conspiratorial grin widened, and she glanced behind them to ensure no one else had entered the corridor. "I'd heard he'd arrived. It's all the other ladies are talking about today. The location of his room is a much-discussed topic downstairs."

"I'd gathered the ladies were excited," Frances agreed, feeling a bit ill to learn that Lord Kendall's bedchamber was a topic of anyone's conversation. Why, she'd been fortunate that she hadn't run into other young ladies hovering about for much different reasons.

"You're not excited?" Lady Julianna gave her a skeptical glance.

Frances let out a long sigh. There was no help for it. "There's every reason you won't believe me, Lady Julianna, but I fear I must tell you the truth or risk you thinking the worst of me."

Lady Julianna's sparkling laughter filled the space around them. "Why, if you're willing to tell it, I'm more than willing to hear it, Miss Wharton."

Frances quickly discarded a few introductions to the subject before deciding to be as direct as possible. "I know it's difficult to believe, but I want to speak to Lord Kendall about his Employment Bill. The one's he's presented to the House of Lords."

Lady Julianna's eyes widened, but ultimately, the look on her face could only be described as...*admiration*?

"I must admit that was the last thing I thought you'd say," Lady Julianna replied, still gently pulling Frances along beside her. They'd only moved a few paces, but they were still headed toward the lady's end of the corridor.

Frances winced and bit her lip. "Do you believe me?"

Lady Julianna patted her hand. "Absolutely, I do."

This time Frances's eyes went wide. "You do?"

Lady Julianna laughed softly. "Of course I do. Who would make up something so unexpected?"

Frances expelled a relieved sigh, her shoulders slumping. "Thank heavens. It is the truth, I swear it."

"Of course it is," Lady Julianna replied, "but you must tell me, what do you intend to say to Lord Kendall about the bill? Now I'm intrigued."

"Do you know anything about it, Lady Julianna?" Frances prompted.

"I'm afraid I don't." She shook her head.

"Well, it's a ghastly bill that will hurt the poor."

Lady Julianna sucked in her breath. She stopped walking for a moment and looked squarely at Frances. "I'm surprised to hear that."

"Why?" Frances asked, frowning again.

Lady Julianna resumed walking. Still clutching Frances's arm, she graced her with another lovely smile. "I've met the Earl of Kendall and he seemed like a decent man to me."

Frances couldn't help but stick her nose in the air. "Well, he isn't. I've never met him but believe me, he's awful. I'm convinced he's pudgy and hideous-looking too."

Lady Julianna's soft laughter followed. "Who told you that?"

Frances gave Lady Julianna a guilty smile. "I'm only guessing based on the contents of his bill."

"Well, I'll leave you to continue to wait for him if you really feel you must, but take care. I suggest you wait over by the chair on the opposite wall. It'll provide you with more of an excuse if someone else happens past."

Frances glanced behind them. Indeed, there was a chair nearly directly across the corridor from Lord Kendall's door. Earlier, she'd been too preoccupied with practicing her speech to notice it.

"That's an excellent idea, Lady Julianna. Thank you."

Lady Julianna dropped her arm and turned to face her. "I've been worried about you, Miss Wharton."

"Worried? About me?" Frances pointed at herself and blinked. She'd no idea until today that Lady Julianna knew her name, let alone would worry about her.

"Yes," Lady Julianna replied softly. "I've seen you at dinner. I'm afraid your mother is doing her best to match you with Sir Reginald, and I don't think you two would make each other very happy."

Frances nodded. "I couldn't agree with you more, Lady Julianna."

Lady Julianna searched her face. "Sir Reginald's favorite subject is himself, while you seem to me to be an introspective, intelligent young woman. I doubt you'd enjoy a life listening to his dull stories."

Tears burned the backs of Frances's eyes. How kind of Lady Julianna to say something Frances needed so much to hear. "You know, for so long I've felt as if I was being disloyal to my mother for not immediately seeing his good qualities...or trying to at least."

Lady Julianna gave her a sympathetic smile and patted her hand again. "Take care, Miss Wharton. I know we ladies don't always have a choice in matters of the heart, but I would hate to see you miserable. You've always been so kind and friendly to my sister."

"Likewise, your sister has been nothing but kind to me as well," Frances murmured.

Lady Julianna drifted away toward the end of the corridor, but not before she waved and said something that Frances was almost certain was, "If Kendall has any sense, he'll scoop you up the moment he sees you on his doorstep. The man's in want of a good wife, you know."

Frances shook her head. No. She couldn't possibly have heard the woman correctly. And besides, even if that was what Lady Julianna had said, the last man she wanted to 'scoop her up' was *Lord Kendall*. She shuddered. No, indeed. She must return to her watch post and recite her speech in preparation for her confrontation with the odious man.

Taking Lady Julianna's helpful advice, Frances made her way over to the chair across the hallway from Lord Kendall's door. She decided to stand beside the chair. That way, she'd be prepared for Kendall's arrival. He wouldn't have a chance to slip inside.

Nearly ten minutes later, she was beginning to have doubts as to whether Lord Kendall actually intended to return to his room before dinner. For all she knew, he could be having drinks with Lord Clayton in his study. Perhaps she should go in search of that room next. She'd just discarded that notion and crossed her arms over her chest when a young man came bounding up the stairs. He was half a floor away and she didn't get a good look at him, but her first thought was that it was Lucas. She was just about to call out to him when she realized it couldn't be Lucas for two reasons. First, he was wearing the clothing of a gentleman, and second, he immediately turned and strode off quite quickly in the opposite direction. Lucas would have greeted her.

She pressed the balls of her hands to her eyes. Dear heavens, she must be tired. Her eyes were playing tricks on her. Perhaps she should actually *sit*. She lowered herself into the chair and had been sitting there silently for several more minutes when a man's voice called out to her from behind.

She turned toward the lady's side of the hallway to see a handsome tall blond man striding toward her. He was dressed in livery, but not Lord Clayton's livery.

"Miss Wharton," he called for the second time.

"Yes?" she said, watching intently as the man approached.

"I'm Mr. Baxter," the man said, "Lord Copperpot's valet. I happened to be in the kitchens a few moments ago when a maid came down asking for a poultice for Lady Winfield."

"Lady Winfield is my mother," Frances replied, worry making her chest tight.

"Yes, Miss Wharton, that's why I came looking for you. Apparently, your mother slipped and turned her ankle in the gardens earlier. She's abed at the moment, but she's asked for you."

"Oh, dear." Frances stood and lifted her skirts. "I shall go to her immediately."

"I think that would be best, Miss. Please let me know if I can send a message belowstairs to get you or your mother anything."

"I'll send Albina if we do need something." Frances had already turned and was making her way toward the opposite side of the floor to find her mother's room.

She got nearly as far as the staircase when she thought to thank the valet. But when she turned around, he was gone.

She turned back toward her bedchamber and made haste. Dear God. She hoped Mama was all right. She couldn't help but wonder if the heavens were paying her back for attempting to break her promise to her mother. No. She shook her head. That was a ludicrous idea. Wasn't it?

She'd had to leave Lord Kendall's door without speaking to him, but he was still somewhere in this house and she would find him before he left if it was the last thing she did. In the meantime, she would just have to wait and see if he deigned to answer her note.

CHAPTER NINETEEN

Lucas made his way toward the library the next morning with a mixture of trepidation and antici- pation coursing through him. He wanted to see Frances. He wanted to talk to her, not just about politics. He wanted to ask her what she thought about a variety of things like steeple chases, and Christmastide, and children. He wanted to hear more of the reasons she disliked the *ton*. After all, they were many of the same reasons he did. She was so honest and open and didn't seem to care what the world thought of her. Everyone could use more of that in their character. God knew he could.

Lucas had been disgusted last night, thinking of Frances married to Sir Reginald. The only thing that comforted Lucas was the fact that she'd clearly decided she would not marry the man, despite her mother's wishes. Of course, if her father demanded it, she would have to go through with the match. Lucas could only hope Baron Winfield would take his daughter's desires into account.

Lucas had been unable to sleep last night for several reasons. He'd nearly stopped breathing when he saw Frances outside his bedchamber door yesterday afternoon. He'd immediately turned in the opposite direction and nearly sprinted away. He'd gone up the servant's staircase to Bell's room and sent the marquess down to lure Frances away from his door. It had been yet another lie, but Bell had been happy enough to deliver it. He'd never met Frances before, and he doubted their paths would cross again during the house party.

At least the ploy had worked, and Lucas had been able to return to his room to fetch the livery he needed to change back into.

But what if Frances was waiting outside his door when he woke up this morning? He'd decided it would be safer to sneak up to his room on the fourth floor with the other servants where Lucas, the footman, slept. At least there he had little chance of being waylaid by Frances looking to confront him about the Employment Bill.

He'd spent the remainder of the night trying to decide how he would handle the note Frances had written him. He'd finally decided the safest thing would be to write back and tell her he needed to return to London immediately, but he hoped to make her acquaintance one day.

It was the cowardly thing to do, but it would serve two purposes: first, it would keep her from an inappropriate meeting with an eligible gentleman that she never should have requested to begin with. Lucas doubted she'd considered the consequences that might occur if such a meeting were actually to take place and they were seen together alone. Second, it would keep them both from an ugly scene in the middle of Clayton's home. If he were to meet with her and confess all, no doubt such a scene would be the result.

Lucas would tell her the truth. Someday. But for now, he needed to extricate himself from the complicated charade he had orchestrated with as few repercussions as possible.

Besides, it was not as if Frances was dreaming of a future with Lucas, the footman. That would be impossible and they both knew it. Her heart might sting for a bit (as would his), but they would move on, eventually. And he would never make a mistake like this again.

He was still contemplating the bittersweet moment he would see her for the last time when he entered the library. She was already seated at the table near the windows smiling at him, her face aglow with happiness. He immediately imagined that same sweet face crumpled in confusion and anger. The inevitable result if he told her the truth.

"There you are," she called. "I was beginning to wonder if you were coming this morning."

He forced himself to paste a smile on his face. "Good morning, my lady."

"Why weren't you serving dinner last night?" she asked.

He was prepared for that question. "Lord Clayton assigned me elsewhere for the evening."

"Hurry with the logs," she continued, clearly accepting that excuse. "I have a great deal to tell you today. I'm not certain where to begin."

He quickly finished his chore and made his way over to the table. "What do you have to tell me?" he asked, hating himself for being deceitful. He slid into the seat next to her.

Her eyes were bright with mischief. "For one thing, Lord Kendall is here. He didn't attend dinner last night, but there is no doubt he's here."

"How do you know?" Lucas asked, his brow furrowing. Had word of his arrival already got out at the party? If so, he would have to keep his head down.

"Sir Reginald of all people told me. I wonder why Kendall didn't come to dinner."

"Perhaps he's averse to large *ton* gatherings," Lucas conjectured, knowing that was precisely why Lord Kendall didn't come to dinner. That and the fact that Frances would have recognized him immediately.

"Perhaps." She shrugged. "But I picture him as more of a man who likes to be the center of attention."

Lucas succumbed to a coughing fit. Frances had to pound him on the back. When it was over, his eyes were watering profusely. "My apologies, my lady."

"Are you quite all right?" Concern was etched into her features.

"Yes, I'm fine. What else were you going to tell me?" he asked, purposely changing the subject.

She tipped her head to the side. "I had the strangest interaction with a man who claimed to be Lord Copperpot's valet. Do you know anything about him?"

"Lord Copperpot's valet?" Lucas repeated, tugging at his neckcloth.

"Yes, he found me in the corridor last night waiting for Lord Kendall. He told me my mother had turned her ankle."

Lucas did his best to feign concern. "Is she all right?"

"That's just it. When I went to Mother's bedchamber, she was perfectly fine. She hadn't turned her ankle at all. Isn't that strange?"

Lucas tugged at his neckcloth. "Perhaps he mistook you for someone else."

Frances shook her head. "I don't think so. He specifically called me by name, and he knew Mother's name."

"That is strange," Lucas replied woodenly. He cleared his throat and forced himself to broach a subject he dreaded. "What were you doing outside Lord Kendall's room?"

Her eyes gleamed. "Waiting for him, of course. Sir Reginald told me they had a meeting yesterday afternoon. I wanted to talk to him about the Employment Bill."

Lucas couldn't let on that he knew she'd sent him a note. Instead he asked, "Did you speak to him...Lord Kendall?"

She shook her head. "No, after I got to Mother's room and realized she was all right, it was time to begin dressing for dinner. I thought better of returning to Lord Kendall's door."

"I think that's wise," Lucas said. "You don't plan to return then?"

"No. I sent him a note asking him to meet with me."

"You *what?*" He did his best to summon the appropriate amount of outrage.

"I know it's inappropriate." She tugged at her bottom lip with her teeth. "But I signed the note with my initials so he wouldn't know I'm a woman."

Lucas did his best to give her a stern stare. "What do you intend to do when you meet with him? Disguise yourself as a man?"

Another gleam came into her eyes. She sat up straighter in her chair. "You know, that's not a half-bad idea."

"I was only jesting," he hastened to add.

She laughed. "Of course you were, but if I thought it would help me gain a meeting with him, I just might try it."

Guilt was now a song singing loudly through every vein in Lucas's body. He may not have had answers to half a dozen questions at the moment, but he knew one thing as certain as he knew that eight bells meant the end of a four-hour watch: he needed to stop this madness as soon as possible.

He'd already decided that he was through with this game. He had one more day to answer Sir Reginald. The only reason he hadn't told the man to go toss himself yesterday was because he hadn't trusted his own temper at the time. He also wanted his friends' counsel as to how to best handle the knight's request. As soon as he answered Sir Reginald, Lucas intended to leave the house party.

It would be cruel to disappear without saying good-bye to

Frances, however. He would speak to her one last time in the library tomorrow morning. He'd make up some excuse for why he had to go. What did one final lie even matter? He would say good-bye to her and then he'd leave this damnable house party, forfeit the bet, and let Worth and Bell compete for the win. He wished he'd never agreed to the blasted bet in the first place. He certainly never would have had he known the depth of dishonesty to which he would sink.

Lucas had wrestled all night with whether to tell Frances the truth now or leave and tell her later. He could either tell her the truth and watch her feelings for him fade beneath the lies, or he could leave with a beautiful memory of a beautiful lady...and hope he never encountered her and whoever was lucky enough to be her future husband about town. Damn it. Both choices were wrong to some extent. He would cause her pain, one way or the other.

He glanced at the clock. It was time to go, for now at least. If he stayed here with her any longer, he would only make things worse. He would only add to the pack of lies he would have to account for in future. If he stayed, he would only...want to kiss her again. And that would be unfair, to both of them.

"I have to go now, Frances," he managed to say. "I...have some additional chores to attend to." As excuses went it was particularly lame, but under the circumstances he thought it best not to invent any more elaborate stories.

She nodded, but he could see the disappointment in her eyes. "Of course," she said. "Will you meet me here tomorrow?"

"I...yes, I will. Tomorrow." His voice sounded melancholy, hoarse. He would do at least that much for her, promise to see her one last time. Say good-bye.

"Lucas, are you all right?" She bent her head to look at him. He was staring unseeing at the tabletop.

He lifted his gaze to hers. "Will you promise me you won't go looking for Lord Kendall again?"

Her sharp intake of breath made him look up. "No, Lucas. I cannot promise you that. Please don't ask me to."

He nodded. "You have to do what you must." He stood, pushed his chair beneath the table, and turned toward the door. Guilt gripped his heart. He began to walk away slowly.

"Lucas, wait," she called.

He turned on his heel to face her. She'd already caught up to him and was standing directly behind him when he turned. "You cannot leave without a kiss."

She lifted herself up on her toes, wrapped her arms around his neck, and touched her lips to his.

CHAPTER TWENTY

This kiss was unlike the others she'd shared with Lucas. At first, he seemed frozen, unwilling to participate. Frances was just about to release him and beg his pardon for mistaking the matter when she felt his resistance give way. His arms snaked around her back and he pulled her tightly against him, his mouth slanted over hers, his tongue sliding hot, wet, and warm, deep into the recesses of her mouth.

Relief swept through her. Thank heavens. She *hadn't* been mistaken. He wanted this as much as she did. Desire coursed through her body. His large frame was trembling when his hand reached up to cup her breast and—

The library door creaked open.

They jumped apart immediately, each taking a large step back. But they were breathing heavily and no doubt looking exceedingly guilty when Albina, of all people, stepped into the room.

The moment Albina saw the two of them together, her eyes narrowed to slits for the barest hint of a moment before returning to their vacant stare.

"There ye are, Mr. Lucas. I've been looking for ye," Albina called.

Frances watched as the maid came waltzing up to Lucas as if it was perfectly normal for her to have just found her employer and the man she fancied standing conspicuously alone in the library together, panting.

Frances scrambled to think of something relevant to say. "What are you doing here, Albina?" It wasn't a particularly remarkable question, but it was the first thing that sprang to mind.

Albina turned innocent blue eyes to Frances and blinked at her. "I've a message for Mr. Lucas from Lord Clayton."

Frances watched in disbelief as Albina made a show of pulling a slip of paper from between her breasts. She clearly intended for Lucas to watch. Appalled at the maid's shocking lack of decorum, Frances stood with her mouth open, staring at Albina. For his part, Lucas shifted from foot to foot, scratching at the back of his neck, and looking nothing if not entirely uncomfortable.

"Here it is," Albina announced, handing the slip of paper to Lucas. "Lord Clayton gave me this ta give ta ye." She laughed and placed her hand atop her *décolletage* again. "O' course, I don't mind coming ta look fer *ye*, Mr. Lucas." She eyed him up and down and licked her lips.

Frances smoothed her hand over her hair and cleared her throat, still trying to make sense of the situation. "Albina, why did Lord Clayton give you the note for Mr. Lucas instead of one of his own servants?"

Albina snort-laughed. "I don't think he realized I weren't one of his maids, milady. And I'm supposin' there weren't no footmen available at the time."

Frances pressed her lips together. The entire situation was odd, but Lucas was already reading the note from Lord Clayton and it appeared to be legitimate. "Is everything all right?" she asked, searching his face for some clue as to the note's contents.

"Everything is fine, but I must go," Lucas replied. "Lord Clayton needs me."

"Of course." Frances nodded.

Lucas bowed to Frances and thanked Albina for bringing him the note before striding quickly from the room.

Frances stood next to Albina and watched him go, her lips still burning from his kiss. She wanted to know if the maid had seen their embrace, but it would hardly be appropriate to ask. Besides, Frances had already got the distinct impression that if Albina *hadn't* seen anything, she certainly had suspected that she'd interrupted something.

Another tug of guilt pulled at Frances's conscience at the memory of Albina telling her that she fancied Lucas. It was madness, but Frances actually felt jealousy, too. She was jealous that Albina was more entitled to him than she was. Frances certainly had no business kissing him. Oh, when had she got involved in such a complicated mess?

"I told ye he were a fine specimen o' a man, didn't I, milady?" Albina finally asked, rocking back and forth on both heels, her hands clasped together in front of her.

"Indeed, you did," Frances replied feeling both awkward and guilty at the same time. How else could she possibly respond to that statement?

"But he *is* a footman, milady," Albina continued, and this time Frances did not mistake the sly, warning look on the maid's face.

Frances dropped her head to her palm and sighed. "I know, Albina." Oh, how well she knew.

CHAPTER TWENTY-ONE

Lucas hurried up the stairs to Bell's fourth floor bedchamber. The note from Clayton had been a request to seek him out there as soon as possible. By the time Lucas arrived, all three of his friends were already in the room. Bell sat on the cot. Clayton sat in the chair in front of the small desk, and Worth sat atop the deep window ledge.

"Ah, if it isn't the elusive Earl of Kendall," Clayton said the moment Lucas entered the room and shut the door behind him.

"Elusive?" Lucas echoed.

"Yes, seems word's got out," Clayton continued. "The gossip mill is well aware of the fact that the *Earl of Kendall* has arrived at the party."

"Blast," Lucas cursed under his breath.

"Well, it goes without saying that Kendall won't be at dinner tonight," Lucas replied with a wry half-smile. After the unsettling encounter with Albina nearly walking in on his kiss with Frances in the library, moments ago, Lucas couldn't seem to focus.

"Thea's at her wit's end trying to come up with excuses for why you haven't joined any of the festivities," Clayton added. "As Kendall of course."

"Sounds like Lucas the footman shouldn't be *serving* in the dining room any longer either," Bell cautioned from his spot on the bed.

"Agreed," Clayton and Lucas replied simultaneously.

"I couldn't do it any longer even if I wanted to," Lucas continued.

"Why's that?" Worth asked, his leg swinging back and forth as usual. "Too much work?"

Lucas shook his head. "No, the chores made me feel useful, actually. I simply no longer have the stomach for lying to Frances about who I am."

"Feeling guilty, Kendall?" Worth asked.

"You've no idea how much," Lucas replied solemnly.

The serious tone of his reply made even Worth go silent.

Lucas shrugged. "Not to mention I don't think I can serve that bombastic clod Sir Reginald again. I'd be as likely to pour gravy onto his lap than his plate."

"I would pay to see that," Worth said with a snort.

Lucas moved toward the cot and dropped onto it to sit next to Bell. "Speaking of Sir Reginald, I have one more meeting with him tomorrow."

Bell frowned. "I thought you already met with him."

"I did, but I haven't yet had a chance to tell you what he said."

"Do tell," Worth replied, settling himself deeper into the window ledge.

"The bastard tried to blackmail me," Lucas began, then he spent the next few minutes recounting his meeting with Sir Reginald.

When he was through, Clayton winced and shook his

head. "It's not particularly well done of him, but there's a fine line between blackmail and political negotiations."

"Is *that* what you call it?" Worth asked, arching a dark brow.

"I call it what it bloody well is...blackmail," Bell said, anger seeping from his tone.

"Perhaps," Clayton allowed, "but you may want to consider Sir Reginald's connection to the prince."

"What does the bloody prince have to do with it?" Worth replied, crossing his arms over his chest.

Clayton took a deep breath and addressed his remarks to Lucas. "Look, you obviously don't want to cater to his disreputable intentions, Kendall, but that doesn't mean you still can't play the game. Tell Sir Reginald you've decided to bow out of this particular match. He can vote on the bill any way he sees fit and may the Chancellor of the Duchy go to the best man. That way, you won't burn any bridges."

"Spoken like a true politician," Worth said with a dramatic eye roll.

"What's your advice, Worth," Bell asked next, "given that you're the subject of this particular attempt at blackmail?"

Worth contemplated his own countenance in the small looking glass on the wall opposite the window for a moment and straightened his cravat before he spoke. "I say you inform Sir Reginald that I will indeed vote for him for the chancellor role."

"Really?" Bell's brows shot up.

"Of course," Worth replied. "Tell him that, Kendall, then I'll maneuver to get the duchy vote moved *after* the Employment Bill vote, and by the time the bastard realizes he'd been lied to, it will be too late." He gave them all a triumphant smile.

"Spoken like a man who doesn't care how many enemies he makes," Clayton retorted, shaking his head.

Bell scratched his chin. "No one's asked me, but for what it's worth, *I* say you tell Sir Reginald he can go straight to hell."

"That's hardly helpful," Clayton replied.

"That's why you're the best politician in the room, Clayton," Worth pointed out with a grin.

Lucas leaned forward, resting his elbows on his knees. He shook his head, staring at the wooden floorboards. "That bastard. I can hardly stand to look at him, let alone speak to him again."

"What do you plan to say to him tomorrow, Kendall?" Clayton prompted.

Lucas lifted his head and met his friend's gaze. "I think I know what I must do. I'll tell you all after I meet with him."

"Well, then," Bell asked, leaning back upon his wrists. "If you're settled on your course of action regarding Sir Reginald, what is your course of action regarding Miss Wharton?"

Lucas expelled a deep breath. "Regarding Miss Wharton, I have one last lie to tell."

CHAPTER TWENTY-TWO

Just one more day. That's what Lucas promised himself when he made his way to the library the next morning. He intended to tell Frances that he had to leave. Lucas the footman's father was ailing in Northumberland. It would be the final lie he told her, and it already sat like a dead weight upon his conscience.

He would leave that afternoon, immediately following his second meeting with Sir Reginald. Leaving was the right thing to do. Lucas was certain of it. He needed time and space. Time to make sense of the last several days and to decide upon the most honorable way to tell Frances the truth without upsetting her more than he had to, and space to stop making additional mistakes such as kissing her again. He would go to his own estate in Kent and think through all of it before returning to London in autumn for the vote in Parliament and his reckoning with Frances. At this point, he looked forward to neither.

He'd promised Frances that he'd meet her today. That promise and his disgust at the thought of leaving her without saying good-bye were the only two things that made him keep walking toward the library.

He'd already written the note to Frances from Kendall telling her he couldn't meet with her. He'd spent the night on the fourth floor in case she decided to wait outside his room again. He would ask James to ensure she received the note the moment his coach pulled away from Clayton's drive.

Lucas was risking something, meeting her today. Her maid interrupting them yesterday had been nothing if not a reminder of the dangerous game he was playing. If the young woman had only walked in a moment sooner, she might well have caught them kissing. As it was, she probably suspected something similar had happened. Lucas had been unable to sleep last night playing the scenario through his head.

What would have happened had Albina caught them in an embrace? They could have asked her not to tell anyone, but could they trust her? The most likely scenario would be that a scandal would result, and Frances's reputation would be ruined. If she was caught kissing a footman, no man in the *ton* would have her. Not even that snake, Sir Reginald.

Of course, Lucas could offer her the protection of his name and marry her, but *telling* her his name would be the problem. She detested who he really was. That would hardly be the answer to such a debacle.

He should have stopped the kiss, shouldn't have allowed it in the first place. He'd come close to resisting her, but in the end, the feel of her soft warm body pressed against his and her lips, insistent and urging, had been his undoing. He wanted her, he always had, and she felt right in his arms, which made the fact that he had to leave her even more loathsome.

When Lucas entered the library, the room was empty. Alarm tingled through his veins. Had Albina seen something after all? Had she told Frances's mother?

In keeping with his usual routine, he set the logs next to the fireplace, removed his coat, and tossed the wood onto the pile.

Perhaps Frances was merely running late. Perhaps she'd decided to wait outside Lord Kendall's room again. He expelled his breath. At least Lucas wasn't in that room.

He finished with the logs, replaced his coat, and wandered over toward the table where she should be. He slid his hands into his pockets and stared out the windows absently into the gardens. Alarm had begun prickling along his skin once more, when a noise from within the alcove caught his attention.

He turned swiftly to see Frances peeking out. She stepped out of the space wearing a pretty white gown, a pink flower tucked behind her ear.

"Well, are you going to join me, or aren't you?" she asked, a beautiful smile on her lips.

Lucas couldn't stop the grin that spread across his face. "I'd no idea you were here." He strode over to her, but stopped just outside the alcove. It was safer outside the alcove. He wouldn't be so tempted to kiss her one last time.

"I could tell," she replied. "It took you long enough to toss those logs on the fire. By the by, what did Lord Clayton say in his note yesterday?"

Lucas dropped his chin to his chest and scratched the back of his neck. "He just needed to see me for a bit." That much at least was true.

"I missed you in the dining room last night," Frances said next, a coy tone in her voice.

Lucas lifted his chin and looked at her again. "I was, ahem, reassigned again." That was somewhat true too. He simply failed to mention that he'd been reassigned to his bedchamber because of his hidden identity.

She plucked at one of the soft brown curls that sat on her

shoulder. "You haven't missed much. It's mostly been a lot of love-sick young ladies swooning over Lord Kendall, who hasn't even had the decency to deign to join them."

"Really?" Lucas asked, clenching his jaw as the guilt gnawed at him. "What excuse was given?"

"None that I ever heard," Frances replied with a sigh. "The only thing Lord Clayton said about Lord Kendall was that he doesn't intend to stay long. But that certainly didn't keep the young ladies from talking about him all night. Both nights." She rolled her eyes.

"Was the conversation more interesting than Sir Reginald's talk about the prince at least?" Lucas ventured, doing his best to smile.

"Hardly, but I wasn't spared that either. Sir Reginald sat next to me again and did an awful job of attempting to be charming. Then he asked me to go walking with him in the garden this morning."

Lucas lifted his brows. "Did you say yes?"

"No, I told him I had already made plans to walk in the gardens this morning, which is why you see this flower in my hair." She laughed, pointing to the little pink bud.

"You're beautiful, Frances," Lucas breathed. "You should always have a flower in your hair."

Her gaze keeping his, she stepped farther out of the alcove and stood not an inch in front of him. "Thank you, Lucas," she whispered.

He tipped down his chin and watched her lips. Just one more kiss? The wicked thought sprinted across his mind. He couldn't ignore it. Without question, a kiss was the wrong thing to do. He would have no excuse when the time came to tell her the truth, but something in him, some primitive part of him that still wished he could have her, told him that he needed one final kiss to remember her by. Afterward, he would have to tell her he was leaving, of course, but first, one more kiss.

He lowered his head and met her soft lips with his. He closed his eyes and relished the scent of her, the feel of her, the sound of her. He would always remember her standing in Clayton's library wearing a white gown with a pink rosebud in her hair. Her image was burned into his memory forever.

His mouth opened and his lips slanted across hers, he pulled her tight against him.

"What do you think you are doing!" The loud shriek jolted Lucas from the cocoon of their intimacy. He pulled away from Frances, who looked equally startled, and spun around to see Lady Winfield standing in the doorway, a look of complete outrage on her mottled face.

The woman shut the door behind her with a loud thud and lowered her voice considerably before speaking through clenched teeth. "I'll thank you to get away from my daughter."

Instead of moving away, Lucas instinctively moved in front of Frances. Clearly, her mother had lost her senses and was even now stalking toward her daughter as if she might inflict bodily harm. He wasn't about to let that happen. A second thought flashed through his mind. While Lady Winfield clearly hadn't looked twice at him while he was serving her meals in the dining room, she might well recognize him if she got a good look at him after he kissed her daughter. So be it. He wasn't about to let the woman hurt Frances, no matter what.

When Lady Winfield reached them, she pushed past Lucas, reached around him, and grabbed Frances's arm.

Lucas moved to block the woman, but Frances cried softly, "Lucas, no."

With a smug smile, Lady Winfield yanked her daughter to her side.

Lucas's nostrils flared with anger, but he stepped aside, not wanting to make this moment any more awful for Frances.

"It's a fine day when I have to come and pull my *daughter* out of the arms of a *footman*," Lady Winfield growled, her voice still low. Lucas could only surmise that she had determined the most prudent course of action would be to keep what she'd seen as quiet as possible. They were the only three in the library after all.

Thankfully for her, Lady Winfield unhanded her daughter, but soon pointed toward the door as she spoke to Frances in a menacing tone. "Walk in front of me. Now. Directly up to your bedchamber. Don't you dare act as if anything is amiss. Do you hear me?"

That confirmed it. Lady Winfield clearly planned to pretend as if this had not happened. The only thing that kept Lucas from ripping off the damned itchy wig and declaring himself in love with Frances as the Earl of Kendall was the certain belief that that was not what *Frances* wanted. She'd made it clear that she thought gentlemen of the *ton* were high-handed when it came to getting what they wanted. The truth was, he wanted nothing more, but he forced himself to watch in silence as Frances walked slowly out of the library, her mother marching behind her.

Lucas cursed and clenched his fist. He cast about with no idea what he was looking for, perhaps something to throw or hit. Either would do at the moment. A small bit of color on the floor caught his attention. He glanced down. The rosebud lay on the rug at his feet. It must have fallen when Lady Winfield yanked Frances away from him. He leaned over, gently scooped up the small flower, and held it to his nose.

Christ, how he hoped that wasn't the last time he'd ever see her.

CHAPTER TWENTY-THREE

Frances sat on the foot of her bed while her mother's lengthy diatribe continued. It had begun the moment they had closed the bedchamber door and it showed no signs of abating anytime soon.

"What were you thinking, you hoyden!" Mama cried, dabbing at her sweating face with her handkerchief.

"Mama, I—"

But her mother was in no mood to listen. The woman continued to pace and wave her handkerchief in the air between dabs. The mottled purple tone of her skin alarmed Frances. The only thing she could be grateful for was the fact that Mama was keeping her voice low, apparently to avoid anyone overhearing and causing a scandal. Their walk upstairs had been perfectly calm and orderly. They'd only seen a few guests to whom they'd both smiled and nodded at as if nothing had been amiss.

"Thank heavens Albina alerted me," Mama continued, her pace increasing.

Frances's head jerked up. She searched the room and the adjoining bedchamber until she spotted Albina peeking through a crack in the door between the rooms. The maid had a sly triumphant smile on her face. When she saw Frances looking, Albina immediately darted behind the door.

"Albina told you?" Frances asked, her eyes narrowing, her hands balled into fists on her lap. "Why, that little, backstabbing—"

"We owe Albina a great debt," Mama insisted. "Do you have any idea what might have happened if someone *else* had walked in on that display in the library? If Albina hadn't sent me looking for you, I might never have known, let alone had a chance to stop it."

Mama continued to pace, while Frances expelled her breath and tried to think of the best way to handle the situation. Normally, when Mama was in such a state, little served to calm her.

"You could ruin your chances with Sir Reginald if he were to find out," Mama said next.

"I don't care if I ruin my chances with Sir Reginald," Frances spit out, still stewing over Albina's treachery. The last thing Frances was worried about at the moment was Sir Reginald's opinion. *On anything.*

Mama pressed the handkerchief first to one cheek and then the other. She looked as if she was about to faint. "How can you say such a thing?" She took a long, deep breath. "You know, I truly believed I was protecting you and your sister by keeping the truth from you, but I now I see I must tell you or you'll continue to sabotage your own future."

"Tell me what?" Frances asked defiantly, her arms still tightly crossed.

"You and your sister have no dowries. None! Not just small dowries. Nothing! Your father has gambled it all away."

Frances's mouth dropped open. "Pardon?"

"That's right," Mama continued. "There's *nothing* left, but Sir Reginald has indicated he's still willing to take you."

Frances closed her eyes. The weight in her chest felt as if a cannonball had just settled in her middle. The news was difficult to hear, but her mother's obvious angst over it was even more difficult to watch.

Frances already knew from experience that attempting to tell her mother that she didn't care if she remained a spinster wouldn't help the situation. Mama was hell-bent on marrying her off. A flurry of thoughts competed for attention in Frances's mind. Could it be that her parents did not even have the money to keep her in their household as a spinster? She'd never considered that before. She was being selfish not to listen to her mother's words. Mama's fear stemmed from the fact that she was clearly worried for her own future.

"Don't you see, Frances?" Mama cried brokenly, coming to a stop directly in front of her. "We *need* you to marry Sir Reginald. He may very well be our only hope for survival. Sir Reginald is wealthy. He's promised us a purse. Your sister is yet too young to marry. I suppose we could consider a match for her sooner than later, but—"

Frances immediately stood and hugged her Mama tightly. Her mother hugged her back, tears streaming down her face.

"I didn't know, Mama. I didn't know how bad it was." She felt like a fool, a blind, selfish fool. She'd known Papa was in trouble, she'd heard the arguments, seen the men come to the house. But she'd foolishly believed Mama when she'd told her they were poor instead of destitute. Frances knew one thing for certain. There was no way she would allow her little sister to be bargained off for a purse. No. If one of them needed to be sold into marriage to save their family, it would be Frances, without question.

"I know you didn't know, dear." Her mother sobbed. "I'm only sorry it's got to this point. The truth is I've spent our last bit of coin bringing you to this house party. Sir Reginald is our final hope."

They both moved to sit together on the foot of the bed. Frances ran a hand over her mother's graying hair, while patting her hand softly. "I'm sorry, Mama. I'm sorry I've been so difficult. Don't worry. Please, don't worry."

Mama dabbed at her wet eyes with the handkerchief she'd finally stopped waving. "Thank you, my dear. Now, will you *please* think of your family and accept Sir Reginald's suit?"

Frances expelled her breath and nodded slowly. However ludicrous the idea that she might somehow have a future with Lucas had been, the notion died an instant death. There was no way she could marry a poor footman. Her family was counting on her.

CHAPTER TWENTY-FOUR

As Lucas dressed for his meeting with Sir Reginald that afternoon, the roil of thoughts that had been racing through his mind all morning since Lady Winfield found him kissing Frances continued to batter against his mind like rain upon a flapping sail.

He was a bounder. He was a scoundrel. He was the lowest form of life imaginable. The worst part was that when he'd first entered the library, Frances had been hiding in the alcove. If only he had joined her there. But, no, *he* had had to stand outside in full view of the doors before acting like an even bigger reprobate and kissing her regardless.

It was all his fault, and the fact that Frances was bearing the brunt of the fallout made him insane. Throughout the day he'd been tempted to search for Lady Winfield's room and declare himself. It was the only decent thing to do. Only he would need to speak to Frances first to find out if she even wanted him to declare himself. And how could he expect that she would want him to declare himself if he would have to admit that he was the detestable Lord Kendall?

That never-ending circle of thoughts tripped over each other, one after the next, until he'd driven himself half-mad.

He glared at himself in the *cheval* glass. Here he was, dressed as an earl once again, in fabric that cost more than Lucas the footman made in a year's time. His clothing hardly mattered. He felt lower than the lowest criminal in Newgate. At least criminals were paying for their crimes. He was walking around completely free. He deserved to pay.

He glanced at the clock on the mantelpiece. It was time to meet Sir Reginald. At least he knew what he intended to say to that sop.

After the meeting in Bell's room yesterday, Lucas had decided upon his own course of action. He appreciated his friends' advice, and he'd considered all of it, but *he'd* always favored reason and logic over plotting and lies, *not* that anyone could tell from his activities of late.

It was time to start over. No more deceit, beginning with his discussion with Sir Reginald.

Lucas straightened his cravat one last time and left his bedchamber. Thank Christ, Frances was not waiting for him in the corridor. He probably didn't have to worry about her being there when he returned, either. Given the level of anger her mother had displayed this morning, he doubted Frances would be let out of that lady's sight for quite some time.

He would make things right with Frances somehow, but at the moment he had a score to settle with a certain knighted blowhard.

WHEN LUCAS WALKED into the drawing room five minutes later, Sir Reginald was standing at the window staring out across the meadow.

"Good afternoon, Sir Reginald," Lucas said, heading straight for the sideboard once again. "Care for a drink?"

"Not today, thank you," Sir Reginald replied, his tone terse.

Lucas poured himself a drink and made his way to the same chair he'd sat in the last time they'd been here for this discussion. Sir Reginald turned and stared at him.

"You all right, Sir Reginald?" Lucas asked, scratching his chin and taking a sip of brandy.

"No. Actually. My back is acting up. It's quite painful." Sir Reginald walked slowly and carefully over to the settee and took the same seat he'd occupied last time as well. He'd barely lowered himself to the cushion before he snapped his fingers and pointed at the footman who stood at attention near the door. "You there. You!"

Lucas's eyes widened and he stared at Sir Reginald, aghast.

The footman, James, took one step forward, clicked his heels together, and bowed. "Yes, my lord, how may I be of service?"

"Fetch me that pillow." Sir Reginald pointed to a pillow that sat literally one hand's length away from him on the settee. He easily could have reached it himself. "My back is aching and I need it for support," the knight finished.

"Of course, my lord." James strode over to the settee and picked up the pillow. He took one small step toward Sir Reginald. Wincing, the knight leaned forward to allow James to position the pillow behind him.

Lucas's gaze caught James's. He'd never been more ashamed to be of the Quality. The man had treated Sir Reginald with far more respect and care than he deserved. Lucas gave James a solitary nod.

"Yes, yes. Now, go away!" Sir Reginald snapped before

sighing and settling back against his pillow. "What were you saying, Kendall?"

"Have you made up your mind about the Employment Bill?" Lucas bit out. He had already decided to get directly to his point. There was no use prolonging this unpleasant conversation.

Sir Reginald's laughter turned into a coughing fit that lasted so long it became uncomfortable. Lucas was just about to ask the man if he needed to be slapped upon the back when Sir Reginald stopped and wiped his mouth with his lacey handkerchief. "Kendall, the better question is, have *you* made up your mind? I thought I'd made my wishes clear when last we spoke."

"I thought perhaps we could talk about the bill itself," Lucas replied, clutching the brandy glass so tightly his fingers ached. He was happily pretending it was Sir Reginald's throat. "There are many facets to consider, you know. Tell me some of the reasons you're against it," Lucas said, ready to have the same discussion he'd had with at least a dozen gentlemen over the past several months yet again.

"Very well, Kendall, we'll play your little game." The knight sighed. "But frankly it would be easier if I were to tell you why I'm *for* it."

"Really?" Lucas lifted his brows. "Go ahead then."

"Well, for one thing, it certainly sounds as if the bill will keep the servant class in their place."

Lucas couldn't help but glance at James. He suddenly felt entirely conspicuous. Even if Sir Reginald felt that way, did he have to say it in front of James? He could well have discreetly asked the man to leave the room or worded his sentence more tactfully.

"On the other hand," Sir Reginald continued, "it does appear to stifle some of the progress we've made with the trade laws. And I can't say I like that one bit."

Lucas frowned. *That* was Sir Reginald's argument? The trade laws had been too archaic even for Charles. Those laws kept the working class from earning any sort of a fair wage and had given them basically no rights against employers who refused to pay them, provide them with any medical care whatsoever, and even beat them. Sir Reginald's argument *against* the Employment Bill was that it didn't make it difficult *enough* for the working class? The repeal of some of the harsher conditions of the trade laws had been the one part of the Employment Bill Frances had actually agreed with. Her words rang in Lucas's memory. *I don't see how anyone with a heart beating in his chest could be for it.* Sir Reginald certainly sounded heartless at the moment.

Lucas forced himself to temporarily swallow his distaste to make his next point. "It will stimulate the growth of tenant farming and help to shore up some large problems with estate economics."

"Yes, but the real beauty of the trade laws was the fact that we don't have to answer to anyone for how we treat our help," Sir Reginald continued. "Why would I choose to vote against my own best interests?"

The House of Lords has the power to defeat this law, but they only vote in favor of themselves and their own purses. More of Frances's words resounded in Lucas's head. He'd actually spent time trying to argue that point, trying to convince her that the male members of upper class did not vote only in favor of themselves and their own purses. But she was right. Sir Reginald was proving her right.

"I suppose you *won't* choose to vote against your own best interests," Lucas managed to bite out. He had only one final thing to say and then he intended to take himself away from Sir Reginald's noxious company and never seek it again. "Look, Sir Reginald, the reason I'm so interested in getting this bill passed is because—"

"We all know why you're so interested in getting it passed, Kendall," Sir Reginald interrupted with an eye roll. "Your brother told you to. Now *Charles* was a man with whom one could negotiate. I was hoping you'd be more like him, actually."

Lucas sat back. His chest ached as if he'd been knocked from a ship's crow's nest to the main deck. He couldn't breathe. His throat burned. "What did you say to me?" he growled through clenched teeth.

"I said your *brother* knew how to be a politician. Clearly, he didn't teach you much before he cocked up his toes."

Lucas squeezed his glass so tightly it cracked. If he didn't remove himself from Sir Reginald's presence immediately, the knight's neck would be next.

"On the contrary." Lucas spit the words like nails. "I've always believed the bill would do the most good for the country. But I'm beginning to understand that it actually does the most good for our class and I'm not at all certain any longer that our class deserves it." Lucas stood, drained the rest of the brandy from his ailing glass, set it on the side table, and strode toward the door. "Good day, Sir Reginald."

The knight stared after him, his mouth agape. "Wait a minute," he called. "What about the chancellorship?"

Lucas didn't slow down. "Good afternoon, James, and thank you for your service," he said to the footman on his way out, tipping his head in the servant's direction. "Please tell Clayton I owe him a brandy glass."

"With pleasure, my lord," James replied with a nod and a bow.

Lucas hadn't got three steps down the corridor before he let out a string of muffled curses that he knew for a fact would make one of the most highly seasoned jacks in the Royal Navy blush. What the hell had just happened back there?

Lucas was thoroughly disgusted. Disgusted with Sir Reginald and all the imperious blowhards like him, gentlemen of the *ton*, who went around making pronouncements as if they were gods. But mostly Lucas was disgusted with himself, because he knew that what Sir Reginald had said about his espousing the bill for his brother was entirely true. Frances was right. Noblemen were self-entitled horse's asses. And he was one of them.

CHAPTER TWENTY-FIVE

Sneaking down to the servants' hall without being seen was no small feat. Waiting to find a particular servant and whisper at him to come speak with you without anyone else noticing was an even larger challenge. But Frances was nothing if not determined. If her mother found her, she would be locked in her bedchamber till her wedding day, but she'd had to take the chance. If only to see Lucas one more time. Frances had little idea what she'd say to him when she found him, however. She only knew she had to tell him the truth. He deserved to know what she was going to do.

She'd been hiding beneath the staircase belowstairs for the better part of a quarter hour before Lucas walked past. He had a frown on his face and looked to be in the devil's own mood. She called his name in a loud whisper.

Lucas froze and his eyes widened. He glanced over and narrowed his eyes into the darkness. "Frances? What are you doing here?"

He glanced around to see if anyone else had seen her before hurrying over to join her beneath the staircase. "Are you all right? Your mother didn't beat you, did she?" A thunderous look covered his face.

"No, nothing like that. She cried actually," Frances replied, wringing her hands.

Lucas winced. "I hate to hear that."

Frances took a deep, steadying breath. "I came to tell you something, Lucas," she whispered. "And I fear I don't have much time."

"Go ahead," he prompted. He'd grabbed both of her gloved hands and was holding them, rubbing across her fingers with the tips of his thumbs. His touch gave her strength. But it also made what she was about to say that much more difficult.

She stared up into his handsome face. Oh, dear. This was *not* going to be easy. It seemed even more daunting now that she was standing in front of him, breathing in the scent of his cologne, and wanting to do nothing more than wrap her arms around his neck and beg him to take her away from the horrible predicament.

Lucas squeezed her fingers and searched her face. "Are you all right, Frances?"

She was not all right and she wasn't certain she ever would be again, but she managed to nod. "Lucas, before I tell you, will you...kiss me first?"

His green eyes widened to small orbs and he took a definite step back, still holding her hands. "No!"

She pulled her hands from his and plunked both fists on her hips. "Well, you don't have to be insulting about it," she replied, but her smile belied the content of her words.

He smiled too. "It's not that I don't want to, Frances, believe me it's not. It's just that...the last time I gave into that temptation it ended horribly as you might recall."

"Oh, yes, I recall." She stared wistfully past his shoulder.

She understood why he was reluctant to kiss her again, but she'd just realized it would have been their last kiss.

He rubbed a knuckle against his forehead. "What did you come to tell me?"

She took another deep breath, pressing her palm against her middle as if that simple act would calm the riotous nerves inside. "My parents intend to announce my engagement to Sir Reginald as soon as my father arrives."

"What?" Lucas's eyes scoured every inch of her face. "What do you mean?"

"My mother has unofficially accepted Sir Reginald's suit. We're merely waiting for my father to make it official."

Lucas's eyes were moving so quickly, Frances could tell a hundred thoughts must be racing through his mind. "When does your father arrive?"

"Tomorrow," she replied.

"You intend to marry Sir Reginald?" It was posed as a question, but Frances could tell he was saying it aloud as if to confirm it in his own mind.

She swallowed and nodded. "Yes, it's my choice."

He scrubbed a hand through his hair and searched her face. "You *want* to marry him?"

She turned away from him and bit her lip. "You don't understand, Lucas. My family needs the money. It turns out I have *no* dowry. None whatsoever. My father has gambled it all away."

He blew a deep breath from his pursed lips as if he was trying to control his temper. "All of it?"

She swallowed the lump in her throat and nodded. "Everything."

Lucas's next words came through clenched teeth. "And Sir Reginald, that ass, doesn't care that you don't have a dowry."

She nodded again. "Not only that, apparently he's agreed to pay my parents a significant sum."

Lucas cursed under his breath. His nostrils flared. "So, he's *buying* you?"

She let her chin drop to her chest. She'd expected Lucas would be angry, but she hadn't guessed his words would be so harsh. "I know how awful it sounds. I have no choice."

He paced away from her, his hands on his hips. "When is the wedding to be?" he ground out.

She took another steadying breath. "As soon as possible. The sooner we wed, the sooner my father will get the purse."

Lucas bit the inside of his cheek and cursed again. "Just to gamble it away again, no doubt."

Tears burned the backs of her eyes. "Probably, but what else are we to do? I must think about my family. They'll be destitute without this match."

"Your father should be thrown in debtor's prison," Lucas growled.

Again, she fought the tears that threatened to spill from her eyes. "That's not particularly helpful, Lucas. Debtor's prison provides no options for men like my father."

Footsteps thudded on the staircase above them.

Lucas paced away from her again. "Blast it, Frances. What if...?"

"'What if' *what?*" she asked brokenly, tears sliding down her cheeks. "Please don't say what if you and I were to marry. I cannot marry a footman, Lucas. Unless you happen to have a secret fortune."

He clenched his teeth and pressed his closed fist against his forehead. "Damn it," he ground out, drawing out each word.

She wiped the tears away with her fingers. "I'm sorry, Lucas. I didn't want things to end this way. It's not what I prefer." She swallowed again. "But I'm resigned to it."

More footsteps.

He swiveled on his heel so quickly he nearly knocked her

over. He gently cupped her shoulders to keep her steady. "What if things were different?" he blurted, searching her face. "What if there was another way?"

She shook her head, still meeting his gaze. "What way? What are you talking about?"

"Do you love me, Frances?" He squeezed her shoulders gently. His heart was in his eyes.

Her tears were falling steadily now. She swiped them away with the backs of her hands. "I do love you, Lucas. But what choice do I have?"

The thud of footsteps on the stairs above them increased. Lucas dropped his hands to the sides. "The servants are coming down to prepare to serve dinner. If we stay here any longer, we're certain to be seen. I cannot explain now. It's not the right time. Will you do me one last favor?"

"Anything." Her voice broke. She swallowed yet another painful lump in her throat.

"Will you meet me in the library again tomorrow morning? There's something important I must tell you."

CHAPTER TWENTY-SIX

Lucas rapped three more times on Bell's bedchamber door. The marquess wasn't answering. Where the hell was he at this hour? He had to be inside. He hadn't been down in the servants' hall earlier when Lucas had gone looking for him. It had been a pure coincidence that Lucas had been there when Frances had arrived to find him.

Lucas rapped on the door for a third time, harder and longer this time. He didn't want to wake the other sleeping servants, but he desperately needed to speak with Bell before morning.

Finally, Lucas heard mumbling and shuffling from inside the room. Several moments later, a sleepy-looking Bell clad only in a pair of no doubt hastily pulled-on breeches ripped open the door.

"Kendall?" he groaned. "I mean, Lucas, get in here." He yanked Lucas none-too-gently into the room by the scruff of the neckcloth and shut the door behind him with a loud thud.

Lucas stepped into the darkened room. No candles were

lit, but a full moon shone outside the window illuminating a great portion of the space, including the desk by the window. He strode over to it and sat on its edge.

"My apologies for coming so late," Lucas began.

Eyes closed, Bell ran a hand over his face and sniffed. "What bloody time is it?"

"Two o'clock," Lucas admitted.

"In the morning? That's bloody ridiculous."

Lucas shrugged. "When I was in the Navy, I used to stand watch at two o'clock."

Bell groaned. "Well, neither of us is in the Navy at the moment, are we? I, for one, find this a ludicrous time to be keeping company."

Lucas halfway turned and stared out at the night sky. "I have to tell you something, Bell."

Bell yanked open the doors to his wardrobe and stared blankly inside. "What is it?"

Lucas stood and braced his palms behind him against the desk. "I'm in love with Miss Wharton."

"I know," Bell announced, tugging a shirt from a peg in the wardrobe.

"You know?" Lucas frowned. "How the hell would you know?"

"Of course I know," Bell continued. "As you've reminded me on more than one occasion, I'm a bloody spy for Christ's sake. It's my business to know what's going on in this house."

Lucas tapped his boot against the floor. Very well. Bell already knew, but his friend's revelation didn't change what he'd come here to say. "I've been meeting with Miss Wharton, every day in the library. We talk about politics, life, …the Employment Bill."

"I know," Bell said, tossing the shirt over his head.

The frown remained on Lucas's face. "You know that, too?"

Bell turned to face Lucas and pointed both of his thumbs toward himself. "Spy."

"Very well." Lucas ran both hands through his hair. "Do you also know I've kissed her? Several times. She kissed me too, actually, but please don't spread that about."

"I *didn't* know that," Bell admitted, tucking his shirt into his breeches, "at least not the 'several times' bit. Of course I won't say anything, you bloody fool, spies don't tell secrets."

Lucas nodded. That was why he was here. In addition to giving sound advice, Bell was an excellent secret keeper. You could tell the man anything, and even the French couldn't torture it out of him. Lucas had known before he'd opened his mouth that Bell would keep this conversation entirely confidential.

"The question is," Bell continued, "why do you find it so important to tell me that you love her at this hour?"

Lucas tugged at the ends of his hair. "Because of what Sir Reginald said."

Bell adjusted his shirt on his shoulders. "What does Sir Reginald have to do with it?"

"She's going to marry him." Cold dread gripped Lucas's chest. It wasn't until he'd said it aloud that he realized how sickened he was by the notion.

"Pardon?" A furrow appeared between Bell's brows.

Lucas nodded. He crossed his arms over his chest. "Her father arrives in the morning. They intend to announce the betrothal tomorrow night."

Bell narrowed his eyes. "Baron Winfield is coming here?"

Lucas gave his friend an are-you-quite-serious look. "Yes, but that's hardly the point."

"What's the point?" Bell scrubbed a hand over his face. "That Frances Wharton is marrying Sir Reginald?"

"No. That Sir Reginald said the only reason I'm interested in passing the Employment Bill is because of my brother."

Bell stopped scrubbing and pressed one palm against a closed eye. "You're not making any sense, you know? And I *don't* have the impression that you're foxed, which means you have no excuse for not making any sense."

"I'm *not* foxed," Lucas replied with an eye roll.

Bell cocked his head to the side. "Then please explain to me what Miss Wharton marrying Sir Reginald has to do with the confounded Employment Bill."

"Nothing," Lucas replied, tossing a hand in the air, "other than I've made a mess of the entire affair."

Bell blinked repeatedly. "How so?"

"Courting Frances, espousing the bill, and now leaving." Lucas counted off his transgressions on his fingers.

Bell frowned. "You're leaving?"

"Yes, in the morning. After I speak to Frances one last time."

Bell shook his head. "What do you intend to say to her?"

"I don't entirely know yet. But I must tell her the truth."

Bell shook his head some more and rubbed his forehead. "You're giving me a megrim, Kendall, and I don't get megrims. Let's begin again, shall we. You talked to Sir Reginald about the Employment Bill?"

"Yes. Yesterday afternoon."

"And what did he say?"

"He still wanted a bribe, but then he said I only was interested in passing the bill for my brother's sake."

"Of course you're doing it for Charles' sake," Bell scoffed. "I thought you already knew that."

Lucas roughly scratched at his cheek. "I knew I was doing it for Charles, but I honestly thought *I* believed in it too."

"You *don't* believe in it?" Bell asked, his sharp blue eyes narrowing on Lucas.

"No. Not any longer."

Bell raised a hand in the air. "Thank God, you've finally seen reason."

"What?" Lucas frowned.

"The Employment Bill is hideous. I never intended to vote for the thing myself."

Lucas stared at his friend as if he didn't know him. "This whole time you've known that, and you didn't tell me?"

Bell stepped forward and wrapped his arm around Lucas's shoulders. He walked him over to the cot that rested against the wall and they sat down, side-by-side. "Kendall, I've known you since we were barely more than children ourselves. You are honest, trustworthy, and kind. You're one of the best men I've ever known. But you've never been cut out for politics. You're far too loyal. And far too decent."

Lucas took a deep, bracing breath. He was about to admit something to Bell he'd never admitted to anyone. He stared down at his boots in the shadows. "The truth is, I've always felt as if I wasn't supposed to be—"

"I know." Bell nodded sagely. "You weren't supposed to be the earl."

"You know that, too? Bloody hell man, you *do* know everything." Lucas couldn't help his half-smile, but the truth was his friend was one of the most perceptive people he'd ever met.

"Perhaps not *everything*," Bell replied with a smile of his own. "Look, you may not be earl by birth order, but I say destiny doesn't make mistakes. Whether you were born to the position or not, you're the earl now, and you have the power to make large decisions, decisions that affect others, decisions that affect the country. Your brother was a decent man, but he never saw beyond his own nose, I'm afraid. You, you're different. You see two sides to a story. You empathize with others. You care about them. All you need to do now is trust yourself."

"'Trust myself,'" Lucas echoed, mocking the words.

"Yes, trust. Yourself. You'll have no better counsel in life. You've always known the right thing to do. Now you simply must do it when it comes to Parliament and the vote."

"And Miss Wharton," Lucas added, expelling his breath.

"And Miss Wharton," Bell echoed, grinning at him.

Lucas groaned and rubbed a knuckle against his forehead. "I've spent the better part of the last year arguing *for* the bill with anyone who would listen."

"And you only have a month or two to argue against it," Bell pointed out. "But something tells me with Miss Wharton at your side, you're certain to win."

Lucas clenched his jaw. "She won't be at my side. She's going to hate me when she finds out who I am."

Bell lifted his brows. "Even if she learns you've changed your mind about the bill?"

"It doesn't change the fact that I've lied to her a dozen different ways." Lucas bounced his fist atop his knee.

Bell nodded, slowly. "All you can do is tell the truth, Kendall, and leave the future to the stars."

Lucas took a deep, steadying breath and looked out the window at the night sky. "Tell me, Lord Bellingham, when did you become so wise?"

Bell shrugged. "I'm even wiser at a decent hour."

CHAPTER TWENTY-SEVEN

L ucas got to the library early. He hadn't been able to sleep, so he'd tossed off the blankets and got out of bed. He'd dressed himself, quite deliberately, as the Earl of Kendall, managing to do so without the aid of a valet.

The Clayton livery was packed in his trunk. He fully intended to burn the odious clothing at his first opportunity. No. He wouldn't burn it. He'd give the clothing to one of his servants. His time belowstairs had taught him the importance the working class placed on valuable items discarded upstairs. It often contributed greatly to the income of a servant fortunate enough to receive such a gift from his master.

His own time as a servant had come to an end. He'd tossed his last log on the fireplace.

This was it. No matter what else happened, he intended to tell Frances the truth today. He was through with lies. If she hated him, so be it. It would be better than living with the regret of not knowing what could have been between them. He'd planned this carefully. As Lucas, he'd asked her in the servants' hall yesterday to meet him here today. As Kendall, he'd replied to her note this morning, writing that he looked forward to meeting with her before he left.

He was sitting at the table, the windows to his back, when Frances entered. She wore a butter-colored gown and matching slippers. Her dark hair was twined around the crown of her head in two braids. She'd never looked more beautiful, and he was about to hurt her.

His chest tightened. He clenched his jaw.

She rushed straight to him, a string of words already flying from her pink lips. "Lucas. Lucas! You won't believe it. Lord Kendall sent me a note saying he'll meet with me. But he didn't give any details, the coward. No matter. I intend to go looking for him directly after this." She stopped short, really looking at him for the first time since she'd come in. "Why are you dressed that way? Where is your wig?" Her smooth forehead wrinkled into a frown.

He'd stood to greet her and moved to the side of the table. Pulling out the last chair for her, he gestured to it. "Please sit down."

Watching him carefully, the frown still perched upon her brow, she tentatively stepped forward and lowered herself to her chair. "You're frightening me, Lucas."

Standing behind her, Lucas closed his eyes, then slowly opened them again. "You don't have to go looking for Lord Kendall."

"What do you mean?" The quiet innocence in her tone made him even angrier with himself. Regret clawed at his insides.

Lucas took a deep breath. It was now or never. He stepped to the side so she could see his face. He would not hide from her when he told her the truth.

"Are you all right, Lucas?" she asked, lifting her face to watch him. "You look...troubled."

"Frances, there's something I must tell you. I've been remiss not telling you 'til now."

She searched his face. "I'm listening. What is it?"

"I—"

Both doors to the library swung open and a group of no less than a half-dozen young ladies and one of their mothers came hurtling into the room. They were dressed in gowns of a variety of pastel colors and their talking and giggling filled the space.

Lucas cursed under his breath and dropped his chin to his chest. Damn it all to hell. He shouldn't have chosen the library. People were always coming into the *bloody* library. It might as well be a public house.

The moment the pack of ladies saw Lucas, their chatter increased.

"Is that him, Mama?" one of the young ladies asked, pointing directly at Lucas.

Her mother nodded vigorously. "That's him, darling."

The pack immediately came streaming over, their giggles and laughter increasing until it was a cacophony.

"There you are, my lord," one of them called. She sidled up to him and wrapped an arm around his, pulling him away from the table and Frances. "Don't you know we've all been looking for you for two nights now." The young lady had a fake pouty look on her face.

Blast. This was just the sort of thing he'd been desperately hoping to avoid.

Lucas tried to locate Frances in the crowd, but the ladies had managed to push him back several paces and Frances was still sitting at the table as far as he knew. He tried to dodge a few of them and make his way back to her.

"Miss Wharton!" he called, mindful that they had an audience.

"Lucas?" Frances called back. He could barely hear her

over the din, but her voice was definitely filled with confusion. "Lucas?"

The cacophony came to such an abrupt and total halt. You could have heard a flower petal fall to the carpet.

"You're calling him by his Christian name?" another one of the young ladies said to Frances, her hand on her chest, her eyes wide with surprise.

Lucas took the opportunity to plunge back through the herd until he stood directly beside Frances again.

Frances shook her head. She glanced around at the ladies. "What are you talking about? Why are you all here?"

"We're here to see the Earl of Kendall, of course," a third young lady explained, giving Frances a look that clearly indicated she thought she'd lost her mind.

"Won't you come for a walk in the gardens with us, my lord?" A fourth young lady said to Lucas, tugging at his arm.

Lucas cleared his throat. "Frances, I—"

Frances turned to stare at him as if she'd never seen him before. "Why do they keep calling you 'my lord'?" Her voice held a note of apprehension, and the look in her eyes was wary.

Oh, God. She knew. She'd asked, but she already knew.

"Frances, please, let me explain," he began.

Her jaw hardened and she glanced around until she caught the attention of one of the girls standing next to her. "Who is this man?" Frances pointed to Lucas.

The young woman rolled her eyes. "Miss Wharton, honestly. You don't know you were sitting next to the Earl of Kendall?"

CHAPTER TWENTY-EIGHT

Tears blurred Frances's vision. Bile rose in her throat. She lifted her skirts and ran from the library. Lucas's voice called after her, but she didn't stop. She ran into the corridor, down the long hallway, around the corner and out into the foyer.

She was at the bottom of the grand staircase about to take her first step when he caught up with her.

"Please stop," Lucas begged.

She hesitated only because she had no intention of causing any more of a scandal, and being chased up the staircase by the Earl of Kendall would no doubt cause the grandmama of scandals.

Frances clenched her jaw, refusing to look at him. She kept her chin lifted, her gaze trained on the top of the staircase. If she turned her head, he would probably see the tears in her eyes. She refused to give him that. "Don't follow me upstairs. My reputation won't stand it," she ground out.

Two of the faster debutantes had already caught up with Lucas and were standing on the edge of the foyer, their mouths agape. Frances could see them from the corners of her eyes.

"Frances, please give me the chance to explain," Lucas said.

"Explain what?" she bit out, refusing to allow the heavy tears to fall. She would *not* cry over this man. She would not cry over the confounded Earl of Kendall of all people.

At least not until she made it to her bedchamber.

"Explain why I lied to you," he said in a rough whisper.

She closed her eyes. There it was. His admission. Whatever hope she'd held out that this was all somehow a crazy mistake and perhaps he just *looked* like the Earl of Kendall was dashed to bits.

"Does it matter? Does it really matter?" She felt her nostrils flare with each word. Her emotions were riding a runaway horse, a mixture of anger and sadness and jealousy and a host of other things she didn't even want to think about. She had to get away from him quickly or he would see her tears and so would the bevy of young women congregating at the foyer's entrance. Two more had joined the first two and they were jockeying for position to get a better view of the show.

Lucas reached for her and kept his voice low. "It may not matter to you. But it does to me. Please, Frances, let me explain everything. It's not what you think."

That was it. Her head snapped to the side as if he'd slapped her. He might as well have, the insult was just as brutal. "How could you *possibly* know what I *think*?" She swallowed the painful lump in her throat and forced herself to keep her gaze trained on him. Tears or no, she wanted him to see her face when she said, "Don't you *ever* speak to me again, Lucas." She paused for a moment, swallowing again. "Wait. Is that even your name? Lucas?"

He lifted his chin. His voice was hoarse, his face had lost its color. "Yes, it's my Christian name."

She put one hand on her hip. Anger spreading through her veins like poison. "Is that the only thing you *didn't* lie about?"

"Nearly." He lowered his gaze to the polished marble floor.

She took a deep breath, still fighting like hell to keep the unwanted tears at bay. Just one minute longer. Just one minute more. Then she could leave his presence and never see him again. "I only want to know one thing." She clenched her jaw so tightly it ached. "*Why?*" she breathed. "Why in the world would you dress up like a footman and pretend to be a servant? It makes no sense at all."

He raised his gaze to hers. It was filled with something akin to regret, but at the moment she couldn't even acknowledge it. "I fear my explanation would make even less sense," he began. "You see, I made a bet with my friends and—"

The wind was knocked from her chest. Pain wrenched her insides. She clenched her fists and turned her head away from him, clenched her eyes shut. "Stop. Just stop. A bet? That is the most disgusting thing I've ever heard." She forced herself to reopen her eyes, but refused to look at him. Instead she kept her gaze focused on the bannister this time. "You played with my life, my *emotions* over something as crass as a *bet*?" She practically spit the last word.

His voice remained low, obviously to keep the ladies from overhearing. "That's not how it started, Frances. You've got to believe me. I—"

Still refusing to look at him, she faced the top of the staircase and lifted her skirts. "Go," she demanded. "Just go. It makes me ill to look at you. I never want to see your face again."

It took all her strength to climb that staircase without

running, but she did it. She didn't know how she did it and she had no earthly idea how long it took, but by God, she never once looked back.

By the time she made it to the end of the corridor and her bedchamber, she was a quivering mess. She opened her door, stepped inside, shut it behind her, leaned back against it, and slid all the way to the floor in a crumpled heap. Sobs racked her body and she cried until she had no more tears.

~

ALBINA CAME TIPTOEING into Frances's room from the adjoining bedchamber. "Are you all right, Miss?"

"I'm fine, Albina," Frances said, grasping the door handle and forcing herself to stand. The last thing she needed was that tell-all Albina running off to inform her mother that she was laying on the floor crying. "I'm just going to lie down for a bit."

"Yes, Miss," Albina said before tiptoeing back out.

Frances walked to her bed on wooden legs. She'd no idea how much time had passed. It could have been moments, it could have been minutes. She pulled herself atop the mattress, and sat on its edge, staring numbly at her sodden handkerchief.

How? How could Lucas, the footman, the man she'd met the first day—no, nearly the first *moment* she'd stepped foot on this property—be the Earl of Kendall? How could he be the man she'd detested since learning last year that he was the sponsor of the Employment Bill? How was that possible? And more importantly, how had she managed to *not* know it? She'd always thought of herself as reasonably intelligent, but somehow, she'd failed to see what was happening. She was an utter fool.

No. That was not true. She *was* perfectly intelligent. The

man had lied to her. He'd deliberately deceived her. Any normal person might have been duped if they'd been placed in her position. But *why*? Why had he lied? And why to her? Had he singled her out? The other young ladies at the party obviously knew who he was. Why had he chosen *her* to deceive?

The questions just kept coming, one after another rolled through her mind like waves upon the seashore. Why would an earl pretend to be a footman? What good did it do? What purpose did it serve? He'd mentioned a bet with his friends. That implied it had been a jest. A lark. She swallowed yet another painful lump in her throat. Had she just had her heart smashed into a thousand little pieces by a group of noblemen trying to outfox each other for a few lousy coins? Dear God, Kendall was even more of a bastard than she'd guessed. He could rot in hell as far as she was concerned.

Anger at herself seeped into her thoughts next. She'd been far too emotional downstairs. She should have told him she didn't give a whit who he was and given him a piece of her mind about the Employment Bill. She'd told him she never wanted to see him again. She wouldn't have another chance to tell Lord Kendall precisely what she thought of his abominable bill. In addition to having her heart broken, she'd missed her only opportunity to rail at the bastard. She ripped at her handkerchief with both hands. Blast. Blast. Blast.

Then the conversations they'd had in the library came back to haunt her, one-by-one. Oh, God! The things she'd said to him about the *ton*, about nobility, about gentlemen of the Quality. And all the while he'd smiled and nodded and pretended as if he agreed. He was a liar and a fake! The lowest of scoundrels.

What sort of man did something like this? What sort of man took advantage of a young lady the way he had? Why, she should have Papa call him out. Lord Kendall deserved no less. She quickly discarded that notion. She didn't want Papa to die. Besides, she'd had a part to play in this turmoil, too. She'd never had any business meeting with a footman in the library each day. She would accept that much of the blame. But she wasn't the one who'd lied about her identity. He was.

Dear heavens. He must have been laughing at her the entire time. And their kisses. Their kisses! Were they even real? Or had he merely been pretending to want her in order to win his silly bet? Good God. He'd touched her, he'd kissed her, he'd— No. She couldn't think about that. If she did, she'd go mad. She had to pretend that had never happened or she couldn't stand it. Not today. Perhaps not ever.

He'd lied about *everything*. From his name at first, to his job, to his relationship with Lord Clayton, to his stance on the Employment Bill. Oh, God. When he'd supposedly been playing devil's advocate for the bill, that hadn't been pretending at all. He *was* in favor of it. Her stomach lurched. She was going to vomit. She slid off the bed and ran for the sideboard, barely making it to the chamber pot in time.

Afterward, she sat in silence as every single word she'd ever spoken to him came back to taunt her. Again and again, she asked herself why? His only answer continued to throb inside her brain. *Because of a bet.* That was the cruelest part of all.

Darkness had descended outside Frances's window when her mother came sailing in from the adjoining bedchamber. "Oh, dear, there you are. Your father's just arrived. He's already spoken to Sir Reginald, and he agrees we should proceed with announcing the betrothal at dinner tonight."

CHAPTER TWENTY-NINE

There were not enough bottles of brandy in the world as far as Lucas was concerned. He'd had the better part of one and half of them and he intended to continue until the earth ran dry. Or at least until Clayton's estate did.

Lucas was sitting on the cot in Bell's fourth floor bedchamber again. Worth and Clayton had joined them.

"Pour me another drink," Lucas demanded, slamming his fist atop the table next to the bed.

"Don't you think you've had enough, Kendall?" Worth asked, from his preferred perch on the window ledge.

Bell sat on the cot next to Lucas, and Clayton, once again, sat in the chair in front of the desk. Just like the last time they'd been here, it was a tight squeeze, four grown men in the small room, but they weren't particularly concerned with their accommodations at the moment. They were much more interested in drinking. Clayton, who'd brought the brandy with him, was in charge of pouring.

"I agree with Worth," Clayton said, replacing the glass

stopper on the brandy bottle. "You've had enough for the time being."

"I have not had enough," Lucas replied, blinking. "I am a horse's arse. I'm a scoundrel. I'm a cur."

"You're certainly making a good case for being a horse's arse," Worth replied with a laugh. "I won't disagree with you there, old chap."

Lucas let his forehead drop to his palm and groaned. "I've made a mess of everything."

"Come now, not everything," Worth replied. "You weren't involved in *everything*."

Lucas's head snapped up and he glared at Worth. "I will fight you with one hand tied behind my back if you besmirch her honor." He lunged toward the brandy bottle.

"Good God. No one is besmirching anyone's honor." Worth reached down and pulled the brandy bottle out of Lucas's reach. "Who knew you were such an angry drunk? I must admit I've never seen this side of you before, Kendall."

"None of us has seen this side of him before," Bell pointed out. "The man's heart is broken."

Bell wasn't telling a secret. In the hours since he'd last seen Frances in the foyer, Lucas had gathered his friends, began drinking heavily, and poured out his whole sad, sordid story to the lot of them.

None of them seemed particularly surprised.

"Is a broken heart the reason he's like this?" Worth scoffed. "I thought he was merely angry with himself for losing the bet."

"If I could reach you, I'd take a swing at you right now," Lucas growled at Worth.

"Well, then it's a good thing the desk is between us then, isn't it?" Worth replied with a smug smile. He lifted his own brandy glass in salute and took a taunting sip.

Lucas pushed himself angrily back on the bed and leaned

his head against the wall. "Damn you, Worth. I didn't lose the bet."

Worth nearly spit his drink. "The devil you didn't. Half the ladies at the house party saw you trying to stop Miss Wharton from running away from you this morning."

"Kendall is right," Bell pointed out. "He hasn't lost the bet."

"How is he right?" Worth wanted to know, resting a wrist atop his propped-up knee.

"The ladies saw the Earl of Kendall trying to chase Miss Wharton up the staircase. They had no idea they were also looking at Lucas, the footman," Bell said.

Clayton's sharp clap of laughter filled the room. "By God, it's true. Somehow Kendall has managed to keep his identities separate even still."

"Except for Frances," Lucas pointed out, tipping his already empty glass back toward his mouth. Realizing it was again empty, he cursed and tossed the glass onto the cot.

"Except for Miss Wharton, of course," Clayton agreed. "And please have a care for my glassware. You've already ruined at least one snifter."

"Well, fine then." Worth crossed his arms over his chest. "I suppose Kendall's still in the game."

"I don't give a seafarer's rope about the stupid bet," Lucas grumbled.

Bell picked up the empty glass and sat it on the floor next to his boot.

"Oy," Lucas yelled. "Give that back."

"I will do no such thing," Bell replied. "Dinner is only a few hours away and you'll need to be sober by then. Or at least much more sober than you are at present."

"I don't give a damn about dinner. Brandy is my dinner," Lucas insisted.

"No, it's not," Bell replied, shaking his head.

Clayton winced and tugged at his cravat. "Yes, well, you know what's going to happen at dinner tonight," he said, giving Bell an urgent look.

"The betrothal?" Bell replied, blinking at him innocently.

Clayton rolled his eyes. "Fine then, if we're going to speak about it in front of him. Yes, the betrothal. I received a note from Baron Winfield just before I came up here. He's arrived and they fully intend to proceed with the announcement tonight."

"Has Sir Reginald heard about the to-do in the foyer between his *fiancée* and Kendall here?" Bell asked Clayton next.

"I'll punch Sir Reginald in the eye," Lucas announced, waving both fists in the air.

"Yes, we'd all like to see that," Bell said, forcing Lucas to lower his hands.

"He's heard about it," Clayton reported, "but according to Thea, who heard it from the servants, who heard it from the guests' servants, who heard it from the guests...no one took the incident in the foyer this morning particularly seriously."

Bell arched a brow. "What? Why not?"

"Apparently, our friend Kendall here did a fine job of keeping his voice low. No one could hear what he and Miss Wharton were saying to each other. And—" Clayton winced. "No one can countenance the fact that the Earl of Kendall would actually be interested in Miss Frances Wharton."

"I'll punch them all in the eyes," Lucas declared next, hoisting his fists in front of his face again.

"Now. Now. You're talking about ladies here. I don't think it would be good form to go about striking any of them," Bell said, patting Lucas on the back.

"They have no right to be discussing me and Frances," Lucas retorted.

"I agree with you there, Kendall," Bell replied evenly. "But violence doesn't seem like the best response. I, for one, think a far better decision would be for you to attend tonight's dinner."

"What?" The other three men all said the word simultaneously. Lucas's mouth fell open, Worth's eyebrows shot up, and Clayton frowned.

"Why shouldn't he?" Bell asked, his gaze traveling around the room.

"He's foxed for one thing," Worth said with a laugh.

Clayton cleared his throat. "And the last thing he needs is all of those debutantes and their mothers trying to throw themselves at him if he wants Miss Wharton to think better of him."

Lucas had leaned over on the bed and was holding up his head on one hand, his elbow braced on the mattress.

"I didn't say he should go as *Lord Kendall*," Bell pointed out. "I think he should go as Lucas, the footman. After he sobers up that is." Bell stood. "And to that end, help me get his face in the washbowl, lads."

APPROXIMATELY THREE HOURS and three dunks in the washbowl later, Lucas was considerably more sober, but Bell still hadn't convinced him to attend the evening's dinner as Lucas, the footman. Clayton had already left to see to his guests and Worth had returned to the stables after wishing Lucas a hearty good luck.

Bell was shrugging into his coat. "It's time for me to go help Lord Copperpot dress for dinner," he announced.

"What purpose would it serve for me to go to the dining room as a footman?" Lucas asked a final time. "Frances would recognize me immediately. Besides, you heard Clayton. Sir Reginald and Frances intend to announce their engagement tonight. It's too late."

Bell adjusted his collar and smoothed his hands down the front of his liveried coat. "I can think of several purposes it would serve and you could too if you'd stop and consider it," he replied. "Meanwhile, if I were you, I'd bloody well go to the dinner in one form or another and ensure the woman I love didn't betroth herself to another man tonight."

CHAPTER THIRTY

Frances was forced to enter the dining room far behind the Prince Regent. Since George's arrival, the party's standards had become much more formal. The prince walked in with Lady Clayton, while Lord Clayton escorted George's sister, one of the Royal princesses, who had come with him. Frances, being the daughter of a baron, stood toward the end of the queue.

While the entire set of guests was buzzing about either the prince's arrival or spotting Lord Kendall in the library this morning, Frances sat at the far end of the table and stared at the wall as if in a trance. Sir Reginald was on her right, her mother on her left, and her father sat on the other side of her mother. Frances had no appetite. The only thought that briefly floated through her mind was gratitude that Albina had produced some sort of paste that had reduced the puffiness of Frances's eyes. They were still slightly red and bloodshot, but at least they weren't bloated, making it obvious she'd spent the afternoon crying in her bedchamber.

Frances had forgiven the maid for her betrayal. After all, what difference did any of it make now? Her betrothal to Sir Reginald was soon to be announced.

Mama had insisted Frances wear her most costly gown tonight. It was one they'd purchased before the Season began, a light pink sheath with puffed sleeves, an empire waist, and lace around the neckline. No doubt Mama had paid for it with credit. Credit that Sir Reginald would be honoring, apparently. Frances could barely stand the thought. At Mama's urging, Albina had created a ring of flowers for Frances's hair. She'd rubbed her cheeks with a bright, happy-colored rouge. On the outside, Frances was dressed up for the announcement of her betrothal, but dread clawed at her insides.

Sir Reginald was doing his best to keep her engaged in the tedious conversation, but tonight the most she could manage in reply was a grunt or an *mmm hmmm* to most anything he said. Of course, that cowardly horse's arse, Kendall, hadn't bothered to attend dinner. In fact, she had no idea if he was still at the house. Half of the table was gossiping about how they'd heard he'd left this afternoon in a coach bound for London. If that was true, good riddance.

Two courses had been served. Frances had been doing nothing more than pushing the food around on her plate until it was removed from her presence. She had every intention of treating the rest of the courses in a similar manner.

Course number three was watercress soup, normally something she enjoyed. She had been paying no attention whatsoever to the footmen who were serving until a familiar voice sounded in her ear. "Soup, my lady?"

She froze. She didn't have to glance up to know it was him. Lucas. No, not Lucas, *Kendall*. Her breathing hitched. Her breaths came in short, anxious pants. She slowly lifted her gaze. *Please God, let me be mistaken.*

She was not that fortunate. It *was* him. *What the devil was he doing here?* Anger began to bubble through her veins.

"No, thank you," she bit out. She smugly glanced around the table waiting for the first person who would recognize the ass. Yes, he had on livery and a powdered wig, but *still*.

It seemed like time had stopped. The table's occupants were laughing and talking and eating and carrying on without the slightest bit of recognition. She glowered at Lucas. He shrugged almost imperceptibly and continued to the next diner, while Frances continued to glare at him as if her eyes could set him on fire.

What sort of sick game was he playing this time? Was *this* part of his idiotic bet? She glanced around at the other diners, silently urging first Sir Reginald, then her mother, then her father, to notice that the *Earl of Kendall* was traipsing around the table offering them soup. Should she say something? Should she point him out? It was as if she was trapped in a nightmare from which she couldn't awaken. Had the entire world gone mad? What was wrong with everyone? How could the same man half of them had been swooning over earlier be completely invisible to them now? It made no—

Frances sucked in her breath. *Wait a moment.*

If he was the Earl of Kendall, why hadn't any of them recognized him all the *other* nights he'd been serving dinner?

Disbelief and disgust swirled in her middle. But the truth was right in front of her. The people he was serving were so oblivious to servants they hadn't even noticed him. They still didn't.

Had *that* been part of the bet?

She glanced at him. He looked tired. Good. *Oh, botheration.* She shouldn't have looked. He looked at her, too, which meant he saw her look at him. She immediately dropped her gaze to her plate, cursing softly under her breath.

Frances continued to ignore her food and give monosyllabic replies to the people sitting next to her until Lucas came around with the fourth course, a roasted duck.

"My lady?" he asked.

"No, thank you," she intoned again, staring directly ahead. This was some sort of torture and she'd no idea what she'd done to deserve it. She kept hoping she would wake up from the nightmare, but it was only too real.

Lucas dropped a napkin onto the floor next to her chair and bent to retrieve it. The scent of his soap hit her nostrils. She froze and pressed her lips together. Why was he here? Why was he tormenting her like this? Why did his cologne still make her pulse quicken?

As he stood up, his mouth brushed past her ear. "Meet me in the blue salon after dinner. I must speak with you."

She kept her gaze fastened on her plate. "Never," she replied in a sweet whisper.

He'd made his point. As a servant, he was completely unseen by the same people who would fall at his feet if he were sitting next to them dressed in his regular clothing. But if that were the point he was trying to make, why was he in favor of the Employment Bill, for heaven's sake? The entire thing was confusing, but she refused to play into his game.

The fifth course seemed to arrive much more quickly, and Frances was beginning to feel as if she had an imminent appointment with the hangman's noose. Her betrothal announcement was impending and the blackguard who'd tricked her into falling in love with him under false pretenses was making her life hell.

Fine. She could admit it to herself. She *had* fallen in love with Lucas. That's why he'd been able to hurt her as much as he had. She'd even admitted it to him, which made her ill to think about now. What an ignorant emotion love was. She'd thought she'd found someone she could talk to, someone with whom she could share her thoughts, someone who respected her. Instead she'd found a charlatan who'd used her feelings as an archery target.

The sweetmeats Lucas brought around next didn't tempt her. And when he lowered his head to fill her wine glass and said, "Please meet me," she couldn't help the seething anger in her reply, "Go to hell."

NEARLY AN HOUR LATER, Frances had long ago given up the hope that any of the others at the dining table were going to notice that the Earl of Kendall had been serving them all night. She steadily drank from her wine glass and pointedly glared at the one person she knew was in on this ludicrous game. Lord Clayton met her gaze every so often before hastily glancing away and gulping more wine from his own glass. The man was obviously guilty over his part in Lord Kendall's ruse. Good. No doubt Clayton was in on the bet, too. He had to be.

At least Lucas had stopped asking her to meet him after his third failed attempt. Though he continued to serve the table inconspicuously.

The dessert plates were being cleared when Sir Reginald finally stood and clinked his fork against his wine glass.

"I would like to call for a toast," the knight intoned as the table quieted down. Sir Reginald was wearing a bright-blue jacket and matching pantaloons. His white shirt boasted a riot of lace around the throat and a similar amount of lace flopped at his wrist as he lifted his glass aloft. Frances couldn't help but think he looked exactly like a peacock.

Frances forced herself to swallow the dread and panic

that rose in her throat, threatening to strangle her. She met her mother's gaze. Mama's gray eyes were wide and feverish. She smiled encouragingly. Frances couldn't remember the last time she'd seen her mother so pleased. Too bad it was at Frances's expense.

She *tried* to catch her father's gaze, but he was staring at his lap, busily folding his napkin in one direction, then the other. She'd barely said two words to him since he'd arrived. If her father felt guilt over forcing his daughter into this situation, he certainly didn't intend to acknowledge it.

Frances attempted to pin a smile on her face, but the best she could muster was a blank stare. She lifted her glass along with the others as Sir Reginald continued to speak.

"Tonight, my friends, I'd like to share some happy news."

The table rang out with cheers and "hear, hears" as everyone watched Sir Reginald, clearly interested in what he was about to say.

Frances couldn't help but glance at Lucas. He stood perfectly straight with his back to the wall next to the sideboard, his hands folded behind him. His eyes locked with hers momentarily. She darted her gaze away as if burned and, taking another sip of wine, did her best to concentrate on Sir Reginald's speech.

"I would like to announce that *I* am engaged to be married," Sir Reginald continued, a lop-sided grin on his face.

Surprised conjectures reverberated throughout the room.

Frances sipped her wine more quickly.

"I know. I know," the knight continued. "Many of you were quite convinced that I was a confirmed bachelor. And I suppose I was, for a bit. But someone with my breeding, title, and fortune ought not to go to waste, wouldn't you agree?"

Laughs and claps bounced about the room while Sir Reginald afforded them all with a self-satisfied smirk. "There-fore," he continued, clutching his wine glass in one hand and his lapel in the other, "I am beyond pleased to inform you all that I have asked for a special lady's hand and she has graciously accepted."

Frances nearly spit her wine. What was he talking about? He hadn't asked *her*, and she'd never accepted. It had been nothing more than a business arrangement with her parents.

"I am the luckiest man in the kingdom tonight and I dare say she is the luckiest lady." Sir Reginald gave the crowd a sly grin.

Frances had to force herself not to wince. Sir Reginald was really spreading the jam on the toast, wasn't he? As far as she was concerned, she was the exact *opposite* of the luckiest lady in the kingdom. She stared straight ahead, but she could feel the knight's eyes on her, beaming at her. He might not have said her name yet, but it had to be obvious to the entire table that *she* was his betrothed. Still, she couldn't bring herself to meet his gaze. He clearly intended to draw this out for both effect and attention.

Frances's gaze darted to Lady Julianna Montgomery who sat near the center of the table with her handsome *fiancé* who'd also just arrived. Lady Julianna's sympathetic look made tears sting the backs of Frances's eyes. She tried to manage a smile to reassure the kind woman, but the best she could muster was a resigned nod.

"A toast to the future Lady Francis!" Sir Reginald finally finished, raising his wine glass even higher. "Miss Fra—"

"Stop!"

Frances's head snapped up and her eyes went big as dinner plates. A collective gasp went up around the room.

Lucas had stepped up on the chair next to the sideboard. "Sir Reginald, I bid you to stop."

The room fell silent. From the chair, Lucas stepped atop the sideboard and stood towering over the dining room, still dressed in his footman's livery, powdered wig and all the rest.

"Dear me, he's going to send me to my grave," Mama huffed in Frances's ear, already fanning herself with her napkin.

Frances glanced at her mother. The poor woman was the color of a ripe rutabaga.

"What is the meaning of this?" Sir Reginald demanded. He turned to Lord Clayton. "My lord, I demand you do something about your impertinent footman."

"I am no footman," Lucas pronounced, lifting his chin. "I am the Earl of Kendall." He ripped off his wig and tossed it into the soup tureen near his feet.

Screams and shrieks went up around the room and one of the young ladies fell out of her chair in a dead faint. Two of the other footmen rushed forward to carry her away.

The rest of the diners stared in fascinated horror as Lucas shed his livery jacket and stood there clad in his waistcoat, white shirt, and breeches.

"By God, it *is* Kendall!" one of the gentlemen shouted.

The Prince Regent dabbed at his nose with an ornate handkerchief. "I was wondering earlier why the Earl of Kendall was serving us all soup," he drawled.

Frances covered her mouth with her bent fingers. If the entire thing hadn't been so horrifying, she might have burst out laughing. Of all the people in the room, the only one who'd recognized Kendall was the prince? The prince who never appeared to notice anything beyond his own nose? Now *that* was humorous indeed.

"That's right," Lucas continued. "I've been serving you, all of you, for days now. I've filled your wine glasses, I've ladled your soup, and I've placed your napkins on your laps."

"The devil you say," another gentleman added.

Lucas put his fists on his hips. "I've done all of this with no other change to my appearance than some livery and a powdered wig. And do you know what I've learned?"

The entire table was silent, staring up at him in rapt fascination.

"I've learned that our class is the most self-centered, vapid, inattentive, uncaring lot of horses' arses there ever was. Not *one* of you recognized me, because not *one* of you took the time to look at my *face*."

The table remained silent. Frances glanced around. There was a mixture of guilt and confusion on nearly every countenance. The tiniest hint of a smile tugged at her lips. Her anger at Kendall had not abated, but even she had to admit it was delightful to gaze around the room as the entitled diners each realized he was right. The man was a horse's arse, but this speech was precisely what these people needed to hear and she couldn't have said it better herself.

"That's all fine and good, Kendall," Sir Reginald snapped, anger and impatience etched on his features, "but you interrupted me in quite an important moment. I was about to announce my engagement to Miss Wharton."

"I interrupted you on purpose," Lucas shot back, "because I haven't had a chance to ask for Miss Wharton's hand first."

Another gasp went up around the room and all of the dining table's occupants swiveled their collective heads to stare at Frances. She took a deep breath. She could happily strangle the blackguard for making such a scene.

"Well, then," the Prince Regent prodded, addressing his remarks to Lucas. "Go ahead, man, ask for her hand."

Sir Reginald shot the prince a positively wounded look.

Apparently, Lucas needed no other encouragement. He jumped to the floor and swiftly made his way to Frances's seat. When he got there, he dropped to one knee.

Her throat was closing. She could not breathe. The walls of the dining room seemed to be closing in on her.

"Frances Regina Thurgood Wharton," he said, grasping her gloved hand in his. "Will you do me the honor of becoming my wife?"

CHAPTER THIRTY-ONE

Lucas felt Frances's hand trembling. Indeed, upon closer inspection, he realized her entire body was shaking. Her teeth were chattering, and she looked as if she might cast up her accounts.

"Are you all right?" he whispered to her, suddenly alarmed.

"I cannot breathe," she gasped.

"Get her some water!" Sir Reginald called to no one in particular.

Frances ripped her hand from Lucas's grasp and ran from the dining room.

Lucas jumped to his feet and made to follow her, but Sir Reginald lunged in front of him, blocking his path.

"Would you please shut up and leave?" Sir Reginald demanded, stamping his foot.

"No," Lucas retorted. "I won't."

Yet another collective gasp went up around the room as the diners watched the back and forth between the two men as if it were a game of battledore and shuttlecock.

Sir Reginald lowered his voice so only Lucas could hear him and spoke through clenched teeth. "I'm warning you, Kendall. If you don't shut your mouth and go away now, you will *not* get the votes you want on your precious Employment Bill. I can promise you that."

Lucas took pleasure in allowing a slow smile to spread across his lips. "I don't give a toss about the bleeding Employment Bill, Sir Reginald, and *you* can go straight to hell."

Lucas pushed the knight aside and strode from the room, grinning to himself. The look of pure shock on Sir Reginald's face would remain in his memory forever.

SHE WAS NOT in the foyer. She was not in the blue salon. Lucas doubted she'd made it up the stairs already. Instead, he took a chance and made his way to the library.

He pushed open the door, the familiar creak making his heart thump harder. He stepped inside and shut the door. The room was dark save for a few candles that burned throughout the space and the fire that was nearly out. The candles gave an ethereal glow to the large, dark, expanse.

Lucas took a deep breath and made his way directly to the spot he hoped she'd be. He'd never been a praying man, but with every step he said a silent prayer. *Please let her be there. Please. Please.*

He turned the corner to the alcove and caught his breath. At first he thought she wasn't there, but then his eyes adjusted to the darkness and he saw her shadowy form. She was sitting on the floor, her knees drawn up, her arms wrapped around them, rocking back and forth.

Relief swept through him. If she'd come here, she must

have thought he would find her. She must have—dare he hope—*wanted* him to?

"Frances?" he whispered, her name a stark plea on his lips.

When she lifted her head and looked up at him, his hopes were dashed. Even in the dim light he could see that anger burned in her eyes. She hated him. He'd made a mistake.

His chest ached and every breath was a struggle. He crouched down next to her.

She was still shaking, her teeth still chattering.

"Are you cold?" he asked.

She nodded.

"I'll be right back."

He quickly strode over to the desk and opened the bottom drawer. The shawl she'd left the first day he'd met her was still there. He'd brought it back down a few days ago and put in the drawer again so he wouldn't forget to give it to her. He grabbed it and hurried back over to the alcove. "Here," he said, draping it over her shoulders.

She clutched it and wrapped it more tightly around herself. "Th...thank you," she managed. "I thought I'd lost this."

"I think I kept it on purpose. It reminded me of you. Will you hear me out?" he asked softly, crouching down once more.

"Do I have a choice?" Her voice was monotone.

"Of course you do, Frances. You'll always have a choice with me." He searched her profile, wanting nothing more than to reach out and trace his fingertip along her cheekbone.

Her jaw tightened. "Then, no, I don't want to hear you out. I just want to ask you one question."

He closed his eyes briefly. "Anything."

"Wh…why did you ask me to m…marry you?"

"Because I want to."

"How c…can you w…want to marry me? I stand against everything you stand for."

He bit the inside of his cheek and expelled a breath. "The Employment Bill is not what I stand for."

She tugged the shawl closer around her shoulders. "Tell the truth, you only asked me to marry you out of guilt."

"No, I didn't." He said the words with all the sincerity he felt in his heart.

"Yes, you did." Her voice sounded resigned, lifeless. He couldn't bear hearing her like this. "You know I'm marrying Sir Reginald for money and you're trying to save me because of your guilt."

"That's not why. I—"

"But what I cannot understand is why you would ever think I'd accept you." She turned her gaze to him. Her eyes were shards of dark glass.

He swallowed hard. "If you'll give me a chance, I can explain everything. Try to, at least."

"You lied to me. About everything. Everything you did was a lie."

"No, Frances, I—"

"Of course I see it all clearly now, but at the time, I'd no idea. Like the time I tried to give you a coin for carrying my trunk to my room. You tried to give it back to me."

He bit the inside of his cheek, hard.

"And the time you called Lady Clayton by her Christian name. It's because you are friends."

He clenched his jaw.

"'*A footman who likes to read?*' I said. You let me feel guilty for saying that and for mentioning that your voice was cultured too. Of course it's cultured."

"Frances, listen to me. I—"

"I was *such* a fool." She shook her head. "And you let me be. Dear God. You even asked me if I was *in love* with you?"

Lucas took a steadying breath. He knew his next few words could decide their future, their fate. "Frances, I'm not about to deny that I've made a mistake, a tremendous one, but I can make this right, I promise you."

"Make it right?" She laughed a humorless laugh. "By marrying me?"

He nodded.

She turned her head to stare straight forward into the darkness again. "I suppose next you're going to tell me that you love me. That you merely forgot to say it that night under the staircase in the servants' hall." Her tone turned wistful.

He opened his mouth to say just that. "I didn't want to tell you until you knew who I really was."

She put up one hand. "Please. Don't." Tears sparkled in her dark eyes.

He scrubbed a hand through his hair and nearly growled with frustration. How could he get her to understand? How could he convince her of how he truly felt? She was choosing to see the worst in him.

She didn't want to hear them, but the words *I love you* incinerated on his tongue.

His throat burned. He shook his head. For the first time in his life, words completely failed him.

She struggled to her feet, declining the hand he offered. "I can't believe you. If you told me you love me, it might be just another lie."

Tears streaming down her cheeks, she brushed past him and raced from the room.

Lucas watched her go and along with her, his hopes and dreams for a marriage full of love with a woman who he knew without a doubt would have been true to him forever.

CHAPTER THIRTY-TWO

"**I**'ve come for the brandy bottle." Bell threw open the door to Lucas's guest bedchamber on the second floor. It had been over an hour since Lucas's scene in the dining room, and Bell had obviously got wind of it.

Lucas blinked calmly at the ceiling from his position lying prostrate on his bed. "There is no brandy bottle."

Ignoring him, Bell proceeded to search around the mattress, beneath the pillows, in the bedside drawers, and even under the bed. "The devil you say," he finally conceded, taking a seat in a large chair near the fireplace that faced the bed.

"I'm not jug-bitten," Lucas replied woodenly, staring at the ceiling, his arms folded neatly on his middle.

"I can see that," Bell replied. "But I must say I'm surprised."

Lucas let out a loud groan. "What good would getting foxed again do?"

"An excellently rational point. I do believe there's hope for you yet." Bell grinned at him.

"I'm certain you've heard," Lucas drawled. He was lying

diagonally across the mattress, still fully clothed as a footman, save for the wig and jacket he'd discarded in the dining room.

"Heard that you made a preposterous scene in the dining room earlier? Or heard whether you're betrothed to Miss Wharton?"

"I am decidedly *not* betrothed to Miss Wharton, and I *did* make a preposterous scene in the dining room earlier."

"Is it true that you threw your wig in the soup?" Bell sighed. "Seems overly dramatic to me, but what do I know? Spies tend to like things quiet and drama-free."

"Yes, well, *you're* the one who suggested I serve dinner tonight," Lucas pointed out.

Bell rested one booted foot atop the opposite knee. "True. But I had no idea the soup would suffer."

"Who gives a toss about the soup?" Lucas bit out.

"Clearly not you," Bell retorted, "but I digress. I've come to ask you what you plan to do next."

Lucas frowned at the ceiling. "What do you mean, what do I plan to do next?"

Another sigh from Bell. "I'm no matchmaker, but even *I* can tell that your courtship with Miss Wharton appears to be going poorly at the moment."

"She hates me."

"Hmm." Bell tapped his cheek. "Perhaps *poorly* wasn't a strong enough word then."

"I cannot blame her for hating me." Lucas lifted his palms to rub his eyes. "But she wouldn't even give me the chance to explain."

"'Love is your master, for he masters you. And he that is so yoked by a fool, Methinks, should not be chronicled for wise,'" Bell recited with a flourish of his hand.

Lucas rolled his eyes. "Spare me your Shakespeare quotations at a time like this."

"On the contrary, I believe a time like this is the perfect opportunity to quote Shakespeare. But my question still stands, what do you plan to do next?" Bell folded his hands together in front of him and blinked at Lucas as if expectantly waiting.

Lucas dropped his forearm across his brow. "I plan to bloody well get the hell out of here tomorrow morning. That's what I plan to do next."

"Quit?" Bell's voice held a note of surprise. "That doesn't sound like a Navy man to me."

Lucas arched a brow and glared at him. "There is a difference between quitting and admitting obvious defeat. Refusal to do the latter can result in accusations of delusion."

"Given the right circumstances, we all suffer from delusion from time to time. I still say that's not an excuse to quit."

Lucas pushed himself up on his elbows to glare at Bell. "Perhaps you didn't hear me? She hates me. She told me she never wants to see my face again."

Bell plucked nonchalantly at his sleeve. "Perhaps you should write to her then."

"She's marrying Sir Reginald. She told me I'm an arrogant horse's arse."

Bell scratched behind one ear. "None of this sounds particularly promising, I agree. But where there is a will, there is also a way."

"Not any more. I tried. I served dinner. I stood up on the bloody sideboard for Christ's sake."

"I heard about that, too. I did like that touch. I've no doubt it added an air of the theatre. By the by, my thanks for making my and Worth's future more difficult. No doubt every guest in this house will be searching the servants' quarters for noblemen now."

"You'll both be fine," Lucas replied.

Bell blinked again. "How could you possibly know that?"

"For one thing, they'll never suspect there's more than one of us being this mad, and for another, you're limited to Lord Copperpot's bedchamber for the most part and Worth is out hiding in stables."

Bell shrugged. "You do have a point."

"I wish you luck, my friend. Between you and Worth, may the best man win."

Resting his elbow on one of the arms of the chair, Bell propped his chin on his fist. "Never thought I'd see the day when I had to call you a quitter, Kendall."

"It's over," Lucas's voice rose. "The entire bloody dining room knows I was pretending to be a footman."

"Not quit the bet, you dolt, I mean quit your attempt to win over Miss Wharton."

Lucas grabbed a nearby pillow and hurled it toward Bell. "Damn it, Bell, get out of here and leave me in peace."

The pillow fell to the floor short of his chair. Bell hadn't flinched and he continued to blink at him. "I still say you should—"

"I should what?" Lucas's voice shook with anger. "I've tried everything I can. You're talking to the wrong person. Perhaps you should try speaking to Miss Wharton. She's the one refusing to hear me out." He grabbed a second pillow and pulled it over his head. "Now, good night!"

CHAPTER THIRTY-THREE

When the door to the library opened the next morning, Frances couldn't keep her traitorous heart from wishing for just one moment that it was Lucas. It was wrong of her to have come to this room. This place held nothing but bad memories for her. But, as if her feet had a will of their own, they'd brought her directly here this morning. She'd pulled one of the chairs closer to the windows and was sitting, staring out into the gardens, her pink shawl wrapped over her shoulders. Dark thunder clouds roiled outside. A horrible storm was brewing.

The familiar creak of the door made her turn with a start, her heart thumping faster.

But it wasn't Lucas.

Her pulse returned to its normal rhythm.

She blinked. In fact, it was the same valet who'd come looking for her to tell her her mother had turned her ankle. She eyed him with mistrust as he came to stand next to her.

He bowed to her. "Good morning, Miss Wharton. I thought I'd find you here."

"Have you come to tell me my father has taken ill this time?" she prompted; her eyes still narrowed on the man.

"No. In fact, first, I would like to apologize for being dishonest with you the other night."

"That's big of you." She lifted her chin. "The question is...*why* were you dishonest with me the other night?"

The valet straightened his shoulders. "Allow me to introduce myself. I am the Marquess of Bellingham, but I do hope you'll keep that to yourself for the remainder of your stay."

Her jaw dropped. "You're a marquess?"

"Yes, but at present I am pretending to be a valet. Much like our friend Kendall was pretending to be a footman."

Frances shook her head. Was she still in a nightmare? "Oh, now I see why you lied. You're *his* friend."

"It's true. I was trying to get you to leave the area so Kendall could return to his room without you recognizing him."

"Yes, I understand perfectly now," she said sweetly. "And pardon me for saying so but you're all quite mad."

"Perhaps." He shrugged. "Or *perhaps* we have our reasons."

"Reasons to lie to people?" She crossed her arms over her chest and gave him a condemning glare.

He folded his hands behind his back. "There's a funny thing about not knowing people's motives. It tends to make one assume the worst."

Her eyes shot daggers at him. "Are you seriously going to attempt to blame *me* for Lord Kendall's deception?"

"Absolutely not," Lord Bellingham replied. "But I am going to tell you a story."

She rolled her eyes. "I don't think I want—"

"Oh, come now, Miss Wharton, everyone loves a good story." He lowered himself to the chair next to her. "And this one is particularly interesting."

She wanted to hate this man, too, but there was something oddly compelling about him. It was as if he'd never met a stranger and knew exactly what to say in any situation. She still didn't trust him, of course, but she had to admit, if only to herself, that she was interested in hearing his story.

Lord Bellingham stretched his long legs out in front of him and settled into the chair as if the tale would be a lengthy one. "Once upon a time," he began, "there was a decent young man, who was honorable, kind, and noble."

Frances watched him carefully, her eyes still narrowed. She assumed he was talking about Lucas, but she wasn't entirely certain.

"This young man was from a fine family. He was the second son who'd spent the majority of his life in the Royal Navy," Lord Bellingham continued.

Very well, he *wasn't* talking about Lucas. Lucas was an earl, not a second son, and she'd never heard a word about him being in the Navy.

"The young man worked hard and rose in the ranks. He became a Commander in the English Royal Fleet in the amount of time it takes most young men to become a sub-lieutenant."

She raised her brows. A high-ranking officer? He couldn't *possibly* be speaking of Lucas. Could he?

"As young men do, this particular young man fell in love with a beautiful young lady and he asked for her hand in marriage."

Frances frowned. Surely, he was *not* speaking about Lucas. Lucas had never told her he'd been engaged to be married. Although Lucas had also never told her he was pretending to be a footman either, if one wanted to be precise about it.

"The wedding was set for Spring and most of the *ton* was invited. The young man was scheduled to return from the Navy on leave a fortnight before the wedding."

"Are we speaking about *you*, Lord Bellingham?" she couldn't stop herself from asking.

Instead of answering her, he merely cleared his throat. "On the night before he was to travel home for the wedding, the young man received a letter from his beloved."

Frances found herself scooting toward the edge of her seat, leaning toward Lord Bellingham. "What happened?"

"The letter informed the young man that his betrothed had received a better offer, one from a man who was a *first* son, a baron."

Frances gasped. "Don't tell me." She shook her head.

"She broke off the engagement and left the young man to come home and tell his family and all of the guests that there would not be a wedding after all."

Frances snapped her mouth closed. "She sounds hideous," she declared.

"She was, believe me," Lord Bellingham replied, breaking off from his story for a moment.

"Then what happened?" Frances prompted. She was so anxious to hear the rest that she was tapping her slipper nervously against the rug.

"The young man came home, but the young lady had already married the baron. It was too late."

"Are you quite serious?" Frances frowned and shook her head. "That is atrocious. But I say good riddance to bad baggage."

"Indeed, that is what all of the young man's *friends* said as well," Lord Bellingham continued. "But the young man was heartbroken and began to feel as if his family connections and money were the only things that mattered to young ladies of the *ton*."

"And?" She searched Lord Bellingham's face.

"And so, the young man went back to the Navy and worked even more diligently. He rose to the rank of

Commodore. And when he came home on leave, he refused to attend events of the *ton*, for he didn't trust that he would ever find a true wife." Lord Bellingham cocked his head to the side and scratched the back of his neck.

Frances continued to frown. "Is that the end? If so, that's an awful story."

"There is a bit more," Lord Bellingham conceded. "Not long after, the young man's older brother died quite unexpectedly from consumption."

"No!" Frances clapped her hand over her mouth.

"And the young man became an *earl*," Lord Bellingham added.

Frances expelled her breath. Oh, dear. Just as she'd feared, he *was* talking about Lucas. "There are obviously so many things I don't know about him," she finally said, staring, unseeing down at the rug.

"You know the important things, Miss Wharton."

"Which are?"

"That he's noble, kind, and loyal, just to name three of his qualities."

She shook her head. "I still don't see how that story explains why he lied to me for so long."

"Might it not seem reasonable, that a man who'd had such a thing happen to him decided to find a lady who wanted him for himself, and not his title nor his fortune? Especially given the fact that once he became a bachelor earl, he also became one of the most hunted men the *ton* has ever known. Every marriage-minded mother and her miss threw themselves into his path at every turn."

She arched a brow. "You want me to feel sorry for Lord Kendall?"

"No. I want you to know the truth about Kendall. He's one of the best, most noble, most honest men I've ever known."

"Except for when he was lying to me," she replied curtly.

"Yes, frankly. Except for that." Lord Bellingham shrugged. "The fact is, he came here as a servant because he was trying to do better, make a better choice, find true love, and I cannot blame him for that. And frankly, you shouldn't either."

Frances leaned forward and met the marquess's gaze. "Tell me, Lord Bellingham, why are *you* pretending to be a servant? Are you also looking for true love?"

He sat back quickly and barked a laugh. "Me? Heavens, no. I am here because I am a man and when men are in their cups they say and do stupid things and the night Kendall decided he needed to find a true wife, we all decided to pretend to be servants along with him and see who could last the longest."

For the first time since she'd heard about the bet, it actually seemed a bit less awful to Frances. She shook her head but couldn't help the smile that popped to her lips. "Are you telling me there are more of you lords pretending to be servants here?"

A sly smile tugged at the corner of Lord Bellingham's lips. "One more, but I'm not at liberty to reveal his identity."

She laughed at that. "You're right. Men do stupid things."

He laughed too. "You'll get no argument from me."

"Is that why you are here, Lord Bellingham? To tell me this story in the hopes that I'll forgive Lucas?"

"No. It's not for me to ask you to forgive him. I merely came to ask you to ask *yourself* an important question."

She eyed him warily. "What's that?

"Are you cutting off your nose to be revenged of your face?"

She sat back and sucked in her breath. "What?"

"Have you asked yourself why you won't forgive him? Granted, what he did was silly and wrong, but would you rather spend the rest of your life as Lady Frances Francis in order to live with your resentment, because frankly, you strike me as a much more intelligent young lady than that."

She leaned forward and stared Lord Bellingham in the eye. "Why do you say that?"

Lord Bellingham shrugged. "Because anyone astute enough to realize what drivel the Employment Bill is, must be clever."

She sat back in her chair. "Not that it matters. The bill probably has enough votes to pass after all."

"I don't know about that. Kendall denounced it, do you know?"

She turned to face him. "Denounced what?"

"The Employment Bill," Lord Bellingham replied.

Frances sucked in a breath. "What? When?"

Lord Bellingham tipped his head to the side. "After you ran out of the dining room last night. He told the whole lot of them the bill was rubbish, and I happen to know that *you* were the reason he thought so."

Frances touched her fingertips to her lips. "Truly?" she breathed.

"That's right. After Kendall left the room, the Prince Regent vowed to vote against it. Which of course means Sir Reginald will as well."

Frances dropped her hand into her lap. She studied Lord Bellingham's face. "Why did Lucas denounce it?"

Lord Bellingham propped his elbows on the arms of his chair. "Because he never believed in that drivel to begin with. He wasn't the one who introduced the law. His brother did. Charles died over a year ago. Lucas was merely carrying out his wishes."

Frances stared at him. Was that true? She searched her memory for the bits of gossip she'd heard about Lord Kendall. Yes, his brother had died. But she hadn't been out in

Society then and hadn't known much about the man. The only Lord Kendall she'd known of was the current one and he had always been linked to the Employment Bill. But it stood to reason that the bill had been around before Lucas had taken up the earldom.

"The truth is," Lord Bellingham continued, "you're the one who was able to show him how wrong he'd been about the law, Miss Wharton."

The marquess could have knocked her over with a piece of parchment. "Did he tell you that?"

"I'm not at liberty to say, but if there's one thing I know it's that the world is not black and white. There are many shades of gray, Miss Wharton, and if you had let Kendall explain why he did something as seemingly insane as pretend to be a footman at a house party, you just might begin to see the gray."

She furrowed her brow. Now the man was speaking in riddles. "What gray?"

"Kendall wanted to find a lady who was kind to servants, who thought about others, and who loved him for himself. He found that in you."

"He didn't have to lie to me."

"No, but think about what happened from his perspective. He only intended to serve dinner. To see which young ladies he might want to meet later. He never expected a young lady to catch his attention so thoroughly by asking him to look out into the hall for her. Then he saw her again the next day while trying to do his chores in the library. They struck up a conversation and he began to look forward to talking to the young lady."

Frances shook her head. Tears blurred her vision.

"He began to realize he'd found the young lady he was looking for," Lord Bellingham continued. "Only how exactly does one admit that one has been pretending to be a footman?"

Frances sat blinking at the marquess for several seconds. Before Lord Bellingham had entered this room, she would have told anyone who'd listen that she wouldn't forgive Lord Kendall until her dying breath, but now she was actually beginning to question herself. "You're confusing me, Lord Bellingham. I can no longer decide if I'm perfectly right or if I'm being petty and merciless."

Lord Bellingham steepled his fingers together in front of his chest. "Have you ever made a mistake, Miss Wharton? One you wished with every bone inside your body that you hadn't made?"

Frances blinked at him again. She shook her head. "I don't think so."

Lord Bellingham let his head fall back against the chair cushion. "You're fortunate then. Because I have, and let me tell you, there's not a day that goes by that regret is not my constant companion."

"That sounds awful," she breathed, staring out into the gardens again.

"It is. Take it from me. The moment you make the decision you'll regret for eternity can also feel very much like being perfectly right."

CHAPTER THIRTY-FOUR

Lucas sat at the desk in his second-floor bedchamber at Clayton's estate. He had just finished writing the final letter to the last of the members of the House of Lords asking him to reconsider his vote for the Employment Bill. He'd also written a letter to the Chancellor, asking him to stop the vote. He was sending all the letters out by courier at his own expense so they would get to London as quickly as possible.

Lucas intended to return to London immediately as well. He hoped to beat the storm that was gathering outside. He would have to tell his mother his decision about the law. She wouldn't like it, but he didn't care. He was through trying to live his dead brother's life. From now on, he was going to be himself, make his own decisions, and the devil take the consequences.

A knock at his bedchamber door interrupted his thoughts. "Come in," he called, already annoyed. No doubt it was Bell come to blather on with more unwanted advice. The man could be a complete nuisance when he wanted to be.

He heard the door open slowly behind him.

"If you're here to tell me some more drivel about how I'm a quitter I don't want to hear it," he said brusquely without turning around.

"What did you quit?"

Lucas's heart stopped beating. He swiveled quickly in his seat to see Frances take a small step inside the room. She was wearing an ice-blue gown with silver trim. Her dark hair was swept up in a chignon and she'd never looked more lovely.

He swiftly stood. He couldn't believe it was her, standing there, looking gorgeous and actually talking to him. "I...I thought you were someone else."

"Who?" she asked. Was it his imagination or was a slight smile riding her lips?

"One of my idiotic friends," Lucas replied, rubbing a palm across the back of his neck. He was half-mad with worry. If he said the wrong thing she might leave.

"Lord Bellingham, perhaps?" she asked next, primly folding her hands together in front of her.

Lucas narrowed his eyes on her. "You know Bell?"

"I do now," she replied with a slight laugh. "Are you... alone?" she asked next.

All Lucas could do was nod. If he took a step toward her, he feared she would disappear like an apparition he'd conjured from his imagination.

"No one saw me come here," she said, shutting the door behind her. She took one more small step forward. "At least I didn't see anyone in the corridor."

Another nod. He felt like a damn fool, but for the second time in his life, he was completely tongue-tied. She did that to him.

"I wanted to...speak with you," she began, biting her lip.

Lucas allowed himself to take two tentative steps toward her. He reached a hand toward her, wanting to do nothing more than grab her up in his arms and spin her around. "Frances, I—" He swallowed. No. He needed to *listen* to her for once and stop trying to explain himself. "What did you want to say?"

She tossed back her head and lifted her chin. A gleam of determination shone in her eyes. "I...came to ask if...your offer still stands."

Lucas's heart thudded in his throat. His pulse raced. "My offer?" He had to be certain of what she meant. He couldn't risk raising his hopes only to have them dashed again.

"Yes." She nodded, not looking away from his gaze. "A wise man came to visit me. He told me I should reconsider before I undermined myself."

"Bell?" he breathed, closing his eyes. By God, he would give Bell his entire fortune, his estate, anything the man wanted.

"Yes. However, he had to admit he wasn't just Lord Copperpot's valet." She arched a brow.

"He's pretending to be a valet," Lucas offered.

"So I gathered. Apparently, it's a popular game for the noblemen of the *ton* of late." She arched a brow.

"Frances, I—"

She lifted a hand to stop him. "So? Does your offer still stand or not?"

Relief swamped Lucas's body. It was as if a dam had broken and pure joy released into his blood. He closed his eyes. "Yes," he breathed. "My offer still stands. Always."

She crossed her arms over her chest. "I don't have a dowry, you know?"

He shook his head. "Darling, I'd pay *you* to marry me."

She laughed, but quickly clapped her hand over her mouth. "You may have to depending on what my mother says. I've no idea how much Sir Reginald offered them."

"I'll pay triple what he offered. I'll—"

"Not so quickly," she said, her tone matter of fact. "I do have some questions for you first."

He searched her face and nodded. "Ask me anything."

Frances folded her arms across her chest and stepped forward until she was able to walk around him in a circle. This interrogation would be anything but simple. And he deserved it. Every single word.

"Did you think about telling me?" she asked. "Before that day in the drawing room, I mean."

Lucas wanted to reach for her so badly his hand trembled, but he understood these answers were important to her and he owed her the truth. He clenched his hands into fists to keep them at his sides. "I thought about it nearly every day. I hated myself for lying to you. But then you told me how much you detested Lord Kendall and I...was frightened that I would lose you."

She stopped circling for a moment. Her skirts swished against her ankles. "I didn't think about that. I did tell you I detested Lord Kendall, didn't I?"

"Yes, but I still should have told you," he continued, turning his head to look at her. "I never should have allowed it to go on for so long. I have no excuse other than...I loved spending time with you. Loved talking to you. Loved—"

"Kissing me?" she offered, quirking a brow, her arms still crossed.

He tugged at his lower lip with his teeth. "Yes, that too. Very much."

She resumed her circling. "Didn't you think I was a fool when I told you how much I hated noblemen?"

"No." He smiled at her and shook his head. "I thought you were magnificent and honest. And unique. How many ladies would say something like that?"

"I *thought* I was talking to a footman," she replied, her tone stern.

"That might be true, but you *are* magnificent and honest, Frances. You're also unique."

She resumed her steps. "What about the time I said gentlemen of the Quality were the most boring lot of over-bred stuffed shirts you could imagine?"

Lucas shrugged. "I couldn't argue with you, and I came to believe you were correct. I only hoped you didn't find *me* to be an overbred stuffed shirt."

She tapped one fingertip along her jaw. "And when I said the talk at *ton* events was boring?"

"I agreed with you." He held out one palm. "Why do you think we never met during the Season? I loathe that endless round of meaningless social events."

She came to a stop directly in front of him and eyed him carefully. "You didn't think I was foolish?"

"Never," he breathed. "But it wasn't just those things you said, Frances. It was much more. I like to talk to people about the things that really matter, too. You made me see how wrong I've been on half a score of issues."

Her brows shot up. "For example?"

"Well, I intend to revoke the Employment Bill and write a new proposal, one for a bill that repeals the worst of the trade laws and provides more safety and rights for servants and the working classes."

A huge smile spread across her face. "Truly?"

"Truly." He nodded.

She clasped her hands together at her side. "Oh, Lucas. I do think that's an excellent idea."

He couldn't stop himself any longer. He reached for her elbow and gently encircled it with his hand, caressing her skin just above where her glove ended. "I have *you* to thank for it, Frances. Will you help me write it?"

She stopped and stared him in the eye, her lips forming a

small O. "Are you quite serious? There's nothing I would like more."

He laughed and pulled her into his arms, hugging her close before lifting her up and spinning her around. When he sat her back down, he said, "I thought you might say that. With both of us working on it, it's certain to be the best law in the land. Though I sincerely doubt we'll win Sir Reginald's vote."

She laughed. "That's a risk I'm quite willing to take."

"Me too."

Frances stared up into his eyes, a pensive look on her face. "There's one more thing I wanted to ask you."

He placed the back of his fingers along her cheek and gently stroked her skin. "What's that, my darling?"

"Do you love me, Lucas? I mean...Ken—"

He rubbed her shoulders. "I am Lucas. I always was the man you fell in love with. And yes, I love you madly."

"I'm awfully glad to hear that." She gave him a pretty smile. "I love you too."

He lowered his gaze to look into her eyes. "Does this mean...you'll marry me?" His words were tentative. By God, she hadn't said yes yet.

"It depends," Frances replied, batting her eyelashes at him.

"On what?" He held his breath. His chest felt so tight he thought it might burst.

"On whether you ask me again. I was a bit preoccupied that last time."

He expelled his pent-up breath in a heated rush and pulled her against his chest, pressing his cheek against hers as he whispered in her ear, "Frances Regina Thurgood Wharton, I love you more than words could ever say." He dropped to his knee in front of her, clasping her hands with his. "Will you please, please say you'll marry me?"

Her eyes filled with tears. She nodded. "Yes, Lord Kendall. I'll marry you."

He jumped up and pulled her tight again, then lowered his head and kissed her as if he would never let her go.

Moments later, he pulled his lips from hers and declared, "I'm going to make you the happiest countess in the land."

"I intend to hold you to that promise," she replied, laughing.

He spun around in a circle, energy coursing through his veins. "I want to shout our engagement announcement to the rooftop!" He squeezed her hand and brought it to his lips to kiss the back of her glove. "Should we go tell your parents right away?"

She shook her head. "Not quite yet. I think there's something *else* we should do *first*."

He searched her face. "What is it, my love?"

Her cheeks flamed. She cleared her throat and glanced away, plucking at each of her fingers. "I…suggest you…ravish me…just in case Mama objects to the engagement."

He frowned. "You think she'll object?"

"Let's see, me marrying one of the most eligible men in the *ton*? I'm certain I can talk her into it, but I can't say that being ravished doesn't hold its own appeal."

He arched a brow and allowed a wide grin to spread across his face. "Your wish is my command, my lady."

WHEN LUCAS PULLED her into his arms and kissed her once more, a shiver made its way down Frances's spine. She'd been slightly worried that he wouldn't do this. She thought perhaps he would insist upon doing the noble thing and refuse, but instead, he pulled her close and kissed her. Then he scooped her up into his arms and made his way over to the giant bed. He laid her carefully atop the mattress and then left her momentarily while he went to lock the bedchamber door.

As he returned to the bed, his gaze caught hers. He untied his cravat and another shudder went through her body. She was about to see him completely naked and there was nothing she wanted more. She sat up on the bed and pulled off both of her gloves, then kicked off both slippers. Next, she began plucking hair pins from her head. Unlike the gloves, which ended up on the floor, she laid the pins carefully on the bedside table. She would need those later if she ever hoped to leave this room with a modicum of dignity.

Grinning, Lucas sat on the edge of the bed. While he pulled off first one boot and then the other, Frances didn't remain idle. She slid across the mattress until she was on her knees behind him. He'd already discarded his cravat and as he began unbuttoning his shirt, she wrapped her arms around him from behind and gently bit his earlobe as he had done to her once in the library. She slipped her tongue along the crevice of his ear. His powerful body trembled. She reveled in the feeling of power. To make this strong, capable man tremble was a heady sensation, indeed.

She helped him pull his shirt over his head. He tossed the garment on the floor before he turned toward her again and slowly pushed her back onto the bed. He was naked from the waist up, with only his breeches on. He kissed her again, deeply, and she wrapped her arms around his neck. Soon, he pulled away from her and she let her eyes wander over his broad chest with its smattering of dark hair, and his muscled abdomen.

"What do you think?" he asked, nuzzling her collarbone.

"I think you're magnificent," she breathed.

His hands had traveled behind her back and were steadily undoing the long row of buttons on her gown. When they finally were free, she sat up and helped him pull the gown over her head. It, too, met the floor with haste and she was clad only in her stockings and shift.

"I've never done this before so I'm not entirely certain how to proceed," she admitted, her cheeks burning. She felt it best to be honest even if it made her feel like a ninny.

"Don't worry," he said, biting his bottom lip in a way that made her want to kiss him again. "I have and I do."

"Good then," she said, nodding like a complete fool.

But when he kissed her again, lowering her onto her back once more before moving down her body to caress her breast through her shift with first his fingers, then his tongue, she was mindless. She moved against him, her hips rocking of their own accord.

"What would you have me do next, my lady?" he asked in a husky tone.

She lifted her head and looked down at him through lust-fogged eyes. "Is that Lucas, the footman, talking?"

He gave her a roguish smile that made her squirm. "Your wish is my command."

A hundred thoughts raced through her mind, each one more tantalizing than the last one. He was at her service...in bed? What could possibly be better? She searched for the perfect response and finally breathed, "Pleasure me."

His eyes flared and he inclined his head toward her, the roguish smile still on his lips. "As you wish."

Frances sucked in her breath. Truthfully, she had little idea what she'd meant by 'pleasure me.' She'd once read something along those lines in a book she probably shouldn't have been reading. It seemed like the appropriate thing to say to one's lover while in bed. She only hoped *he* knew what it meant. Fortunately, he hadn't hesitated or given her a strange look or anything, so she was fairly certain he knew what to do next.

Moments later, Lucas shifted his weight farther down her body. She had scant idea what he was planning to do until she felt her shift moving up along her thighs. His handsome face was hovering just above the juncture between her legs. He couldn't possibly mean to—

Oh, God. His strong warm hands pushed up her shift until she was completely exposed to him. Then he lowered his head and Frances forgot to breathe. She was resting on her elbows watching him with wide eyes until the first hot lick pushed through her folds. An involuntary moan escaped her lips and her head fell back, her hair spilling onto the pillows behind her. The second lick made her thighs tense. The third made her knees fall apart. The fourth made her groan his name. In her entire life she'd never imagined anything like this. *Pleasure me*, she'd said. She'd had *no* idea.

Lucas's tongue found a spot at the apex of her thighs. He rubbed it, once, twice. She cried out. He rubbed it again and her hips jerked. Then he sucked the tiny nub into his mouth and she nearly came off the bed. His large hands held her hips tight and pressed them back onto the mattress, pinning her in place as his mouth tormented her. He licked her again, giving her just a moment to catch her breath, before his tongue circled the sensitive spot again and again. His tempo increased and her fingers grabbed at his dark hair. She wanted to pull him away because the feeling building between her legs frightened her, but at the same time she wanted him never to stop. She grabbed at his broad shoulders, trying to tug him up to her.

"Let me love you more, Frances," he breathed against her, just before his tongue descended into her wetness again.

"Lucas!" she called, panting so heavily she thought her lungs might burst. "Lucas."

His tongue continued its gentle assault and he slid one finger into her wet warmth. She shuddered, contracting around his finger. His tongue brushed roughly again and again over the nub while his finger worked its way inside of her until he found a spot so sensitive that when he pressed it, she cried out and clasped his head hard with both thighs. His tongue kept up its rough lapping, while his finger returned to the spot and pressed again. She lifted off the bed, crying out. She bit the back of her hand to keep from being too loud as her body shuddered with wave after wave of rippling pleasure.

Good God, what had this man just done to her?

In the aftermath, she fell back against the pillow, her entire body feeling as if she'd gone boneless. Her breathing wasn't right, and she wasn't entirely certain it ever would be again. Leaving her shift bundled at her waist, Lucas moved up to pull her into his arms against his hard chest. "Well?" he asked, kissing her ear. "Did I pleasure you?"

"Did you pl—?" she breathed. "Lucas, I can honestly say I've never felt such pleasure before."

He kissed her earlobe and nuzzled her neck. "I cannot tell you how pleased I am to hear that, my lady."

The words 'my lady' gave her a devilish idea. She plastered an equally devilish grin on her face and turned her head slightly to look at him. "Is my wish still your command?" she asked, arching a brow at him.

"Yes, my lady," he said. He pulled her fingers to his lips and kissed them one by one. "I'll do whatever you want me to." The look in his eyes was positively roguish.

"Good then." She pulled away from him and sat up, pulling her shift back over her thighs.

He frowned when she covered herself.

"Would you rather I be naked?" she asked.

"What would *you* prefer, my lady?"

"At the moment," she replied. "I want to pleasure you."

His eyes flared.

She let her fingers trail down his flat abdomen. "Which means, I demand that you tell me what you want me to do to pleasure you the way you just pleasured me."

"No." The word shot out of Lucas's mouth. He grabbed her hand to stop it from going any lower.

She lifted both brows. "Did you just say *no*? Is that any way for a footman to treat a lady?"

He shook his head. "No, but, Frances—"

"Ah, ah, ah." She waggled one finger at him. "I believe you said my wish was your command. Do you still mean that?"

"I do," he replied, bowing his head.

A thrill shot through her. He was going to do this with her. He was going to let her be in control of him, let her tell him what to do. Only she needed his help. Well, she would just have to ask for it.

"First," she said, warming quickly to her topic. "We're both going to get naked, you and I."

His eyes flared again, and he expelled a deep breath.

"You first," she demanded, only because she didn't think she could stand to be the first one naked. She might be enjoying this, but at the moment she was still too shy.

"Take off your breeches," she demanded, quite enjoying her ability to get him to do whatever she said.

"At your service," he replied, his gaze not leaving hers.

She watched as he pushed himself up on the bed until he was on his knees. Good heavens. She was quickly becoming aroused again with this playacting.

He unbuttoned his breeches slowly. He pushed them down his thighs until she saw dark springy hair and his manhood, thick and heavy, in the center. It was so...large.

He sat back on the bed and quickly discarded the breeches altogether. "What next, my lady?"

She had to take a deep, shaky breath to right herself. "Next, I want you to lay down on the pillows."

He arched a brow at her but did as she commanded. His big strong body rested atop the mattress; his dark hair splayed against the white pillow. This man was magnificent. And he was going to be her husband. A shudder racked her body.

She quickly pulled her shift over her head, deciding that the faster she did it the less self-conscious she would be.

The moment he saw her nude, he sucked in his breath sharply and Frances was suddenly proud of her body, something she hadn't thought much of before.

"Do you want to touch me?" she asked, not entirely certain where that question had come from. Apparently, it had come from the place inside of her that wanted to enjoy every single moment of this.

"Yes," he breathed.

"Touch me," she ordered.

"Where?"

"Kiss me...my breast." She rolled onto her back and he joined her, lying half atop her he trailed his lips down her throat to her breast until his mouth fastened on one nipple and she called out. He licked her, sucked her, and drew his thumb against her until she was nearly mindless with need.

"Wait!" she called.

His mouth came off her breast and he met her gaze with his own questioning one.

"This wasn't how it was supposed to happen," she finally managed to say.

"There's not exactly a rule book," he replied with a chuckle.

"No, but I want you to show me how to give *you* pleasure." She cleared her throat, intent upon not allowing him to distract her again. "On your back again," she demanded, then added, "please."

"Very well." He rolled over onto his back and propped up his head with both hands beneath it, a huge grin on his lips.

She let her eyes travel over the entire length of his body. His gorgeous face, wide shoulders, muscled chest, flat abdomen, and his long legs covered in dark, coarse hair. His member still stood at attention, but the man seemed positively at ease with his nakedness. As he should be. He was more beautiful naked than he was clothed, and she hadn't thought that possible.

She had little clue what to do next, but she let instinct guide her. She rolled over atop him, her naked breasts pressing against the dark hair on his chest. He sucked in a breath and was about to pull his hands out from beneath his head to touch her, when she said, "No!"

He froze. "No, what?"

"No, don't move your hands. Keep them under your head," she said in her most commandeering voice.

"You cannot be serious," he said with a groan.

"I'm entirely serious," she replied pertly, trailing one fingertip down his side to stop at his hip.

She rubbed her nipples along his chest to see the reaction in his eyes. Flames leaped in their depths. She smiled to herself. Next, she kissed her way along his flat belly the same way he'd done to her earlier. His groan told her she was doing the right thing. She finally moved down between his legs until the musky scent of him filled her nostrils and she was staring at his manhood.

Taking a deep breath, she leaned forward and kissed it tentatively. He groaned. *Oh, he must like that.* She pushed herself up, her palms against the mattress on either side of his hips and kissed the tip of it. He sucked in his breath, hard. *Ooh, that must have been even more pleasurable for him.* She stared at it for a few seconds, contemplating what else might give him pleasure before deciding to touch the tip with her tongue.

His hips nearly came off the mattress. She smiled to herself, immensely pleased with her discovery. Her tongue gave him the *most* pleasure. Duly noted.

She wrapped one fist around him and held him in place before descending again to lick the tip.

"Please can I move my hands?" he begged.

"No," she replied simply. "Not unless you tell me what else would give you pleasure."

She heard him swallow hard.

"I—"

"Yes?" She licked the tip again. He groaned.

She licked again. "I cannot possibly be doing this correctly. I need you to tell me what else to do."

"Jesus. You're doing it correctly."

She licked him once more before adding, "Tell me what else to do. I insist."

His voice was filled with half-pleasure, half-pain when he choked out, "Slide…slide me into your mouth."

Frances blinked. Of course. Why hadn't she thought of that? She wasted no time. She pushed herself up on her knees and lowered her mouth so that she was just above his member. Then she kissed the tip once more before opening her lips and sliding him into her throat. His moan made her shudder. The farther she took him into her mouth, the louder and more intense his groan. When she nearly reached the hilt, she pulled her lips back up slowly.

"Oh, my God, Frances," he gasped.

It was official. She was drunk with power. To have this gorgeous strong man at her mercy. She did it again and again as his hips thrashed. Then she pulled her lips off of him with a sucking noise. "What else should I do?" she whispered breathlessly, wildly. "To give you pleasure."

He moved one hand down to the back of her head and guided her back to his manhood. "Suck me," he breathed.

The wet warmth between Frances's legs increased. She wanted to rub herself against him, instead she put her lips back over him and took him into her mouth again, this time sucking as she went. His hand stayed on the back of her head, gently guiding her as he trembled.

She kept up the motion, again and again until she felt him tense.

"Frances, please," he begged.

She pulled her lips off of him. "What is it?" She searched his face.

"I can't take much more. Please let me make love to you."

She tugged at her bottom lip with her teeth and smiled. "Very well." She moved away from him and rolled onto her back. "As *you* wish."

He wasted no time moving atop her. His mouth returned to her breast and he pulled her nipple between his teeth, making her arch her back and wrap her arms around his neck.

He pushed her legs apart with his knee and she felt him probing against her wet warmth. She reached down between them to guide him and wrapped her hand around his manhood. He shuddered and groaned.

Then he was sliding into her. He stopped when she made a little hitching noise in the back of her throat.

"Am I hurting you?" he asked, kissing her cheek.

"No, I just didn't think it would fit," she admitted, her nose scrunched up.

He smiled against her shoulder. "I love you," he breathed, sliding in all the way.

Frances blinked. She'd been expecting pain. Mama had told her to expect pain. But all she felt was the hot glide of him inside of her. When he rocked his hips, she forgot to breathe. Then his hand moved down between them and he found her sensitive nub once more. He circled it with his thumb again and again until she called out his name as she fell over the precipice.

Lucas pushed inside of her again and again until he called her name and collapsed against her.

Several moments passed in which they were silent. Rain pelted against the windows. The storm outside had begun in earnest and they hadn't even noticed. Finally, Lucas pushed himself off of her and leaned up on his side to look at her. He pulled her against his chest and cuddled her to him. "That was the most amazing thing I've ever experienced," he whispered against her hair, kissing the top of her head.

"You don't have to say that just because—"

He lifted himself up over her until she was staring into her eyes. "Frances, listen to me. I promise to never lie to you again and I would never lie about something like that. I meant every word I said."

She smiled and snuggled back against him again. "Very well. I believe you, but while we're on the subject of your, ahem, playacting, why didn't you tell me?"

"Tell you what?" He kissed the side of her neck and a shudder went through her.

"That playacting is quite fun," she said, trailing her hand along the outside of his thigh.

He grabbed her hand, pulled it to his lips, and kissed her knuckles. "You know we can do that again whenever you'd like," he whispered against her ear.

"Ooh," she said. "Next time, can I pretend to be a housemaid?"

"Whatever you wish, my lady." He kissed her long and deep, then pulled her against his chest and cradled her in his arms. "I was serious. I'll double, no triple, whatever purse Sir Reginald offered your parents."

"No doubt *that* will convince my parents," she replied. "Only I'm afraid Father will just gamble it all away again."

"I've no intention of letting your father have the money," Lucas said. "I'll set up an allowance for him through my solicitor so he can't plough through it, at least until your sister is wed."

Frances lifted up and turned to face him. "How did you know I have a sister?"

He winced. "I sort of did an...investigation of your family. After I realized how much I was beginning to like you."

"You spied on us?" She blinked at him.

He lifted his shoulders. "Spying is such a complicated word."

She arched a brow at him. "Is that how you learned my full name?"

He nodded guiltily.

She laughed. "Well, what else did you find out?"

Lucas settled back onto the pillow. "I learned the details and sums of your father's debts. I'll be paying them all off, and don't worry, I fully intend to settle a sizable sum on your sister when it comes time for her debut."

Frances caught her breath. "Truly?"

He nodded. "Of course. Why wouldn't I?"

Her eyes filled with tears. She cupped her hand against his cheek. "That is the loveliest thing anyone has ever done for me."

Lucas pulled her hand to his lips and kissed her knuckles again. "I love you, Frances, more than words can say. I'd do anything for you, and I know I already said it, but I promise you, I'll *never* lie to you again. Thank you for showing me what was right in front of my eyes."

She frowned. "What do you mean?"

Lucas rubbed a fingertip against his temple. "The glaring difference between the classes. I'm ashamed to admit that I'd never stopped to think about it deeply until I was playacting at being a footman and talking to you about the Employment Bill."

Frances sighed. "I'd like to say I can't believe the guests at the party didn't recognize you when you were serving them, but the truth is I shouldn't have found it surprising in the least."

Lucas nodded. "It may have begun as stupid, drunken bet, but I've learned more from this experience than I imagined, and I've gained far more than I deserved." He touched his nose to her cheek and kissed her.

"I should thank you, too, Lucas. You and Lord Bellingham, I suppose," she added with a laugh.

"For what?"

"Through our disagreement I realized something about myself."

"What's that?" he asked.

She winced and ducked her head under the covers.

Lucas laughed and pulled down the sheet to reveal her guilty face. "What?" he prodded.

"Well, this *may* be difficult for you to believe, but I tend to think I'm always right."

"No!" he exclaimed, a mock-horrified look on his face.

She laughed and pushed at his shoulder. "Yes. I was so convinced I was in the right about you, I wouldn't even let you try to explain yourself to me. I might have let you go and married Sir Reginald out of spite. That's madness."

"I thought I'd lost you forever," he breathed, squeezing her hand gently.

"That's just it. Lord Bellingham made me realize that things aren't always as obvious as they appear to be." She shrugged. "Apparently, there is gray in this world. Not just black and white."

"Hmm." Lucas stared at the ceiling and narrowed his eyes.

"I believe I've heard Bell's 'gray' speech before. It is a good one."

"I was convinced I knew everything," Frances continued. "But I've learned that I've been wrong about a great many things. And the best part is that I'm happy to have been found wrong."

Lucas furrowed his brow. "A great many things?"

"Yes, in addition to realizing that you might actually have worthy reasons for behaving the way you did, I learned I was wrong about love and marriage. I was planning to marry Sir Reginald to keep my father from debtor's prison, but I plan to marry you for one reason alone." She leaned over and dropped a kiss on his forehead. "Love."

Lucas pulled her atop him. "I'm awfully glad to have changed your mind."

Frances kissed him soundly on the lips. Then she wiggled down and propped her chin on his chest. "Now, you must tell me something that Lord Bellingham wouldn't."

He ran his fingers through her hair. "What's that, my love?"

A sly smile curved her lips. "Who is the third nobleman pretending to be a servant at this house party?"

Lucas let out a crack of laughter and clasped his arms around her back. "Would you believe me if I told you it's the Duke of Worthington?"

"No!" Her eyes widened. "Are you quite serious?"

Lucas nodded. "Yes, he's pretending to be a groomsman in the stables and apparently Lady Julianna Montgomery has already spotted him."

Frances gasped. "No!"

"Yes, trouble's brewing there, I can tell," Lucas replied. "But now that you know about Worth and Bell, you're sworn to secrecy of course. We've yet to see who'll win the bet."

Frances laid her head against his chest and stroked his

shoulder. "Very well. I promise not to say anything now, but someday I intend to write a story about this entire outrageous affair. Otherwise, our grandchildren won't believe a word of it."

He dropped a kiss atop her head. "'Our grandchildren.' I quite like the sound of that. What will the title of the story be, my love?"

She giggled and squeezed his muscled shoulder. "I'm going to call it *The Footman and I.*"

∽

Thank you for reading *The Footman and I*. Please page forward to see related books, my biography, and how to contact me!

Valerie

ALSO BY VALERIE BOWMAN

The Footmen's Club

The Footman and I (Book 1)

Duke Looks Like a Groomsman (Book 2)

The Valet Who Loved Me (Book 3)

Save a Horse, Ride a Viscount (Book 4)

Playful Brides

The Unexpected Duchess (Book 1)

The Accidental Countess (Book 2)

The Unlikely Lady (Book 3)

The Irresistible Rogue (Book 4)

The Unforgettable Hero (Book 4.5)

The Untamed Earl (Book 5)

The Legendary Lord (Book 6)

Never Trust a Pirate (Book 7)

The Right Kind of Rogue (Book 8)

A Duke Like No Other (Book 9)

Kiss Me At Christmas (Book 10)

Mr. Hunt, I Presume (Book 10.5)

No Other Duke But You (Book 11)

Secret Brides

Secrets of a Wedding Night (Book 1)

A Secret Proposal (Book 1.5)

Secrets of a Runaway Bride (Book 2)

Thank you for reading *The Footman and I.* I so hope you enjoyed Lucas's and Frances's story.

I've had the idea to write a series involving noblemen who pretend to be servants for quite some time and these two characters and their Employment Bill were always set to be the first.

I'd love to keep in touch.

- Visit my website for information about upcoming books, excerpts, and to sign up for my email newsletter: www.ValerieBowmanBooks.com or at www.ValerieBowmanBooks.com/subscribe.
- Join me on Facebook: http://Facebook.com/ValerieBowmanAuthor.
- Reviews help other readers find books. I appreciate all reviews whether positive or negative. Thank you so much for considering it!

Want to read the other Footmen's Club books?

- Duke Looks Like a Groomsman
- The Valet Who Loved Me
- Save a Horse, Ride a Viscount

ABOUT THE AUTHOR

Valerie Bowman grew up in Illinois with six sisters (she's number seven) and a huge supply of historical romance novels.

After a cold and snowy stint earning a degree in English with a minor in history at Smith College, she moved to Florida the first chance she got.

Valerie now lives in Jacksonville with her family including her two rascally dogs. When she's not writing, she keeps busy reading, traveling, or vacillating between watching crazy reality TV and PBS.

Valerie loves to hear from readers. Find her on the web at www.ValerieBowmanBooks.com.

facebook.com/ValerieBowmanAuthor

twitter.com/ValerieGBowman

instagram.com/valeriegbowman

goodreads.com/Valerie_Bowman

pinterest.com/ValerieGBowman

bookbub.com/authors/valerie-bowman

amazon.com/author/valeriebowman